Hadn't she dis~~ ~~ already?

But Jack just stood there, eventually letting go of the ladder and strolling to the fence a few yards away. "Well, how about I stay here a few minutes longer, until you get the hang of it?"

"Oh, no, please, you don't have to," Samantha said. She could figure this out on her own.

He said nothing, just hoisted himself up on the top bar of the fence and sat there.

"You're not leaving, are you?" she asked in disbelief.

"Not at the moment." He smiled at her pleasantly.

"Fine, suit yourself." Knowing she sounded a bit like a peeved child, she turned toward the ladder. While he was still as gorgeous as he was yesterday, evidently he was a bit of a chauvinist, too. She didn't appreciate all his worry. She thought of her work in San Francisco—people there knew that she could handle pretty much anything the world threw at her, including some rickety old ladder. But, if the man had nothing to do today but watch her pry boards off her windows, that wasn't her problem.

Dear Reader,

I am a very happy person these days, but several years ago, I wasn't. I had taken a few wrong turns in my career and my personal life, and I felt pretty lost. There were days when I wished I had the courage to get in my car and drive away, into some new kind of life.

A Ranch to Keep was born from that fantasy. What if I did get in my car and drive away? Who would I hope to meet and what kind of place would I end up in? Since I didn't feel as if I could actually leave my life behind, I created Samantha and sent her on that journey instead.

Samantha loves her life in San Francisco and the career that gives her the stability she didn't have as a child. She likes to be independent, and keep her life simple and predictable. Then she inherits her grandparents' ranch in the wild and scenic Sierra Nevada, and finds herself on unfamiliar ground, in plenty of situations that she can't handle on her own. And the last person she wants help from is the gorgeous cowboy next door who makes her feel way too many complicated emotions!

That cowboy has been nursing a bruised heart for a long time now, and Samantha's arrival disturbs Jack's peaceful world in more ways than one. For one thing, she's thinking about selling the acres he's leased for years. If she does, his business will be ruined. He needs to make sure that if she sells, he's the buyer. But her beauty and determination are inspiring feelings he's pretty sure he'll regret when she heads back to the city. He loves the land, but is it worth risking his heart again?

I hope you enjoy this story about two people who find love in the wrong place, with the wrong person. But maybe two wrongs can heal old wounds and make their lives just right?

And as for the unhappy-me of several years ago? Well, I got in my car and drove to my first Romance Writers of America conference! Writing brought a new joy into my life. And eventually my own all-wrong hero showed up, and just like Samantha, we left the city behind, not for a ranch, but for a cottage by the ocean, which is just right for our own happily ever after.

With gratitude,

Claire McEwen

PS—I love to hear from readers. Please visit my website, www.clairemcewen.com, or find me on Facebook or Twitter!

CLAIRE McEWEN

—

A Ranch to Keep

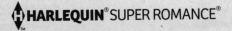
HARLEQUIN® SUPER ROMANCE®

Recycling programs
for this product may
not exist in your area.

ISBN-13: 978-0-373-60829-4

A RANCH TO KEEP

Printed in U.S.A.

HARLEQUIN®
www.Harlequin.com

ABOUT THE AUTHOR

Although teaching, bartending, dancing and farming were all wonderful jobs, Claire McEwen thinks writing novels is her best career yet. She always dreamed of becoming a writer and *A Ranch to Keep* is proof that dreams can come true! She lives by the ocean in Northern California and, when not writing, can often be found digging in the garden, playing on the beach with her son or dancing with her own romantic hero, also known as her husband. Claire enjoys getting to know her readers and can be reached on Facebook, Twitter or at her website, www.clairemcewen.com.

For my family—

Melanie, Beth, Sally, Danny, Steve, Cisco,
Sallie, Melia and Linnea,
thank you for years of crazy plot ideas and laughter
and for your boundless enthusiasm for this book.

Mango, sweetest pup ever,
you were my loyal friend and writing buddy
and always made sure I took my walks!
I miss you every day.

Shane, you inspire me to pursue my dreams
and so much else that is wonderful.

Arik, you gave us a love story that is more romantic
than anything I could possibly imagine.
You believed in me, you believed in my writing
and you made me believe in true love.

CHAPTER ONE

THE EASTERN SIDE of the Sierra Nevada Mountains was the perfect setting for fleeing a funeral. The high drama of the granite peaks rising abruptly from low, jagged hills, the earthy scent of sagebrush and pine, the open space of the high desert, were naturally suited to thoughts of life and death.

Grandma Ruth had loved these mountains. She'd lived most of her life in them. Driving down the scenic highway, marveling at each gorgeous view, seemed a much better way to celebrate her life than sitting in a musty Reno funeral chapel. Samantha still wasn't sure how she'd ended up on this impromptu road trip. One minute she'd been listening to the pastor's words, and the next an outraged voice was screaming in her head that this service wasn't doing justice to Ruth. The rote text didn't describe the loving, vibrant grandmother she knew. Samantha couldn't stand it anymore, so she'd fled.

Running away wasn't like her. Samantha felt her forehead, wondering if she was getting sick. She was known for showing up, helping out and always doing the right thing. But instead she'd abandoned the funeral and then, from the parking lot, called work to let them know she wouldn't be in today. She'd cancelled all her meetings and now, instead of the many things she should be doing, she was speeding down this scenic highway to the ranch outside of Benson.

Her ranch. That idea would take some getting used to. Samantha smiled. In the past few years, Grandma Ruth had tried to get her to be more adventurous. Maybe leaving her the ranch was her last attempt to shake her granddaughter up a bit. "Well, Grandma," Samantha said aloud to the mountains, "you have definitely stirred things up this time."

Samantha turned up the volume on her iPod and let the strains of opera soar. Maybe it was melodramatic, but it had seemed like the only music appropriate for the splendor of this drive, the sadness in her heart and the emotion of this homecoming.

A few tears insisted on rolling down her cheeks. Samantha brushed them off and took a deep breath. All this crying wasn't her usual style. More evidence that it would do her good to be away for a few days, to see something other than the crowded streets of San Francisco and the busy conference rooms of Taylor Advertising. She pictured the ranch as she remembered it from childhood. It might make her sad to be there without her grandparents, but how amazing to see the ranch again after so many years. Growing up, it was the closest thing to a home Samantha had known.

She glanced at the keys on the seat beside her, hooked on a ring neatly labeled Rylant, Ranch House. What would the old house be like? Ruth had moved to Reno ten years ago—what had she left behind? And in what state? The will had promised Samantha four thousand acres of ranch: barns, house, outbuildings "and all items found on the premises therein." She hoped some of those items included furniture or it was going to be a long night.

CHAPTER TWO

JUST PAST THE highway sign for Benson, population five hundred seventy-five, another weather-beaten sign read Blue Water Mercantile-Groceries, Beer, Fishing. Under the letters, a painted and peeling fish jumped out of faded water with a smile, holding a beer can in its chipped fin. The local store beneath the fish looked the same as it always had, just smaller and lower, as if it was retreating into the earth. It had been years since she'd been here, but she still remembered climbing down from Grandpa's truck, holding on to his strong hand and hurrying him indoors to get a popsicle or a soda.

An old pickup was parked in front of the store and a man in a battered cowboy hat was leaning on the cab door, talking on a cell phone. As she pulled her car up to the curb, Samantha caught a glimpse of long legs in faded jeans, broad shoulders in a plaid shirt and white teeth that flashed when he talked. A perfect, modern Western scene, she thought, taking in the contrast of the cowboy, the old truck and the cell phone.

She smiled to herself. The sight of a good-looking

man in a cowboy hat in San Francisco generally meant one thing—he was not interested in women. Out here that stereotype might not apply, and she couldn't help but glance again at the stranger, appreciating his silhouette. Then she remembered Mark and turned away with a stab of guilt. The last thing she should be doing was looking at another man when she already had a boyfriend—even if that boyfriend hadn't been around much lately.

Samantha crossed the small parking lot and reached for the handle to pull open the glass door of the shop. She jumped, startled, as a much larger hand swooped over hers to pull it open for her. "I got it," said a deep voice in her right ear, and she recognized the navy plaid shirt on that long arm and knew it was the same man she'd seen in the parking lot. Glancing up to voice her thanks Samantha froze, her breath caught in her teeth.

Tall, she thought incoherently. *He's really tall.* Her gaze slid down to a wide chest underneath faded flannel. Everything else was just a series of impressions—a silver belt buckle, lean muscle, fair skin tanned to gold, dark blond hair that was a little shaggy under the hat, curling a bit at the collar. She looked up quickly and met blue eyes with a brilliance in them that caught the light. Dark honey lashes surrounded them, thick and long. He looked like a man who spent plenty of time out in the elements. There were creases from sun and smiling etched on his angular face. Samantha hadn't known a man could be so beautiful. She just stood there like a fool, staring, trying to remember how to breathe.

The cowboy regarded her with a wide grin, as if he knew just what she was thinking. Then he took a long, slow look at her before saying "You're not from around here, are you?"

It took another attempted breath to get her heart beating again. Glancing down at herself she saw what he saw…the long, black pencil skirt, the high, spiked heels on her boots, the chunky gold ring on her hand, the black cashmere sweater. She was definitely not dressed for life in a small mountain town.

With an embarrassed smile tugging at her mouth, she forced herself to look up at those eyes and act as if they weren't paralyzing her. If her friend Tess were here, she'd have the perfect, appropriate-yet-sexy reply, not this vast blankness that had taken over her mind.

Finally she managed, "Nope, I guess not," and pushed past him into the store, hoping he couldn't see her heart pounding through her sweater. She heard him laughing softly as he closed the door behind them with a clang of the bell.

Samantha grabbed a basket. This was ridiculous. Losing Grandma Ruth must have destroyed her confidence. She shopped at the Marina Safeway, for crying out loud, the most notorious singles pickup spot in all of San Francisco! She was used to fending off men asking for cooking advice in the pasta aisle. Back home she brushed those men off easily, but walking to the back of the dusty store, she felt the cowboy's glance lingering on her and just prayed she wouldn't trip and fall.

Samantha heard him greet someone at the counter. She forced herself to focus on her shopping.

Everything about the store brought back a memory. She smelled the unforgettable combination of dust, firewood and the faint odor of the bait sold out of the freezer in the back. There was the ice cream case, and the small section of toys. And in the air there was something she hadn't felt in years—the peace of childhood summers, solidity and home. Tears prickled for what must have been the twentieth time that day and she blinked them back quickly. She was an emotional wreck, one moment running out of Ruth's funeral, the next lusting after some random guy in a cowboy outfit, and now missing her grandparents so much it hurt! Disgusted with herself Samantha turned her attention to filling her basket with provisions and cleaning supplies, and kept her mind busy with plans for opening up the long-neglected farmhouse.

A man in a fishing vest sat behind the counter. She noticed his face was lined and weathered, much like the sign in front of the store. He smiled at her with a "Morning, ma'am," and she smiled back, dumping her basket onto the counter.

There was no sign of the cowboy she'd met at the door. He'd probably left, and Samantha gave a small sigh of relief at his absence. The last time her heart had pounded that fast was during her first formal pitch at work…about five years ago? It wasn't a pleasant feeling and not one she felt like repeating anytime soon.

"You look like you mean to stay awhile." The grocer's friendly eyes twinkled at her from beneath his gray brows. "You here for the fishing?"

"It's been a long time since I tried it." Samantha pulled out her credit card as he totaled her purchases on an archaic-looking cash register. No scanners and barcodes at the Blue Water. He took her card, set it in the holder and began to place a paper slip over it. Reading the name on the card, he stopped and looked up at her in surprise.

"Rylant? Are you any relation to Ruth Rylant?" The lump she'd suppressed rose in her throat again. She hadn't thought this through, hadn't taken into account all the people in Benson who'd known Ruth. Figuring she'd better get used to it, and quickly, she swallowed the lump yet again and stuck out her hand to the beaming face across the counter.

"Yes. I'm Samantha Rylant, Ruth's granddaughter," she told him as she shook his hand. "I'm not sure you heard, but Ruth passed away earlier this week."

She heard the emotion in his voice. "Yes, I did hear…stupid of me not to give my condolences right away. Ruth was a fine woman. We all missed her when she moved away. I'm sorry to hear she's gone." They were silent a moment and then he continued, "Well, but here you are and I'm being impolite. I'm Dan Sanders, owner of this fine establishment. Welcome to Benson, Samantha. You staying in town?"

"I thought I'd stay out at the ranch."

Dan's gaze shifted down to her hands, eyeing the bold rings and the manicured nails. "Oh, I see. Have you been out there recently? You might want to try the hotel for a while until you can get someone in to clean up the place."

"Believe me, I called, but it's full. A fly-fishing tour. But it's okay, I'll figure something out. I guess I'm just going to have to clean the house up myself." At Dan's incredulous look she pushed on, needing to explain, maybe to herself as well. "She left it to me…so I guess I just want to spend some time there, figure out what I've got on my hands. I haven't been out there since before she moved away."

"Wait a minute!" Dan interrupted. "I remember you now! No wonder you stopped here—you know this place. I remember Ruth bringing you in here from time to time when you were just a kid! And your grandpa, he always used to buy his fishing license here. If I remember right he'd take you fishing right along with him." He grinned and stacked her groceries in a paper bag as he continued. "You were just a skinny little thing, all big green eyes and arms and legs."

"Not much has changed since, has it?" The cowboy's deep voice spoke right behind her. Samantha nearly jumped out of her skin. She turned quickly, hitting her elbow against a rack of sunglasses. "Whoa, steady there!" He caught the wobbling rack and Samantha grabbed her elbow, wincing at the pain sizzling up her arm. "Are you okay? That looked like it hurt."

Her traitorous heart thumped and her pulse raced at top speed as she stared at him, momentarily stunned into silence. What was wrong with her? "I'm fine, really," she managed. Time to gather the shreds of her dignity.

She pulled her eyes away from his handsome face and drew herself up to her full five-and-a-half feet, forcing herself to let go of her stinging elbow. She deliberately turned her back to him and gave Dan the most dazzling, confident smile she could muster, ignoring the cowboy's presence behind her. "Mr. Sanders, it was nice to meet you. I look forward to seeing you soon. Thank you for your kind words."

If Dan noticed the flushed cheeks and contrived dignity he said nothing. He took her hand, a kind expression on his face. "You come on by if you need anything, Samantha. And don't pay attention to the clown behind you. He's just fond of causing trouble. If he wasn't one of my best customers I'd kick him on out of here for you!"

There was another laugh behind her, courtesy of the gorgeous cowboy. Samantha gathered her bags and turned to go. Mr. Perfect stepped out of her way, tipping his hat in her direction. She refused to look at him. Brushing past his broad shoulder she turned to Dan. "Oh, don't worry, I won't pay attention to him." More laughter, deep and warm, crested behind her like a wave that prickled her skin and washed her out the door into the bright fall sunshine.

THE PHONE TRUMPETED a faint snippet of Beethoven's Fifth and Samantha pulled the car onto the gravel shoulder, reaching for her purse. Hopefully it was Mark, dutifully calling to apologize for not attending the funeral with her. Or, more likely, he'd be calling to talk about work. Still, maybe his familiar voice would banish the memory of the handsome cowboy, whose laughter still echoed in her ears. Ugh.

The screen was flashing her mother's name.

Ignoring the stab of disappointment that her boy-friend continued to be AWOL, she answered.

"Samantha! Are you okay? How's it going?" Her mother sounded revved and excited. She always did, especially before any type of global travel.

"Mom, I'm not even at the ranch yet, but almost. It's nice here." She looked around at the ridges rising above her. "Peaceful. Beautiful."

"Wow, you're making me miss it." Samantha could hear an unfamiliar, wistful note in her mother's voice.

"Really? You *know* you never liked it here. No one speaking Swahili, no volcanoes erupting, nothing exciting enough for you."

Her mom laughed. "You're right. It's a little tame for your father and me. But gorgeous, nonetheless. Speaking of Swahili, we're at the airport now. We should be back in Kenya by tomorrow."

Samantha had spent most of her life on a different continent from her parents, but the familiar pang returned. No matter how often she reminded herself that they were happy this way, traveling the world and making their documentary films, a part of her never stopped wishing they would just stay in one place at least for a little while. She opened her door and stepped out of the car, wanting fresh air to blow out the ghosts of accumulated disappointment. Her foot landed in something unexpected, soft and yielding. She looked down in horror. "Oh, no!"

"What's wrong, honey?"

"Mom, you won't believe this. I just stepped in a cow pie."

Her mother's giggles filled her ear as Samantha tried to extricate her foot from the clinging green mass. "No, it's not funny! It's disgusting!"

"I know dear, it's just so ridiculous is all. Welcome to the country. And I bet you didn't follow my advice and pick up some hiking boots before you drove down?"

"I tried mom, but they were all too ugly. I just couldn't do it."

"Well, unfortunately Manolo Blahnik doesn't make anything suitable for ranch living but…"

Samantha listened to her mother's good-natured teasing as she hobbled over to the grass at the side of the road and attempted to wipe the manure off her boot, trying not to worry about the butter-soft Italian leather she'd paid way too much for. It was awkward, trying to get cow poop off stiletto heels, and she was bent over, using a stick to scrape at it when the last voice she wanted to hear said, "Do you need some help there?" causing her to jump at least three feet in the air. She turned and faced her intruder.

"Mom," she interrupted, "I have to go. Call you later. Love you." She shoved the phone into her pocket. The store cowboy, alias Mr. Perfect, was leaning against his truck, arms folded across his chest, looking relaxed and confident. How had she not heard him drive up? How long had he been there, watching her hop around in the grass? She felt a blush creeping up her neck again. "That's the third time in fifteen minutes you've startled me like that!" Her voice was shrill, but she didn't care. Sometimes the best defense was a good offense.

"Well, not to be rude, but you seem to scare pretty easily." His eyes were mocking her, again, the lids creased in a smile that she could tell he was trying, and failing, to keep away from his mouth. At least he had the courtesy to *try*. Only then did she realize that she was pointing a stick covered in cow poop at him.

A thought occurred to her and she advanced, stick extended. "Why are you here? Are you following me?"

"Lady, you've been living in the city too long! No, I'm not following you. I live around here and when I saw you pulled over by the side of the road, I thought I'd offer help. That's what we do out here. Maybe you've heard of it? It's called being neighborly?" He paused for a moment and put his hands up, palms out, as if in self-defense. "And how about putting that stick down?"

Could this get any more embarrassing? First she was hopping in the bushes, now she was threatening assault with cow manure? She looked at the stick, then at him. "Er…manure," was all she could manage to say. When he looked at her blankly she stumbled on. "I mean, I stepped in it, and I was, well, trying to…" Oh no, this wasn't going well. Why couldn't she talk around this man? He leaned slightly back and eyed her warily and her face got even hotter. Maybe it was best just to get out of here and clean the cow manure out of the car later.

She set the stick gingerly down on the ground between them. He relaxed and the smile he'd been trying to contain came out in full force and there was actually a dimple in one cheek. It wasn't fair for a man to look so good, especially when she looked like such an idiot. She gestured to her car. "Um…well. I've got to go."

"Wait," he said. "Now that you've put your weapon down…" The glance he gave the foul stick was pure amusement. "I bet I've got an old rag in my truck that you can use." He turned around to rummage in the cab, and she tried her best not to stare at his long back and tight, faded Levi's. It was hard to look away.

Shaking her head, she walked carefully across to her car and braced herself against it, still radiating embarrassed heat but genuinely grateful when he handed her an old Led Zeppelin T-shirt. She bent down and began wiping at the boot, wincing at the pungent smell of cow.

He leaned against his truck, watching. "So, you weren't planning on a trip to the mountains? Those shoes aren't exactly meant for the terrain around here."

Exasperated, she glared at him. "Don't start! I was getting a lecture from my mother on the same topic when you pulled up." She finished wiping her poor boot and stood up. She didn't know what to do with his T-shirt, now covered in filth, so she just held it. "I'm from San Francisco. And you're right. I didn't really know I was coming here when I left home."

He nodded toward the T-shirt. "And you've had quite a welcome."

"Yes, locals keep sneaking up on me, and the resident livestock even left me a welcome gift." He laughed at that and she couldn't help but join him. It was all just so ridiculous. So far, her return to her roots was not going at all smoothly. Jenna, one of her best friends, would say these events were all some sort of sign. If that was true, she should turn around and head back to San Francisco as fast as she could.

"So, *San Francisco,* what brings you to our neck of the wilderness?" The cowboy gestured to the vast peaks unfolding behind them. "I take it you're not a hiker, or a fan of fly-fishing?"

"Don't assume you know everything about me just because you don't like my shoes!" Samantha retorted. She was starting to like this exchange, now that some of the embarrassment was fading. "I've caught some fish around here in my time."

"Hey, I've got nothing against the shoes...they're very sexy." He flushed. "Sorry, I mean they're very...um..."

Oh, how nice to see him at a loss for words for a change! It was tempting to just stand there and watch him bury himself in the hole he was digging. But he'd stopped to offer her help so she took pity.

"Pungent?" she suggested. "Odiferous? Expensive and quite possibly ruined?"

His look was genuine gratitude. "Yeah, all of the above."

"Anyway, you're right. I'm not exactly here for the fishing, or the hiking. I'm here because my grandmother passed away and I was at her funeral in Reno, and I just couldn't stay there anymore. So I left and started driving." Ugh, too much information there. One minute she couldn't talk at all and the next she was telling him all this? She looked away, out at the fence line on the hill behind him. The posts had weathered to silver and were spotted with lichen.

His voice was serious. Soft. "I'm sorry for your loss. But, yeah, funerals can be rough. Most times they don't seem to have much to do with the person who's passed on."

Samantha studied the fence for a moment longer.

The tears were back, blurring her vision. The lump was back, making it hard to speak. She looked down at the messy shirt and he held out his hand.

"I'll take that for you."

She looked up and saw his eyes, and they were no longer bright with laughter but deep with compassion. All she could muster was, "Thanks. Look, it was nice of you to stop, but..." She opened the car door to leave, but he stepped forward.

"Wait." He threw the old shirt into the back of his truck. "Before you go, I might as well introduce myself. I'm Jack Baron." He wiped his hand on his jeans and then held it out.

Samantha shook it, noting rough callouses, and the strength of his grasp. Somehow she didn't really want to let go and the shake went on just a beat too long. She pulled her hand away quickly. "Samantha Rylant," she said. "Do you live around here?"

"Yup, I do. Up this road a bit. Hang on..." He looked at her more closely. "Did you say Rylant? Is...was...your grandmother Ruth?"

"Yes. Did you know her?" Her voice was scratchy but it still worked, barely.

"I only met her a few times, but enough to know she was one of the great ones. I was really sorry to hear that she'd passed away." His glance was sympathetic. Then he shifted and cleared his throat. "Actually, there's more to it." He continued. "I rent...rented...a lot of land from your grandma."

Her tenant? Oh no, this gorgeous guy was her tenant? The lawyer had mentioned a tenant, but when he'd used the word "rancher" she'd pictured an older man with gray hair and a beer belly. Not a man so beautiful he removed her powers of speech! Not this man, who'd seen her looking ridiculous several times in their very short acquaintance. It was mortifying, and she found herself wishing fervently that she'd never stopped at the Blue Water today.

He regarded her with a searching look, waiting in silence for her reply.

"Wow," she finally said. *Wow?* Not a word usually found in her vocabulary. "I'm sorry, you just caught me a little off guard. You see, I inherited the ranch from Ruth. That's why I came today...."

His slow smile was back, creasing his face, lighting his eyes under the brim of his hat. The wider his smile, the unsteadier her legs felt and the tighter she held on to the car door.

"Well, I guess if you've inherited the land from her that means you're my new landlady. So, welcome to the neighborhood, landlady. Guess we'll be seeing each other around." The smile had become a grin, with straight white teeth flashing.

There were definitely butterflies in her stomach at the thought. That was a first. "Yeah, see you," she replied, and quickly lowered herself into the car and shut the door. With an awkward wave she fired up the engine and started on up the road, ready to put as much distance as possible between her and her new tenant. She glanced in her rearview mirror and could swear he was laughing again as he stepped up into his truck.

CHAPTER THREE

FOCUS ON THE ROAD, Samantha commanded herself. But it was hard to focus with her heart beating fast and her glance flicked back to the rear view to note that the cowboy was now driving behind her. For a split second she thought he might really be following her, but reason prevailed. Of course he was behind her—his ranch bordered hers and if she remembered correctly, they actually shared a driveway for a few yards.

She looked down the curving road, trying to see when that driveway was coming up. It had been a long time since she'd driven here and she didn't want to miss it. Despite her efforts, the old mailbox flashed past before she even registered that it was there. She groaned. Now she had a wrong turn to add to her collection of embarrassing moments in front of her new neighbor.

With a sigh she slowed down and looked for a safe place to turn around. At least she was providing Jack with all kinds of stories to tell down at the local bar. They'd definitely be good for a few laughs. She found a turnout and slowed to a stop then U-turned back toward the ranch. As she pulled into the driveway she saw Jack stopped on the left-hand side. He rolled down his passenger window and she pulled up next to him, lowering hers.

His face positively glowed with tamped-down humor. "Everything okay there, San Francisco? I was beginning to wonder if I'd have to go flag you down."

"Thanks for your neighborly concern, Jack." Sarcasm was always a good weapon when deeply embarrassed, she'd found.

"Think you can make it from here?"

She found herself staring at his smile, and the place where his lower lip curled up a bit. Catching herself, she rolled her eyes at him. "Yeah, I brought my compass."

He nodded in mock-seriousness. "I'll rest easy then. Well, nice to meet you again, Samantha." This time he went first and she felt only relief when he turned off toward his own property. At least if she drove into a ditch getting her city slicker car up this old road, he wouldn't be there to witness it.

Taking a deep breath, Samantha revved the engine up the hill. To her surprise, the driveway was recently graded and fresh gravel had been spread. Who'd been maintaining it? Her gaze roved to the pastures sloped down to the main road on either side of her. She knew from what the lawyer had told her that the fields on her left were leased to

Jack. The lawyer had mentioned that her tenant had horses and she could see a mare and foal grazing busily just beyond the fence.

In contrast, the fields to her right were overgrown with weeds and shrubs. No stock had grazed here for a long time and some of the fences were sagging with disrepair. A wave of loss swept over her as she remembered these pastures years ago, when The Double R Ranch had thrived under Grandpa's hands. He'd kept a few sheep and goats down here through the fall to graze the field into an even-cropped, green swath that ran right up to the picket fence of the front yard. He'd have been disappointed to see the state of it now.

She rounded one last turn and the house was in front of her. The well built, turn-of-the-century farmhouse was bathed in the golden light of the late afternoon. A closer look revealed three stories of peeling white paint, boarded-up windows and a sagging porch that ran along all sides of the building. Off to the right it was doing more than sagging—it looked like it might soon detach itself completely.

Samantha turned off the engine and sat, taking in the changes, letting the memories flood over her. Grandma Ruth's wide smile as she came out to greet her granddaughter at the beginning of each summer. The tears she'd tried to hold back as she sent her off again in the fall, with hand-knit sweaters and cookies. Grandpa sitting on that porch mending a harness in the evening while Grandma read to him from the swing that used to hang by the front door—it had been her favorite place to sit. In the past there had always been a border collie or two barking at visitors, romping and jumping with excitement. In contrast with her memories, the silence and stillness of the house was almost oppressive.

Tears slid cool paths down her cheeks while she let the memories run their course. Then she straightened, blew her nose and got out of the car. Staring at the boarded-up windows, panic hit her. What had she been thinking? This place was dirty and dilapidated. She should've just waited for another time, when there was room at the hotel and she wouldn't have to sleep here. "Samantha, get a grip," she said out loud to the silence. She'd grown up living in rural villages, in huts with dirt floors, in countries where the insects grew as big as your hand. Surely she could handle a few years' worth of dust and neglect. Squaring her shoulders, she popped the trunk of the car. It was time to get to work.

Samantha unloaded her cleaning supplies, stacking them on the porch. She unlocked the front door of the old house and pushed it open. The room was dim, with just a trickle of light seeping between the boards on the windows. Samantha stepped in and flipped the switch by the door, relieved when the old bulb in the entryway flickered on. The utility company had kept its promise. She had electricity, and hopefully she'd have water, too.

With each flick of a light switch, the house came alive a little more. Samantha allowed herself just a few moments to wander through the downstairs rooms. It was like stepping back in time.

All the furniture she remembered was still there, shrouded in cloth, waiting to be brought to life. For the first time, Samantha wondered when Grandma had decided that the ranch would be hers. When she left for Reno ten years ago? Knowing Ruth, she probably had.

Samantha imagined her grandmother carefully placing the furniture covers, making sure the house would be ready for her granddaughter when the time came. Friends sometimes wondered where Samantha had gotten her talent for organization. It was hard to trace that back to her parents, whose constant traveling and artistic pursuits had mystified the people of Benson. But Samantha knew that all those traits had skipped a generation and come straight to her from Ruth.

Well, she'd definitely put that organization gene to good use now. She headed back to the porch, ready to start cleaning. Beethoven's Fifth rang out again, jarringly loud in the quiet house. She dug her phone out of her deep leather purse and touched the screen. Still not Mark, but it was good to see her friend Jenna's name on the display.

"Where are you?" Jenna's voice sounded distracted. "Are you home? Are you really sad?"

"I can't quite hear you. Are you there? You're fading." Samantha used her free hand to yank a canvas cloth off the armchair in the farmhouse living room. Bad idea. A small cloud of dust rose from the fabric and she backed away from it. Once the dirt settled, she carried the canvas gingerly through the kitchen and out to the back porch, dumping it off the edge into the long grass below.

"Oh, sorry, Sam, I was doing turns. Warming up for a wedding couple. Oh joy." Jenna taught ballroom dance at a popular studio in San Francisco. She had a love-hate relationship with her job, the love part being the dancing, and the hate part being couples who snarled at each other throughout their lessons.

"You'll be fine. Just wear your referee jersey and bring a whistle."

"You're not kidding." Jenna giggled. "Anyway, what's going on? Did the service go well?"

Samantha took a deep breath. "Well, I'm not home. I didn't go home. I'm in Benson. At my grandmother's ranch." She looked past the overgrown gardens to the gray, granite peaks rising beyond. A patch of snow on a high peak was glowing a crisp white. Long shadows darkened the high valleys.

"Samantha, that's fantastic!" Jenna exclaimed. "I'm so proud of you! I thought you didn't go anywhere that didn't have a Starbucks!"

"Jenna!" Samantha protested, happy to let the familiar teasing chase away the melancholy she'd been feeling. "I go places! I take vacations! Sometimes."

"You deserve some time off after this huge loss. Make that boyfriend boss of yours do some work for once instead of always leaning on you."

"Well, you know me. I brought my laptop and I'll probably work from here. Plus, I'm not sure this counts as vacation. The house was shut up for ten years. It's pretty run-down and dirty."

Jenna's voice faded out for a moment, then came back and Samantha imagined her wafting about the studio, graceful and elegant with her red hair and dancing dress, holding a cell phone to her ear. "Just watch out for mice and dust and stuff. You don't want to get some weird disease."

"Disease?" Samantha joked. "Like old house disease? I didn't know about that."

"You know what I mean!" Jenna giggled down the line and Samantha could tell she'd stopped turning. "Like that mouse disease, the hantavirus? Or tetanus from old rusty nails."

It was Samantha's turn to laugh. "Okay, Jenna, I'll watch out for mice and nails."

"And weird people. You might get some real crazies out there. Hermits, unibombers, survivalists."

And gorgeous cowboys, Samantha added silently to her friend's list. "I'll watch out for them, too."

"Tell me more about...oh, wait, don't tell me more. Mr. and Ms. Miserably Engaged have just arrived."

"There's not much more to tell anyway." Samantha answered untruthfully. "We'll talk later. Don't get in the middle if they start brawling."

Samantha felt so much lighter when she hung up the phone. Jenna and her silly humor were exactly what she needed, and what this house needed. It had gone too long without the life and laughter it had sheltered when Grandma and Grandpa were alive.

Samantha looked around the room. She'd free the furniture first. There was something magical about uncovering the familiar pieces, the worn upholstery emerging like the faces of old friends. It really was a comfort to be in the place that Ruth had loved so much.

Being so sentimental wouldn't help though, Samantha chided herself. The reality was, she'd have to sell this place. There was no way she could keep up this ranch and take care of all these acres. She could barely keep her apartment in San Francisco livable. Better to think of this trip as a way to have some closure. As a way to somehow say goodbye.

Samantha willed herself to be practical. If she spent the rest of the afternoon working hard she could get the kitchen, downstairs bathroom, downstairs bedroom and living room clean by tonight. Tomorrow she'd pull some of the boards off the windows and then she'd have a nice space to live in until she figured out what in the world she was doing here.

Grabbing the rest of the old canvas, she threw it out in the backyard, watching the clouds of dust and memory billow and scatter, disappearing into the high mountain air.

SAMANTHA WIGGLED THE old ladder to the left, then back again to the right, trying to get it stable against the wall of the house. It tipped toward her, and she shoved it back again. When it hit the wall, dirt showered down and carpeted her face, sticking in her hair and eyelashes.

"Ugh!" Samantha spat out what she hoped was just dust and blinked her eyes. She'd been sweating and the dirt added one more layer to the film on her skin. She wiped her face on the shoulder of her T-shirt and for the tenth time that morning wondered why she felt such a strong need to take on this house herself. There was no reason not to hire someone else to do it…in fact that would make the most sense, and leave her free to spend her days here hiking and exploring. But the answer

came back, as it had ten times already. This was
her grandma and grandpa's house and she was responsible for it.

Yesterday she'd cleaned until midnight, and the
entire downstairs gleamed. It felt satisfying to see
the results of her work and good to use her hands.

She'd headed into town early this morning and
found a pair of work boots—she was still coming
to terms with their lack of aesthetic appeal—gloves
and a crowbar, and had returned to the ranch ready
to tackle the boarded-up windows so she could let
in light and fresh air. She'd finished the lower windows on this side of the house, so next up were the
ones on the second floor.

Samantha looked up and the top of the ladder
seemed to disappear into an ethereal distance. Her
heart sped up in an anxious dance and her breath
came with a shudder. She hated heights. Hated ladders. Especially spidery, rusty, rickety ladders leaning up against old houses.

"Come on," she muttered to herself. "You can
run a national ad campaign. This ladder is nothing
to you." She wished she believed her own pep talk.

Taking a deep breath, she tucked the crowbar
under her arm and put a foot on the ladder. So far,
so good. The metal frame was cool and damp under
her sweaty hands as she began to climb. Up and
up, shaking hand over shaking hand, trying to ignore the quivers and groans of the rungs, until she

was at second story window level. Gripping the sill with white knuckles, she looked down and the ground spun beneath her. Quickly she leaned her head against the wall, trying to compose herself and fight the dizziness.

When the spinning slowed to a gentle rotation, she gingerly lifted up her head and moved far enough back from the wall to position the crowbar under the first board. It looked old and rotted, and sure enough, it yielded easily to her prying. So easily in fact that it popped off and slammed into her arm before it fell to the ground, hitting the ladder with a resounding thud on its way down. The ladder moved with the impact and Samantha let out a yelp as she scrabbled for the windowsill, trying to steady herself.

"You okay up there?" The deep voice that rose from the foot of the ladder made her jump again. She gripped the sill even more tightly as she slowly turned her head and looked down.

There was a cowboy hat about ten feet below her. A cowboy hat set on broad shoulders. Jack Baron. Why had he decided to pay a neighborly visit now? "I'm fine, thanks," she called down, trying to sound like she climbed huge ladders on a daily basis. "I was just wondering when you'd show up and startle me, *again!*"

Jack was looking up at her and she saw those slate-blue eyes, lit by mischief, glittering with

humor. His lips were curled into a lazy smile that
flashed a dimple onto a cheek with a day or so of
stubble on it. "Startled you, huh? I was afraid for
a moment there that I was going to have to catch
you!"

"No catching necessary." She knew she sounded
annoyed, but her heart was still racing, whether
from nearly toppling over or from his sudden arrival, she couldn't be sure. "Can I help you with
something?"

"Well, it looks like I might be able to help you
with something, Frisco. Why don't you come on
down here and let me take a turn with that crowbar?"

She didn't want to acknowledge the relief Jack's
suggestion sparked in her. Especially when he was
obviously assuming that she was incapable of a
simple task like this. "That's okay. I've got it!" she
called down to him, forcing her mouth into what
she hoped was an easy smile. She turned a little
more to see him better, suddenly aware of the awkward nature of her position on the ladder, and the
view of her that, by the expression on his face, he
appeared to be enjoying.

"Well then, I'll just stay here and hold this ladder for you. You don't look too steady up there."
His voice was like amber, warm and spiced and
traced with laughter.

"Jack, I don't need help. Thank you for coming

by and offering, but I'm sure you have work that I'm keeping you from."

She thought she'd dismissed him but he just stood there, then let go of the ladder and strolled to the fence a few yards away. "Well, why don't I just stay here a few minutes, until you get the hang of it?"

"Oh no, please, you don't have to."

He said nothing, just hoisted himself up on the top bar of the fence and sat there.

"You're not leaving, are you?" she asked in disbelief.

"Not at the moment." He smiled at her pleasantly.

"Fine, suit yourself." Knowing she sounded a bit like a peeved child, she turned toward the ladder. Well, he was still as gorgeous as yesterday, but he was evidently a bit of a chauvinist. She didn't appreciate all his worry. She thought of her work in San Francisco. People there knew that she could handle pretty much anything the world threw at her, including some rickety old ladder. But, if he had nothing to do today but watch her pry boards off her windows, that wasn't her problem. She turned toward the wall again, and wedged the crowbar underneath the next board, pulling with what she hoped was a professional flourish.

JACK LEANED BACK against the split-rail fence, enjoying the shade of the pine trees and the view of the ladder where Samantha was perched. He'd told himself he was just coming by to be neighborly, but looking up at her determined form on that ladder, he knew he'd wanted to see her again. Something in him refused to leave her alone, even if that's what she'd prefer.

Plus, he figured a view like this was the best argument he could think of for helping one's neighbor. From his vantage point he could see a mile of slim legs ending in tempting curves covered in low-cut jeans. As Samantha reached out with the crowbar, her T-shirt lifted, exposing the pale smooth skin at her waist. Her black hair wasn't straight like it had been yesterday. It was piled in a messy knot of curls at her neck and he already knew he'd love to see it down, tangled around her striking face.

He hadn't meant to make her angry with his offer of help, but he was kind of glad he'd pissed her off. Her eyes had gone from that rich green to a sharp emerald in an instant—the transformation was fascinating.

As Samantha wrenched another board off, a stab of admiration hit him in the gut. She was clinging to that ladder with the determination of terrier, though she obviously didn't like it up there. Samantha wedged the crowbar under the next board, along the rim of the window, and leaned over to get better leverage. The board wouldn't budge and she leaned just a little farther.

He saw it coming but he was just a split second too late. She threw her weight into the crowbar and the ladder shifted suddenly, throwing her off balance. There was a brief, awful moment where everything—Samantha, the ladder and the crowbar—seemed to be suspended in space, and then all three came down with remarkable speed.

It felt like an action film, but unfortunately he was in it. He dodged the ladder as it slammed into the fence next to him and sprinted for Samantha as she hit the grass at the foot of the wall with a sickening thud. It occurred to him as he ran that he hadn't heard her scream. Then all thoughts were banished as he reached her inert form and frantically tried to remember all of the first aid he'd ever been taught.

She was on her side, facing him. He knelt and felt her breath on his cheek in a flood of relief. Her eyelids fluttered. "Samantha!" he called, checking her over for blood. None. Her limbs didn't look twisted, but who knew how this had affected her back or neck. "Samantha!" Damn. He didn't know her. What if she had some kind of medical condition? He reached into his pocket for his cell phone.

"Wait." Her voice was like a whisper and he couldn't remember when he'd been so glad to hear a sound. "I'm okay." She was staring up at him, looking a little startled.

"Stay still," he ordered. "Don't move. You've had a bad fall."

"No, really…" She started to push herself up.

"Samantha, stay still!" he barked, ferocious now with worry. "You don't know what could be wrong with you. I'm calling 911!"

SAMANTHA LAY ON the ground watching Jack fumble with his phone. As far as she could tell, all of her arms and legs were intact, and her breath was starting to come back to her. Embarrassment flooded her as she realized what had happened. She'd pretended to be so capable and confident in front of him, and then had fallen right off the ladder.

Another thought occurred to her. If he called 911, the whole town would know that she'd made a fool out of herself on her first day at the ranch. She wasn't sure why that mattered so much but it did. She was dizzy and her head was pounding but she tried to sit up, ignoring the sharp pain that sizzled in her ankle, and reached for the phone. "Please, don't call an ambulance. I'm fine. I just need a few moments."

It took a minute to convince him that she wasn't about to expire, but he finally put the phone away, checked her pupils, which were, apparently, still the same size, and let her try to stand. She leaned heavily on his arm as they walked around to the front of the house, grateful for his strength. His mouth was a grim line as he sat her firmly on the porch steps.

"Let's get a doctor out here, at least," he said, sitting down next to her.

"I don't need a doctor."

He paused, his brow creased in a frown, and he gave her a long look. Suddenly the frown passed and she knew she'd won. "Fine. No doctor then, if that's the way you want it. But let me get some ice…and do you have a first aid kit around here? It looks like you got a couple of cuts."

She looked at him, puzzled, and he pointed. "On your arm, there."

Samantha twisted her arm around and looked down, seeing the scraped elbow and the gash on her upper arm for the first time. A small trickle of blood was making its way toward her wrist.

She directed him to the car for the first aid kit, and the freezer for ice. He came back and reached for her arm but she pulled away. "I can take care of it."

He caught her chin in his hand, just for a moment, and turned her head to face him. A slight smile tilted his mouth but his eyes were serious, looking intensely into hers. "No 911, no doctor, and now you won't let me help. Looks like you're used to looking after yourself, Samantha. That's great. But out here we like to help out our neighbors. So let me help you. Okay?"

A blue lake on a sunny day. That's all she could think of as she looked into his eyes. A lake you could drown in if you weren't careful. Her brain couldn't form a complete sentence so she mumbled "Okay" and sat quietly while he put a bag of ice on her ankle and opened the first aid kit.

Jack tilted back the lid and let out a laugh as he eyed the contents of the box. "Samantha, you are one of a kind!" He continued to chuckle, obviously amused by something.

She hated to take the bait but she had to know. "What? What's so funny?"

"Your first aid kit! I've never seen anything like it."

She looked over at the neat stacks of Band-Aids, the miniature scissors, the bottles of disinfectant and rolls of bandages. "Don't you have a first aid kit?" she asked, bewildered.

"Yes, but not one that looks like this!" The chuckles subsided a bit. "I'm pretty sure the contents are alphabetized. Are you always so organized?"

Samantha felt herself blushing for what seemed like the millionth time since they'd met yesterday. "Yes, I suppose you could say that." She ignored his teasing grin. "I like to keep things in order."

"I'll bet you do." He was suddenly more serious. "You like to keep things under control." His big hands dwarfed the cotton ball as he covered it with disinfectant, but his touch was gentle as he lifted her arm and stroked the soft, cool liquid over her cuts.

Samantha tried to focus on the conversation instead of the strength of his fingers on her skin. "I guess I do keep things under control," she admitted. "It's actually an important part of my job."

Jack ripped open a bandage. "So, is coming down here and cleaning up this old house on your own a part of getting things under control?"

She winced as the truth of his words hit her. How did a complete stranger know things about her that she hadn't even realized herself? She'd had no control over what had happened in her life lately. She hadn't wanted to lose Ruth, but it had happened anyway. Her parents were off on another continent again and she'd certainly never been able to do anything to make them stay. Even Mark seemed to be disappearing from their relationship lately. And now she owned an enormous ranch that she didn't know the first thing about running. Maybe cleaning it up was her way of imposing order on the chaos of all this change.

Samantha closed her eyes, wanting Jack to keep touching her arm, even if he was just sticking gauze on with some white tape.

Jack tucked the supplies neatly back into her kit and got up to stow it back in the trunk of her car.

The air felt cold on her skin after the warmth of his hands.

"Nice wheels." He grinned as he turned back toward her, patting the BMW roadster appreciatively.

"Thanks!" she answered brightly, grateful that he wasn't going to analyze her personality any further. Cars were a much safer topic.

He came back to the porch and sat down beside her, looking at her with genuine concern. "How's the ankle? Are you able to walk?" His hand came up and brushed back the hair that had come loose from her bun and fallen across her face. He gently tucked it behind her ear, and she froze, caught in the fire of his gaze. She'd swear heat was rippling down her neck from the spot he'd just touched, warming her.

She couldn't breathe. She couldn't think. She could only stare into those blue depths and wait. A breeze gently lifted the sandy blond hair that tumbled down his forehead. Jack's jaw was strong, firm, a little square and definitely stubborn. He leaned closer to her. His fingers wove further into her hair, his strong hand pulling her gently toward him. Samantha felt her mouth part just a little to accommodate her quickening breath. Her lips felt unbearably tender, as if anticipating his touch. The wanting she saw in his eyes intensified and wrapped around her. She leaned slightly in and froze as the shrill tones of her cell phone sang out

Beethoven from somewhere underneath her, jolting her back to reality.

Jack stopped and unfurled his hand from her hair, tilting his head inquiringly in the direction of her rear end. "Expecting any important calls?"

If she spent any more time with this man she would burn up, either from desire or nerves, she wasn't sure which. "Well, at least my phone survived the fall. Excuse me for a moment." She grabbed the cell phone she'd wedged in her back pocket this morning and answered it. "Samantha Rylant." She kept her voice casual, as if she hadn't been about to kiss a man who was essentially a complete stranger. Unfortunately the voice on the other end of the phone was Mark's.

"Mark, how are you?" she asked. There was a strange, squeaky note to her voice.

She looked over at Jack and instinctively got up and walked to the far end of the porch, as if the distance might erase whatever had almost happened just now.

Rather than apologizing for not returning her calls, Mark was complaining. He needed her at work. He was busy and wanted help. Finally, Samantha could stand it no longer and interrupted him.

"Mark, I know you need me, and I've been working remotely as much as possible. But you've got to understand. My grandmother died, and then she left me a ranch! I had to come see it for myself."

She glanced at Jack, who was writing something on the notepad she kept in her car. He set it on the porch, gave her a quick wave and walked to the trail that connected the front yard of the old house with his property. She watched him go as he started up the hill—her annoyance with Mark inexplicably growing with every step Jack took.

Samantha turned away and tried to focus only on Mark. He wanted her to come home and work and she wanted him to be a more supportive boyfriend. It was very clear that they were not going to see eye to eye today.

"Mark, I'm sorry, but I have to go. I'll be there on Monday and I'll see you then." She tried to ignore Mark's sullen reply as she disengaged herself from the conversation and ended the call. Why was he being so pushy? Didn't he, of all people, understand why she needed some time off right now? He was her boyfriend. He should want her to do what she needed to do. He should want her to feel better.

Speaking of feeling things, what had just happened on the porch with her neighbor? She'd practically kissed him, and probably would have if Mark hadn't called. The thought knocked the wind out of her and she sat back down on the steps, putting the ice back on her sore ankle. She leaned over, pressing her head to her knees with a groan of self-disgust.

Mark might have been a little flaky lately, and not the most supportive today, but he was a sweet guy overall and a good boyfriend. He deserved her respect and her loyalty. Not this.

She took a deep, calming breath and raised her head, idly looking out over the front yard, the pasture and down the driveway toward the valley below. She'd just gotten sucked in, that's all. Sucked into blue eyes and a macho manner that was different than what she was used to. Simple as that.

Except it *wasn't* really so simple. She wasn't sure she'd be able to forget the way his hand had felt on her arm, and the gentle way he'd tangled his fingers in her hair. All his movements had exuded strength, yet were controlled to create the softest touch. Just thinking about it made her blood feel hot and uncomfortable in her veins.

Pushing herself up on her feet, she caught sight of her notepad, leaning against the wall of the house. The printing was elegant but strong, with bold black lines and capital letters. Not what she'd expect from a horse rancher, or horse farmer, or whatever you called a man who lived out in the middle of nowhere on a ranch with a bunch of horses. She scanned the page, hearing the humor in the tone of the note.

Frisco,

It seems that the city has caught up with the city girl. I didn't want to intrude. I'll come by tomorrow afternoon to pull down the rest of the boards. Stay off the ladder until then!

Jack Baron

So on top of being unbelievably sexy, he was nice. Great. That didn't make it any easier to ignore what she'd just felt with him. Samantha looked out over the driveway to the shrubs and weeds of her front pasture and sighed. She hated to admit it, but she really didn't want to get up on that ladder again. Jack was right. She was a city girl, and being a city girl meant she wasn't stupid enough to fall off the same ladder twice. She'd finish the rest of the ground floor windows herself and then she'd accept his neighborly help for the high ones. And she'd admire his handiwork from afar because obviously it was hazardous for her to get too close to him.

You're here to clean up, she reminded herself, *not to make a mess.* And what she'd just felt for Jack was very, very messy.

What she needed were goals to keep her mind off the cowboy next door. Clean up. Get this place organized. Those were her goals, and the sooner she got to work on them, the sooner she could head back to her real life in San Francisco. Her real job. Her real boyfriend. Her real home, conveniently and ideally located far, far away from Jack Baron.

CHAPTER FOUR

THE PROBLEM WITH sticking to her goals on the ranch was the ranch itself. It was Sunday morning and Samantha had so much to do before driving home. But the freedom of the surrounding pastures, the grandeur of the sheer peaks pushing up behind them, the bright light and warmth of the fall sunshine, all pulled her away from her tasks.

Almost every window she cleaned provided a view that begged to be admired, and the time lost slowed down her progress considerably. Eventually it was just too hard to stay indoors at all and Samantha abandoned her bucket and mop in the upstairs hallway and headed out the back door.

She'd forgotten the beauty. She'd forgotten the way the air seemed to clean her lungs of all the city grit and lift the stress right off her shoulders. She'd forgotten how it felt to come around the corner of a narrow mountain path and catch sight of a lizard sunning on a granite boulder. And the way her mouth lifted into a smile before she'd even realized the lizard was there, in that fleeting moment between when she saw it and when it skittered away.

She followed the sound of the creek. The mountains were veined with streams that tumbled down the steep slopes and spattered over boulders, making their way down to the Owens River in the valley that ran along the foot of the range. Some were famous trout streams that brought fishermen to the area all summer long. And others, like this one, were just little no-name creeks, not much visited and more beautiful because of it.

When she'd stayed on the ranch during summers, she'd taken this path almost every day. Grandma Ruth would put a battered basket in her hand, heavy with a book, a water bottle and a snack. Those snacks were always delicious. Chocolate chip cookies, apple pie, homemade bread and butter; her grandmother had spoiled her only grandchild during those special summer months.

Samantha tried to remember the last time she'd spent a summer here. It had been just after her freshman year in college, and she'd stayed only a few weeks. Then she'd returned to campus to intern for a professor, pushing herself to reach the solid, stable life she'd so craved. And every summer after that she'd worked and interned and her visits to the ranch had dwindled down to the occasional weekend, and then to nothing.

But her sacrifice paid off. Right after college she'd been hired at the advertising firm, and by carefully saving she'd bought her apartment a few years later. After the many countries and cities and schools of her nomadic childhood, it had been such a relief to finally have a home of her own.

The splash of the creek was getting louder, and around the next corner she came to the small waterfall she'd loved as a girl. Looking at it now, with a grown woman's eyes, it barely qualified as a waterfall, just a spot where the creek took a leap down a few large rocks and formed a small clear pool at the bottom. But when she was young it had been a wonderland where fairies hid and boats made from leaves and sticks crashed down torrents of water on grand adventures. The air felt cooler here, making it a tiny oasis where a few summer wildflowers still bloomed, peeking between the rocks alongside the creek, vying for the precious water.

Her bruised ankle was starting to throb again. It probably didn't help that Samantha hadn't been able to face her ugly work boots this morning. Without them she'd had only the two pairs of shoes she'd packed for Ruth's funeral to choose from. Since her stiletto boots were still recovering from the cowpie incident, she'd gone with her slightly lower, classic pumps, which clearly weren't meant for hiking in the mountains. Luckily she'd had lots of practice walking on the steep sidewalks of San Francisco.

The flat rock she'd loved to picnic on as a child was still there, so she picked her way toward it, kicked off her shoes and sat down, easing her feet into the water. It was ice cold and made her gasp, but she welcomed the numbness that sucked away the heat of the morning and eased her ankle.

She shook her head as she remembered her mortifying tumble off the ladder in front of Jack Baron. She'd met the man less than forty-eight hours ago and had managed to fill that time with more embarrassing moments than she'd had in years.

To make matters worse, all the ridiculous things she'd done had made him smile, and that smile, and the way his eyes lit with humor, were haunting her. Between the memories of that smile and all her embarrassments, it was hard to think of much else. Samantha wasn't used to being distracted and it was an uncomfortable, itchy sort of feeling. Hopefully this walk would help clear her head.

So far, it wasn't working.

Reminding herself that she'd come out here to enjoy the scenery, not think about her neighbor, she turned her mind to the landscape around her. Across the creek, a few pine trees clung to the rocky edges of the waterway, and beyond them was pasture. Or, it used to be pasture. Her grandfather had used this area for fall grazing if she remembered correctly. Now the grass was knee-high and making its way up between all kinds of shrubs and the occasional pine seedling. The mountains were taking back the fields. While it was definitely sad, there was also a feral beauty to it that she admired.

Samantha closed her eyes, listening to the water tumble, letting it numb her sore ankle, and couldn't remember the last time she'd just sat like this, doing nothing but relaxing and enjoying.

Maybe that was the problem between her and Mark right now. With the new clients they'd been pursuing, their relationship had become nothing but work. When she got back to San Francisco tomorrow she would suggest a vacation. Somewhere warm, tropical, romantic and just the two of them. They'd never taken a long trip before and it was time. In fact, maybe this explained all her thoughts about Jack Baron. She hadn't had fun with Mark in a long time, it was no wonder she kept thinking about the cowboy next door.

It was getting close to noon and growing hotter. She looked up at the sky, hoping to see some clouds, some glimmer of a thunderstorm to roll through and cool the afternoon off, but the blazing blue above her held no sign of rain. Sweat ran down her neck and mixed with the dirt of cleaning and the dust of the walk up here, and suddenly she couldn't stand it anymore.

Samantha rolled her jeans up as high as they could go and put her legs into the water up to her knees. It felt amazing, so she yanked off her T-shirt and set it aside. Standing on the gravel floor of the small pool, she cupped her hand to pour the icy water down her back and onto her neck. She splashed a little more on her chest, relishing the way the sweat disappeared and left her skin cool and clean. Inspiration struck and she sloshed carefully through the pool to the tiny waterfall.

If there'd been room to put her entire head under, she probably would've. She settled for scooping handfuls of water over her hair and rubbing it into her scalp. It was better than ice cream, better than a mojito, better than anything she normally craved on a hot day. It was like being a kid again and even her heart felt cooler, less anguished from Ruth's death. The unexpected feeling made her laugh out loud.

"That good, huh?" His voice came from the bank behind her.

Samantha froze. This wasn't possible.

She took her hand out of the waterfall and used it to try to smooth down her hair before she turned around, though it wasn't much use. Her hair had gone rogue and there was no going back until she could tame it with a shower and about a half gallon of hair conditioner.

"You have the worst timing, Jack Baron," she finally said, looking reluctantly over her shoulder at him. He was dressed for work in his jeans, boots and hat. His only nod to the heat was the old Rolling Stones T-shirt he'd put on, instead of his usual faded plaid. He was holding a rope and Samantha looked back to see a horse behind him, looking at her with its ears forward, curiosity evident in its keen glance. Even his horses knew how to make her feel ridiculous. "Hand me my top, please?" she asked.

Jack tied the horse's rope to a sturdy branch of one of the pine trees and picked his way easily over the rocks to the other side of the creek where her shirt was. She noticed he carried an old leather bag over his shoulder. Samantha just stood there. Maybe if she didn't look at *him,* he couldn't see *her.*

"Here you go." He tossed the shirt her way and she glanced back to catch it, catching sight of the grin on his face at the same time.

She pulled the top over her head and turned toward the flat rock, hoping fervently she'd be able to walk gracefully across the treacherous rocks and pebbles lurking underwater. "What are you doing here?" she asked him, trying to sound casual, as if he hadn't just found her half dressed, splashing in a creek. She sat down on the sun-warmed granite and tried to rearrange her hair again, though she doubted there was much hope for it.

"I lost Gideon." He motioned to the horse. "Figured he'd come down this way. He has before."

"Do you often lose your horses?"

Jack smiled and glanced at the bay gelding, who was trying to bite a clump of grass at the foot of the tree. "Just this one. He's an escape artist. I turned my back on him for a moment and he got the latch on the arena gate open."

"He probably sees all this long grass down here and can't resist grabbing a snack."

"He's stubborn as a mule, but he's a beauty." Jack crossed back over the creek and loosened the rope so the horse could actually reach the coveted grass. He gave him a pat on the neck and came back toward her, watching her with that half smile…and those deep blue eyes.

"So I gotta say it's not every day I see a beautiful, half-dressed woman at my favorite lunch spot."

Samantha wondered if Jack might simply attribute her bright red face to sunburn. It was blazing-hot out, after all. "Well if I'd known it was going to get crowded I'd have made a reservation."

Jack laughed. "Hey, don't get me wrong, I'm not complaining." He winked and sat down on the rock next to her. Reaching into his decrepit old bag he pulled out a sandwich and held it out to her. "Hungry?"

"No, thanks. I'd better get going actually."

"I don't mind your company." His eyes were serious for a moment and then the usual humor was back. "Though you might want to consider keeping your clothes on."

Samantha couldn't help it. It was impossible to maintain her casual demeanor. "Enough!" Her voice was pained. "Ever since I got here two days ago I've done one stupid thing after another, all in front of you! It's all been incredibly embarrassing and I just don't get it. This isn't me! I am *not* like this!" She gestured at the creek in front of them.

"You mean you don't usually want to cool off on a hot day? I wouldn't call it embarrassing, Samantha, I'd call it human. If it hadn't taken me so long to find old Gideon there, you'd have probably come across me in this creek. And there'd have been a lot more clothing than just a T-shirt sitting on that rock!"

Samantha stared at him, trying to absorb the image of a stark-naked Jack Baron splashing in the creek. It was an unsettling picture and she tried to banish her visions of lean muscle and golden skin and all the other bits she might have seen. She came back to the present and saw him grinning at her with an enjoyment that told her he knew exactly where her thoughts had been.

His eyes were lit with a mischief and she wanted to stay and look at them longer, but that wasn't a good thing so she decided to go. "Well, I'm going to take my red-faced self back to the house and get some work done before I leave today." She reached for her pumps and started to pull them on.

Jack took one look at her footwear and his grin faded. "Are you trying to sprain your other ankle? Where are your work boots?"

She glared at him. "They're ugly. I couldn't face them this morning."

Jack's expression was half amusement and half

disbelief. "They're work boots, Samantha! They're not supposed to be cute, they're supposed to protect you!"

"My feet are fine." He looked so horrified that she grinned, succumbing to the temptation to tease him. "In fact, these shoes are incredibly useful. If I meet a bear I can just smack it across the head with one of the heels. They're Italian. Well made. Dangerous."

Jack burst out laughing. "That's quite an image. I don't know whether to pity that bear or envy him!"

The naughty reference sunk in and she laughed sharply, surprised at his wicked humor. What was it about him that made her want to dish it right back? "Somehow we always end up talking about my shoes, Jack. I'm starting to wonder about you."

"Wonder away." Jack pulled off his hat and ran a hand through his hair, which the sunlight spun into dark gold. He gave an exaggerated wink. "I'm just glad to know I have a place in your fantasies."

"I'm not sure that's what I'd call them. Concerns, maybe?"

His laugh rang out over the sound of the creek and the little horse, who'd been happily munching by the pine tree, looked up at the sound. Samantha watched him watch Jack for a moment, and then go back to his grass clump. When she looked away, Jack was regarding her intently, the last fragment of his smile still curling his lip. His eyes were serious in contrast.

"You're something else, Frisco."

"Probably." She couldn't move. She'd grown roots, and her body was heavy. All she wanted was to stay there, lost in that look that held her so firmly. Sitting next to him on the rock she was inches away from the bronzed skin of his arm, from the biceps that rose below the sleeve of his shirt, and she could see the way his hair trailed over his collar at the back. He smelled like salt and horse and something else…something comforting.

It had that same feeling from yesterday, on the porch. Liquid heat, as if her muscles had gone soft with wanting him. She was glad she was sitting down. The image of herself collapsing into a puddle on this rock was enough to pull her out of her trance. The last thing she wanted was another embarrassing moment. Or to kiss her neighbor. It was past time to put some distance between her and Jack Baron.

"Well, Cowboy, this has all been very informative but I'd better get back and let you eat your lunch in peace."

"I'm feeling pretty peaceful right now." His eyes darkened, the way she'd noticed they did when he grew serious.

"I need to go." Samantha stood up. She wanted

to turn away from him and run. She wasn't comfortable with the way those eyes made her feel.

"I'll be down to finish the upstairs windows this afternoon." His voice was casual again, the moment of intensity gone so quickly it was easy to pretend it hadn't existed.

"Oh yes, about that," Samantha said. "I have a lot of work to do this afternoon. Would you understand if I didn't come out to help?"

He met her request with his usual wry smile. "No offence, Friso, but after yesterday I was thinking I might be a little safer doing the job on my own anyway."

Relief shifted through her. And just a fleck of disappointment, which she quickly squelched. "I guess I can see why you might feel that way. It seems that prying off boards isn't one of my innate talents."

"Well, I'm sure you have many others," Jack assured her.

"So I've been told." She laughed, glad to have the buffer of humor back between them. "I'll see you later then."

Samantha turned and picked her way down the path toward the house. As she got to the turn in the trail where the lizard had been, she turned to look back. Jack had just finished pulling his shirt off and when he spotted her looking he gave her an enthusiastic wave. Then he splashed into the pool and let out a wild whoop which wafted across the quiet stillness of the hot hillside. Suddenly she wanted, fiercely, to go back there and be with him—to be close to all that light and humor.

Shaking her head at her own inexplicable thoughts, Samantha turned back to the task of picking her way across the rocky ground in heels without breaking her ankle. It was time to get to work. She had hours of cleaning ahead of her, and her email inbox was full enough to cause panic whenever she glanced at it. In the morning she'd pack up early and head back to San Francisco. Six hours of driving and the bustle of the big city should be enough to wipe out this wild and impractical desire to splash in a mountain stream with an undressed Jack Baron.

IT WAS STILL hot. Hotter, actually, thanks to the afternoon sun reflecting back at him from the clapboard siding of the old house. The refreshing chill he'd felt after his visit to the creek earlier was a distant memory. Sweat rolled down his back in rivulets. Jack wiped what felt like steam out of his eyes and cursed the misguided sense of chivalry that had gotten him here, balanced on this shaky ladder alongside the old Rylant farmhouse.

Hoisting the crowbar up, he wrenched a board off the window and was rewarded with yet another shower of wood dust and paint chips. The board hurtled to the ground and landed with a thud amongst its fellow discards. Only one more window to go and then he was heading straight to the shower and the iciest beer his fridge had to offer.

Jack climbed down to move the ladder over and caught a glimpse of Samantha through the dining room window. She was at the old mahogany table, a laptop in front of her, papers scattered all around, and she was talking on the phone. She ran a hand through her tousled curls and tapped her pen impatiently while she listened to the person on the other end of the line.

She looked amazing and completely out of his league. Dark-framed cat's-eye glasses, perfect for a 1950s librarian, rested on the bridge of her nose. He hadn't known that he'd had librarian fantasies before, but he was pretty sure he'd just developed some.

Realizing that his current position bordered on stalking, Jack quickly got off the ladder. Grabbing the sides, he walked it carefully over to the next window and tipped it back against the wall, steadying the legs as best he could on the uneven ground. He climbed up with his crowbar, thankful this was the last round in his fight with Samantha's windows.

As he pried, his thoughts returned to his new neighbor. More specifically, his new neighbor in a lacy black bra, with her hair tumbled and wild, playing in his creek pool…. Well, her creek pool, technically, but in all these years of renting land from Ruth, he'd never seen anyone else there. He'd come to think of it as his. But hell, if she was going to show up there and take a swim in her Skivvies, he was happy to share.

He still couldn't believe he'd almost kissed her on her porch yesterday. And given a few more minutes by the creek he'd have figured out a way to kiss her there. Which would be completely stupid for a long list of reasons. But why such a strong reaction to her? It was frustrating that the first real attraction he'd felt for someone in years happened to be for a woman whose life was firmly entrenched in a city about six hours away.

But damn she was pretty…well, more than pretty. It was all her contradictions that had him so intrigued. With so much spirit in her green eyes and her dark, curly hair cloaking her pale, delicate face, she looked like some kind of otherworldly fairy queen. But as soon as she started talking it was obvious she lived very much in the real world: intelligent, tough and driven.

She had such a cool, controlled demeanor most of the time, but he'd seen that she could laugh at herself, and he liked that a lot. She was tough as nails in there working at the dining room table, or throwing his teasing right back at him, but he'd seen her face at the pool today as she'd watched Gideon. Her expression had been all gentleness and warmth. The controlled, collected woman she appeared to be at first glance was capable of melting, and that thought was making him crazy. He wanted to see what would happen if she truly started to thaw.

The last board was the messiest of all and had him picking splinters out of his eyes. With a choice epithet he tossed the offending board to the grass and climbed down the ladder with a sense of relief and a promise to himself to be more careful about what he volunteered for in the future. Even if the beneficiary of his altruism was the most beautiful and intriguing woman he'd ever met.

Well, none of it really mattered anyway. She wasn't going to be hanging around the ranch much, he was sure of that, and *he* didn't have a lot of free time to spend in San Francisco. So he'd just have to find a way to get all these thoughts of her out of his head. Lucky for him he had a new project starting tomorrow, and it was going to be an interesting one to put it mildly.

Jack usually worked with quarter horses, helping them learn everything from trotting to winning trophies. But a few weeks ago he'd started talking with a guy at the local bar. Over a beer, Todd had told him about the plight of the wild horses that had been living out in the high deserts for generations. Jack had never paid much attention to that particular cause, just because there weren't any herds close by, but Todd had.

The herds were overpopulated so every few years a roundup took place and many horses were caught, and if new homes weren't found for them, they were destroyed. Todd had finally broken down and adopted a handful of them. Now he had a bunch of wild horses in his paddock and no idea what to do with them. Which is where Jack came in. Though he didn't know much about wild horses, either, he figured they were just the wild and crazy relatives of the horses he usually worked with. And he hoped that with enough patience, he'd be able to settle them down.

And now it turned out that Todd's timing was perfect. Taming mustangs, on top of his usual commitments, wouldn't leave much time for thoughts of Samantha Rylant.

He walked around the front of the house to return the crowbar. Just as he rounded the corner, Samantha shouldered through her front door, her arms laden with various bags. She didn't see him, just clicked efficiently across the front porch and down the stairs, moving so lightly in the same heels she'd been out hiking in earlier. The memory of that made him grin, and forget his plan to forget her. She threw her belongings into the trunk and turned to go back to the house. That's when she saw him standing there like a tongue-tied yokel trying to approach a princess.

Her face lit up in a wide smile. "Jack, I was just going to look for you! I wanted to thank you for taking the boards off the windows."

"No problem." She was all business now. In fact she vibrated with an impatient energy that made it hard to even connect her with the woman at the creek, or the woman on the porch yesterday.

He walked toward her and saw her expression change. A hint of laughter twitched at the corner of her perfectly lipsticked mouth, lit her green eyes with a golden light. There—that was the woman he'd been getting to know. "Okay, Samantha, what's funny now?"

"It's… I mean…I think you might have gotten a bit dirty. Would you like to come in and wash up?"

"It's okay, thanks," he answered. "I'm used to dirt." And that was a perfect example of why he and Samantha would never work. She couldn't handle a guy with a little dirt on him, and he spent most days being dirty.

Her mouth twitched a little more. "Well, okay, but…hang on." She went back to the car and rummaged in one of her bags, bringing out a small mirror. "Here," she said, handing it to him.

He peeked into the tiny mirror and instantly knew why she'd been laughing. His face was filthy. Layers of dirt, small wood chips, old paint, probably toxic with lead, had made a mask over his features. Glued there by sweat no doubt. His hair was gray with dust and there was a cobweb across one eyebrow. He grimaced. So much for making a good impression on his beautiful neighbor. He handed the mirror back. "Maybe I'll take you up on your offer, after all."

She opened the front door of the house and he was amazed to see how spotless it was. Everything gleamed and the room smelled fresh, like herbs. No way was he going to track a bunch of dirt across this pristine living room. "You don't mess around, Samantha. How'd you get this place cleaned up so fast?"

"I don't know…I just couldn't stand the dirt, I guess. The upstairs is still a mess. Something came up last minute for work today and I couldn't spend any more time cleaning."

"I can't come through here like this. I'll meet you round back and wash up in the kitchen."

She didn't protest so he walked back around the house and up the rickety steps to the back porch. Part of him just wanted to take off running up the hill toward home, now that he'd seen how filthy he was. But he wasn't a coward, and just because she was dressed to the nines and seemed to have secret housecleaning superpowers, didn't mean he had to turn tail and run. Especially since he'd gotten dirty by way of helping her out.

He kicked his boots off at the back door, and when she opened it he went straight to the big, white farmhouse kitchen sink, turned on the faucet and put his head under. The cool water felt invigorating, and he scrubbed the layers of sweat off of his face and neck and the dust out of his hair. If the sink had been any bigger he would have stripped down and put his whole self in there, just to feel that cool water taking away the remnants of this too-hot day.

Samantha didn't say a word, just handed him an old rough cotton towel when he was finished. He scrubbed himself dry, looked up and caught her staring. Her lower lip was caught in her teeth and her fascinated expression was heated by the desire he could see in her eyes, which had now darkened to the green of pine trees.

Something in his stomach twisted and something lower hardened—he held the towel in front of him just in case. What the hell was wrong with him? Had he suddenly been transported back to junior high?

She suddenly seemed to realize that she'd been staring. Her porcelain cheeks flushed a deep pink and she turned away quickly.

"Can I get you something cold to drink?" she asked, reaching for a glass in the old pine cupboard above the counter.

"Something cold would be great," he managed.

Like an icy shower. She opened the fridge and pulled out a pitcher of water.

"Nothing fancy, I'm afraid. I haven't exactly stocked the cupboards."

"It's perfect," he croaked, reaching for the glass. His hand brushed hers and he couldn't help it, he held it there for just an instant, loving the way her soft skin felt against his, the warmth of her in contrast to the chilled glass. Then her hand was gone and he told himself that it was for the best if he was going to be able to walk out of there without making a complete idiot of himself. He took a long drink of the water, watching her. She had a rag and was swiping at a speck of dirt on the counter that only she could see. She didn't look at him.

"So you're packing the car up," he offered, regretting the words as soon as they were out. Talk about stating the obvious.

"Yes," she answered, and turned, her eyes cautious and veiled, making him wonder if he'd imagined the deep green wanting he'd seen moments ago.

"Heading back to San Francisco?" He wasn't earning any points as a conversationalist, that was for sure, but he wanted to be with her a few more minutes. He had no idea when he'd see her again, and he wanted to know more about this woman who'd invaded his thoughts and held them hostage ever since.

"Not home to San Francisco right away, actually. Los Angeles for a day or two first."

"You're driving to L.A. tonight?" It was almost six hours to L.A. from here and it would be dark soon. He didn't like the idea of her alone at night in the rugged country between here and Southern California.

"Yes, I know, it's a long ways. Not exactly what I had planned, but I got a call that I'm needed at a meeting there tomorrow, and it's a really good opportunity for me, so I said I'd go."

"What kind of opportunity?"

Samantha's face lit up. "Well, I've been with this advertising firm for six years, and last year I was made a vice president. But after putting in so many extra hours, and giving up so many weekends, I think I'm ready to take on more. But—" she paused for a moment, a worried look flitting across her features "—for various reasons, I haven't really felt comfortable asking my boss about it. At this meeting in L.A., I'll be working with my boss's boss, so this will be a great opportunity to show him what I can do."

"You really love your work, don't you?"

Samantha looked at him quizzically. "Well, *love* is a pretty strong word. But yes, I like it. It's what I do."

He studied her, standing in the old kitchen, so strong and independent. She wasn't a big woman, in fact her frame was slight and graceful. He tried to imagine what might happen if she had a blow-out or engine trouble and was stuck on her own on a pitch-black road in the middle of nowhere. The thought made him queasy. "Samantha, I get that you want this promotion, but is it absolutely necessary to drive six hours in the middle of the night?"

Annoyance flashed across her face. "I'm perfectly capable of driving after dark. That's not a skill specific to men, Jack."

"Look…I'm not questioning your abilities. Just drive safely. It's a rough road and there're not a lot of towns along the way. Just make sure you fill your tank when you get to Bishop."

"Thanks for the tip. Now, the sooner I get on the road the less dark I'll be driving in." She'd softened a little, but not much. Questioning this trip had been the wrong move. She was way too independent to listen to some guy she'd just met telling her to be careful. But he knew he'd be up all night thinking about her anyway, and he'd prefer it if that thinking didn't include worrying if she was okay or not.

She'd picked up her last few bags and was heading out to the porch. He rinsed out his glass, grabbed his boots and followed her. The car loaded, she came up onto the porch next to him to lock the front door.

"Samantha." She stopped and looked at him. In

her heels, fancy jeans and leather blazer she looked beautiful and totally out of place. Like some exotic flower that had just sprung up somehow in the old ranch yard.

"Yes?"

"Out here on these mountain roads a lot can go wrong. The roads wind through a lot of wilderness areas. They get washed out and rough sometimes. Do me a favor. Take my phone number and send me a message when you get there? So I know you made it okay?"

Her eyebrows drew together in a scowl and her chin tilted up defiantly. "Jack, obviously you've experienced some sort of trauma with a woman driver at some point in your life, and I'm sorry for that. But trust me, I'm fine! I don't need someone worrying about me like this. I've made it this far through life without it. And I, for one, have great confidence in my driving abilities!" Her eyes were flashing an amazing emerald color, which he'd appreciate more if it didn't mean she was furious with him. He stood wary, choosing silence as his best defense.

"Thank you so much for everything you've helped me with this weekend." The easy familiarity that had been between them at the creek earlier was gone. She was icily polite. "But I don't need your help with this particular task. I'll see you in a week or two." She stepped into her car and closed the door firmly behind her. With a wave, she started the engine and drove the sleek, black machine down the driveway.

Jack turned away, shaking his head in frustration. He admired her stubborn independence, but not when it had her ignoring a common-sense safety precaution like letting someone know when her long drive was over. And he was frustrated with himself. What was wrong with him? Samantha might be beautiful and funny and smart, but she clearly wasn't going to stay around here long, and he needed to stop wanting her to.

A whinny echoed faintly down the valley, reminding him that it was feeding time. Jack started up the rocky trail that separated the two ranch houses, deep in thought. Samantha was a complex woman who'd made him feel complicated things all weekend. And some of those complicated things felt a little too familiar. Like maybe history was repeating itself. What was that old saying? "Those who don't know history are doomed to repeat it"? It seemed like he had some unpleasant memories to study up on. He thought he'd learned his lesson about getting involved with a city girl a long time ago, but apparently he needed a refresher to stop him from wanting Samantha.

Jack covered the last yards of the trail with big strides and stepped with relief onto his own property. His old wooden barn, stripped of paint long ago by the harsh mountain weather, was a welcome sight. He was ready to get back to his own world. It might get kind of lonely at times, but it was far simpler and a whole lot more peaceful.

CHAPTER FIVE

MARK'S TEXT READ delayed—20 mints. Samantha smiled, despite the rising annoyance that he was keeping her waiting even longer. Life Savers? Peppermints? She thought it was kind of cute that despite being addicted to his smartphone, Mark had never really mastered texting shorthand.

She looked around the coffee shop where she'd been sipping her cappuccino and sighed. Just one more hazard in the bumpy road of dating her boss.

They always tried to leave work separately and meet up somewhere a safe distance from the office. Tonight he'd given her the thumbs-up about a half hour ago and she'd closed up the file she'd been working on, said good-night to a few colleagues who were working late, and headed nonchalantly out the door. She didn't think anyone at work suspected, which was pretty miraculous considering that she and Mark had been dating for over a year now.

As much as she cared for Mark, sometimes she wished she hadn't fallen for her boss. All the required sneaking around lost its romantic mystery after the first few months, and now it just felt like extra work sometimes.

Samantha stared out the floor-to-ceiling windows to the gray-green water of San Francisco Bay. The steel towers of the Bay Bridge rose beyond. At least they'd picked an espresso bar with an inspiring view for their rendezvous. And the cappuccino was fabulous. Organic, of course, with the "artisan, micro-roasted" beans ground just before the sleek barista made the coffee, and the milk was fresh from a farm just thirty miles north of the city. This was the Ferry Building in San Francisco after all; the old terminal had been converted to an enormous farmers market, and a mecca for politically correct diners.

She might make fun of it a bit, but she loved the space, with the sky-high ceiling, the warehouse feel and the bay visible through every window. Plus, where else could you get your caffeine with a "coffee-compatible edible," as the sign above her boasted?

Glancing again at Mark's message, she calculated the time until he got here. It took about five minutes from their office to the street below, if the elevator was its usual slow self. And it took another ten minutes to walk from there, which meant that Samantha had at least thirty-five minutes to kill. She could answer emails on her phone, but she hated the inefficiency of poking away at the microscopic keyboard when she knew she could get the same message written in a fraction of the time on her computer. Wishing she'd brought her laptop, though—she hadn't thought she'd need it on a date—she decided to go for a walk.

The damp wind hit her the moment she stepped out the door and onto the waterfront walkway. When she'd first moved to San Francisco she'd been so frustrated with the wind. The fog was always blowing in or out of the bay, and whenever she went out, she always arrived at her destination windblown and messy. After a year or two it occurred to her that this was a trademark of San Franciscans. They blew through doorways with coats pulled around them, hair flying over their faces, looking like they'd been somewhere exciting and perhaps a bit treacherous. It was part of the mystique of living there. At least this is how she consoled herself when she arrived somewhere and glanced in a mirror to find her hair standing on end and her cheeks and nose bright pink from the wind.

Wrapping her wool coat tightly around her and tucking her purse carefully under her arm, Samantha headed south toward the Bay Bridge, savoring the scenery. Treasure Island and the East Bay hills beyond hadn't yet been engulfed by the incoming fog and were lit up with the last bit of sunlight. Dodging joggers, cyclists and even a few salsa dancers with a boom box, Samantha took in the

view and tried to keep her mind in the present—
enjoying her adopted city that had come to feel
like home, and looking forward to finally spending time with Mark. But her mind wouldn't be still,
her thoughts slipping back to the weekend, to the
ranch and to the way she'd felt when she'd been
near Jack Baron.

Maybe it was his eyes, she mused. No one had a
right to eyes that blue, or that compelling. There'd
been a happiness about him, too, a contentment
that radiated, as if he was exactly where he wanted
to be in life. That was something she definitely
wasn't used to. Most people she knew were fairly
happy, but they were always reaching for something
more…a promotion, a relationship, a vacation, or
the mastery of a new hobby. Jack didn't seem to be
reaching. Just enjoying.

It occurred to her that Grandma Ruth had been
content like that, and her grandfather as well. She
suddenly remembered something Ruth had said a
few years ago, on what had turned out to be her
last visit to San Francisco. They'd been sitting in
a Union Street café near Samantha's apartment,
taking a rest from window shopping and watching the weekend crowds stroll by. Ruth had taken
Samantha's hand across the table, patting it gently.
"You've chosen a beautiful city to live in, Sammy,"
she'd told her. "But I look at these people going
by, pushing their designer baby carriages, walking

their beautiful dogs, with cups of fancy coffee in their hands, and I worry about you. All these people have so much, but no one looks very happy to me. No one ever seems satisfied here."

At the time Samantha had teased her grandmother. "Happiness is overrated, Grandma," she'd replied. "In San Francisco it goes along with a lot more, with accomplishment and with living well and doing things the right way. You can see why my perfectionist self fits in so well!" They'd laughed at the truth in that and Ruth had said no more about it.

Now it occurred to her that maybe Ruth had left her the ranch in an attempt to give her the type of happiness she'd enjoyed throughout her own life. But if the core of that happiness was contentment, then how could Samantha Rylant, vice president at Taylor Advertising, ever achieve that on a ranch in Benson? How could she possibly be satisfied living out in the middle of the mountains?

Samantha felt a stab of guilt at the realization that she wasn't going to be able to fulfill Ruth's dream for her, that she was very likely going to have to sell Ruth's beloved ranch.

But Ruth must have also understood that Samantha had a different dream, one with a different type of happiness—more ephemeral maybe, more based on career and accomplishment. With that came a little less contentment perhaps, but wasn't it a lack of contentment that drove people to keep striving and achieving more?

Her phone jangled and she grabbed at it, startled out of her thoughts.

Mark's voice sounded annoyed. "Samantha, where are you?"

Surprised, she immediately turned around and started back. "Mark! I'm so sorry. I went for a walk while I was waiting. I guess I lost track of time!" Lost track of time? That wasn't normal for her. She mentally kicked herself, *and* Jack Baron, for proving to be such a distraction, even from so many miles away. "I'm on my way back now."

"Well, it's getting really late," Mark complained. "We're going to miss the movie at this rate."

His accusing tone grated but she tried to keep her voice pleasant. "Mark, I apologize for not being there when you arrived, but I'm also not the only reason we're running behind. How about we just get dinner and we can see the film another time?"

With a sigh he agreed and hung up. Samantha shook her head. The male ego astounded her. True, she wasn't at their meeting place, but he'd kept her waiting an hour. She dialed the restaurant to change their reservation for the second time that evening and was relieved when the host said that it wasn't a problem. It was hard to even get into the popular waterfront eatery, with its divine Vietnamese-Californian cuisine.

Breathless, she pushed through the doors of the café. Mark pulled her into his side with a one-armed hug and kissed the top of her head. "Hey, Kiddo, been doing some jogging?"

Kiddo? He finally gave her a nickname and it was Kiddo? "Hi, Mark." She reached up and kissed his cheek. "It's so nice to see you in real life again."

"You mean as opposed to office life?" He led her through the double doors and back out into the street, now lit by the glow of streetlights, steering them alongside the docks to the restaurant.

"Yes. Office life doesn't count, really," she joked.

His voice was suddenly serious. "I think it counts a lot, actually."

It always took a while to warm Mark up; though once he shed his professional skin he could be quite sweet and funny. "You know what I mean," she chided him teasingly. "Of course it *counts*. But it doesn't compare to time spent like this, with just us, together."

His mouth relaxed back into a smile as he glanced down at her. "You're right, of course. Sorry about that. It's just been a challenging few days, with you gone for the funeral and then running out on me to go to some ranch. And then going to L.A., where, by the way, you made a pretty great impression on the boss. So you can see, I've had nothing but work on my mind for a while now."

"You poor guy. But I didn't run out on you, you know. I did invite you to come along."

"Well, you know, I've never much enjoyed funerals, particularly of people I've never met." He stopped them for a moment and took her gently by the shoulders, his brown eyes serious beneath his shock of light brown hair. "But I am sorry I made you go alone, Samantha. I realize it was selfish of me." He leaned down and kissed her mouth gently, his lips soft and undemanding. "Forgive me?"

It was hard to resist his apology. "Don't worry about it. It wasn't a very enjoyable event. I didn't actually stay until the end. Plus—" she lightened the moment "—someone had to stay home and pick up all the slack!"

He pulled her toward him for another lopsided hug. "And speaking of all that slack, there's still a bunch of things I need to run by you since we're gearing up for the big pitch next week."

"Now?" Samantha asked.

"Why not?"

Samantha tried to focus as he went through the talking points he was considering for tomorrow's planning meeting, but her mind kept wandering away.

Maybe it was grief over losing Ruth, but one moment she was listening to Mark's discussion of their next brainstorming session, and the next she was noticing how graceful the lines of the old shipping warehouses were. How had she never seen that before? And there was the familiar shape of Coit Tower, all lit up on top of Telegraph Hill, but tonight, wrapped in fog, its lights were blurry, almost mysterious.

Her mind wandered even further away, back to the intense look on Jack Baron's face as he'd placed the Band-Aid on her skin. The memory scorched her. The resulting guilt shook her out of her reverie. What had gotten into her? How could she be picturing him at all when she was on a date with Mark?

Luckily Mark had a lot to say, and with a few well-placed yeses and I-sees they made it to the restaurant without him noticing her distracted state. Soon they were seated at their table right by the water, just as she'd requested, and were ordering exotic cocktails from the menu the waitress placed in front of them.

Noticing the waitress glancing and smiling at Mark, Samantha mentally kicked herself. San Francisco had many wonderful attributes, but a large supply of handsome, single, career-oriented straight men was not one of them. She needed to stop thinking about some random hick cowboy she'd known for a couple of days and start appreciating the good-looking, sweet and successful boyfriend in front of her.

As they ate their meal, she asked him questions about what else had transpired in the office while she was gone, and offered to take on some extra work to ease the burden he was feeling. It would mean that if she went back to the ranch this weekend she'd have to do some work, but there wasn't much to do out there in the evenings anyway.

It wasn't until Mark paid their bill and they were picking up their coats to leave that he finally asked, "So tell me about this ranch you inherited? Did you have fun playing cowgirl over the weekend?"

Samantha started for the door. "I wouldn't exactly call it playing cowgirl. More like playing housecleaner, except unfortunately I wasn't playing."

Pushing the door open for her, Mark looked at her, surprised. "You stayed away the whole weekend so you could clean? You never really did know how to take things easy, hey, Kiddo?"

She winced again at the nickname. Kiddo? Not Beautiful? Or Sexy? Or pretty much anything else that didn't make her sound like his little sister? "Probably one of the reasons you hired me, right, boss?"

"Well, that and the fact that you're gorgeous, of course." He stopped suddenly and swept her into a hug. "Missed you!"

Samantha wrapped her arms around his broad back and returned Mark's embrace. It felt good to be with him again. Sure, maybe they talked about work too much, but she was glad to feel his strong, reliable arms around her. She turned her face up toward his expectantly, but he just planted a playful kiss on her nose then turned and continued walking, pulling her with him.

"I guess you'll need to get a real estate agent, then?" he asked. "I know some good ones. I'll email you their information."

Tension coiled through her, and Samantha sighed, leaning her head against Mark's shoulder. "I don't really want to think about it, but yes, I guess I'll need to sell it at some point."

"I guess? You're not thinking of keeping it, are you, Samantha?"

"Not forever, no. But, Mark, this has all happened pretty fast and I don't think I'm ready to let it go just yet. Not this week, anyway. I'm still wrapping my mind around the fact that she left me her ranch!"

"Look, I understand why you're feeling sentimental, Samantha, but remember, while you're getting used to the idea, the tax bills are adding up."

"I'm thinking of going there again this weekend, actually." Samantha hadn't really been sure until she said it aloud.

"What? You just got back from L.A. yesterday!"

"I know. But it's like you just said. The tax bills are adding up and if I'm going to go through Grandma's things, I should do it soon. Plus, I can't really explain it, but I feel like I need to spend a little time there before I can let it go."

"You're sounding really groovy, there, Samantha. 'Let it go'? Maybe your buddy Jenna's rubbing off on you."

Her temper flared. "Mark, if it was your childhood home, wouldn't it be hard for you to sell it? Wouldn't you need to go through it, pack things up and say goodbye?"

"You're right, Samantha. I'm sorry. It's just that this is a new side of you. I'm used to my practical, efficient Samantha, not this new conflicted one."

"Well, maybe it's a good thing I can still surprise you, right?"

"If you say so. You know me, I'm not too good with surprises. I'm too much of a planner, just like you are...er...were."

She gave his arm a smack, laughing. "Enough! I haven't changed, truly. I just have a ranch...which feels really weird to say, by the way. I'm still me, just with a bit more property."

"Well, I'll miss you this weekend, but I get why you need to go, I think."

"Come *with* me." She blushed as soon as the words were out. Why was she acting like a spineless, needy girlfriend? He'd already declined once.

He stopped, looked down and suddenly his face was clouded and troubled, and Samantha felt even worse. Now she'd made him feel obligated. The last thing she ever wanted was for someone to feel *obligated* to spend time with her.

"Mark, I know you're busy," she assured him. "Forget it."

"I wish I could go with you, Kiddo." He took her hand as they walked and gave it a squeeze. "I have a lot of work to do, especially since my star employee is disappearing into the mountains again."

"No, really, Mark, I get it. It's fine."

"And then Sunday I'm flying to New York, remember? I've got those meetings there until Tuesday night."

"That's right. I'd forgotten. No worries, I'll just go play cowgirl on my own."

"That's my girl." He leaned over and planted a kiss on the top of her head. "That's another thing I appreciate about you. You get it. You get what it's like to do my job and you don't resent the time I spend at it. In fact, you're the only person I've ever met who probably works even more than I do."

She stopped them and put her arms up around his neck. "I'm glad you appreciate all my excellent, understanding-girlfriend qualities." She stood on tiptoe and kissed his mouth, feeling his lips warm and familiar under hers. Instead of kissing her back he looked down at her with a sheepish grin.

"So, perfect girlfriend, can I ask for just a little more understanding?"

She smiled. "Don't push your luck."

He gently smoothed back her hair, looking down at her seriously. "I am really, really beat. I know we talked about me staying over tonight, but would you mind if I just went to my place? I think what I need more than anything is a good night's sleep. In my own bed."

Ouch. Samantha took a step back and fixed a smile on her face. She understood him intellectually, of course. There were nights when she was really tired and wanted to curl up alone in her bed, but she hadn't expected that from Mark. Not tonight at least, after she'd been gone for almost a week. And the previous week he'd been away at a big meeting, and the week before that he'd been really busy as well.

Karma, her guilty conscience suggested. This dry spell was the universe's retribution for lusting after her gorgeous cowboy neighbor. She shooed the thought out of her head. Maybe Mark was right. Maybe she was spending too much time with superstitious Jenna.

"Sure, I get it," she told him. She took his hand and started walking toward the cabs that often waited at the foot of Market Street. "Rain check, okay?"

He pulled her close and leaned his cheek into her hair as they walked. "Absolutely."

A thought struck her. "Mark? Since I'm the most

perfect, understanding girlfriend, can I ask you to be the most understanding boss?"

"Uh-oh," he teased. "What now? More time off?"

"A half day on Friday so I can leave at noon and beat the traffic out of town?" She gazed adoringly up at him, batting her eyelashes in a mock plea.

Mark smiled. "Don't you have to get everyone ready for the pitch next week?"

"We were ready last week. You know I'd never leave something so important until the last minute!"

"Don't we have a conference call at two? You know I'll need you on that."

"Two hours will get me through Sacramento and I can avoid the worst traffic jams. At two I can pull over and take the call from wherever I am."

"Well, I can't argue with that. Just make sure you have reception."

"Mark, I'm a big girl, remember? The one who's landed you three huge accounts in the past six months? Not to mention a bunch of smaller clients, too. Trust me, I'll make sure I have reception."

"Okay, sorry. Didn't mean to patronize. And you know I'm grateful for all those accounts." Mark stopped and pulled her close, pressing her against his torso. "As well as everything else you do for me."

"Does this mean you're changing your mind

about tonight?" she murmured as he bent down to kiss her.

"Sadly for me, no. Believe me, I want to, but it's a busy week and I need my sleep."

A cab pulled up to the curb near them. "Do you want to take that one?" he asked. Cabs were few and far between in San Francisco.

"Hang on," Samantha said and went to the car window. "Can you wait a second, please?" she asked. "Start the meter and I'll be right there." The driver nodded his head and set the meter. Samantha turned back to Mark.

"Hey, I feel bad that I'm leaving again this weekend. Do you want to get together sometime in the next couple days before I go?"

"If I have time," he answered. "Check calendars?"

They pulled out their phones in the familiar ritual, but there was no shared free time in their schedules.

"I think we should take a vacation together," Samantha said. "Let's just get away somewhere warm and relaxing where we don't have to compare calendars like this."

"Sounds great," Mark answered, with a half smile.

Samantha looked up sharply, disappointment growing. "Don't sound so enthusiastic."

"No, Kiddo...don't take it like that! I'm just tired.

A vacation would be nice. But we're both so busy right now. Maybe we can talk about it in a couple of months."

Samantha sighed. She admired Mark's work ethic, but it meant she was going to have to work harder to improve their relationship while closer to home. "You're right. We are really busy. But what about if, in the future, we schedule each other in first? Then make our other plans?"

"That's a big step in modern relationships, isn't it?" he teased her. She knew when she was being dismissed. Well, he was tired. Maybe tonight just wasn't the best night to try to make things better between them.

Mark pulled her in for a last hug and planted a quick kiss on her mouth. "Now get in that cab before I fall asleep right here. I'm tired enough, but it looks like all the doorways have already been spoken for tonight."

Glancing around, Samantha could see that he was right. The city's ubiquitous homeless had staked their claims as soon as the offices emptied of workers. Shopping carts and sleeping bags blocked entries all around them.

Samantha sighed, feeling the familiar helplessness at seeing so many people in such great need. "Ugh. So heartbreaking, isn't it?"

"Sure is. I'll see you at the office."

One last quick hug and Samantha was in the cab.

"Scott Street, near Union," she told the driver, waving one last time to Mark.

The driver sped off and Samantha sat back in the cab, watching as the passing lights unfolded the character of the city around her. The waterfront flashed by, followed by the tawdry lights of the strip clubs on Broadway. Diners still crowded the sidewalk tables of the busy Italian eateries in North Beach. Samantha caught a brief glimpse of Chinatown's dragon statues and colorful lanterns before the cab zoomed through the Broadway tunnel and came out flanked by more genteel neighborhoods.

Here was the San Francisco that tourists imagined: steep, narrow streets lined with old Victorian houses, complete with cable cars clanking through. Down the hill they passed edgy Polk Street, and then the stately buildings of Pacific Heights rose up. Samantha loved this part of town. It was a predictable oasis to come home to amidst the exotic and changeable temperament of the city she loved.

As she let herself into her apartment, she saw the candles she'd set out this morning and the bottle of wine she'd left casually on the counter. Disappointment tugged at her heart. So much for her pathetic attempts at seduction.

SUGAR WAS HIS nickname for the quarter horse mare with a mile-long pedigree and the sweetest temperament he'd encountered in all his years of working with horses. She nickered as Jack approached the stall, uneasy with being kept inside on such a fine morning. Jack set his coffee mug down on the shelf outside her door and slid the bolt, laughing as she nuzzled his pockets for a treat.

"Yep, you're onto me." He smiled as she daintily removed the carrot piece from his outstretched hand.

Jack moved to her side and ran his hand down her right front leg, picking up the foot to remove the bandage and examine the hoof. She'd stepped on something sharp up in the pasture and came in limping a few evenings ago. He'd applied a compress and was giving her a rest in the stall, and it seemed to be helping as she barely favored the leg now.

"Just a few more days of this and we'll have you as good as new." He spoke soothingly to her as he worked, applying the fresh medicine and wrapping new bandages. She nibbled at his jeans and then settled down with a sigh, giving him her weight as she relaxed. As it had in every quiet moment this week, his mind drifted to thoughts of Samantha.

No matter how many times he replayed their last few minutes together, no matter how often he reminded himself that her message to back off had been loud and clear, he still wanted to see her again. He'd tried all week to focus on the work in front of him, but just when he thought he was done thinking about her, the heat he'd felt between them on the porch, and at the creek, would come back to him. And then he'd picture her smile, the relaxed, warm one. And there it would be. That feeling that he wanted to take care of her. That he wanted to get to know her—all of her.

Disgusted with this train of thought, Jack loaded Sugar's manger with hay and left the stall. Grabbing a hay bale, he hauled it out to his truck and threw it in the back for the morning feed. He liked feeding time and today he was grateful to have something else to focus on. Sometimes it was a hassle to be tied to the ranch every day, and have to schedule everything around the needs of thirty equine stomachs. But as soon as he was in the truck, rattling out to the upper pasture, and when he saw the horses' heads come up and their ears prick forward as they jostled and pranced toward the fence line, the rewards were obvious. He was completely in the moment, his entire focus on his horses. Exactly where it should be.

All their personality quirks came through at feeding time. The timid foals hung back from the fray while June, the matriarch broodmare, bit and kicked her way up to the front of the crowd. Larry, his gentle-giant Appaloosa gelding stood aloof and dignified off to the side, knowing a special treat was likely waiting for him in Jack's pocket.

Jack tossed out the alfalfa hay in scattered

piles, making sure June got hers before she could do any actual damage to the younger ones. The horses broke into groups around the hay and Jack reached for the grain bucket and scoop and swung his leg over the rail fence. Making his way from group to group, surrounded by the noise of strong teeth munching, tails swishing and hooves stomping away flies, he delivered the mixture of oats, corn and molasses while at the same time looking over his little herd.

When the bucket was empty, Jack drew himself up to the top of the split-rail fence and watched the sun rise over the valley below and the early-morning shadows brighten into day. He could smell pine and sage and for that moment it was enough just to watch, listen and breathe in that fine dawn air.

It had been a good week. He'd learned a lot about mustangs, and had a bunch of aches and pains to prove it. There was a long way to go with them, they were wild to the core, but he welcomed the challenge and the hard work. Anything to stop him from wasting time on thoughts of Samantha Rylant.

A crunching of gravel under tires had him looking up. Walt was coming up the lane in his blue pickup. Walter knew more about horses than anyone Jack had ever met. He was sort of a legend on the rodeo circuit, where Jack had ridden his fair share. After Jack had bought the ranch, and began leasing some of Ruth's pastures, he'd gone out to find Walter, knowing he wanted him as his main hand. He'd found him drunk in a bar in South Texas. He'd hauled him out, sobered him up and paid off a few of his debts. Walter had made the bunkhouse on Jack's property his own and could be found during most of his waking hours puttering happily in the barns or helping to gentle and train the young colts.

Walt's truck slowed to a halt and he leaned out the driver's side window. "Morning!" he grunted, a cigarette stub between his teeth.

Jack went around to the driver's side window. "You better stop smoking those damned things, old man," Jack said half humorously, reaching in and grabbing it out of Walt's teeth. He threw it on the gravel and ground it out beneath his boot. "They'll shorten your life and I need your sorry ass around here."

Walt gave a wheezing cackle and cuffed him on his shoulder. "My life's been too damn long already!"

"No way, you're not getting off that easily. You still got a lot of work to do around here before you check out. You heading up to the training ring?" Jack asked.

"Yep. I had Shadow up there yesterday, trying to get him to accept that damn saddle. That colt sure don't want no one to ride him." He chuckled softly. "Almost took me out with one of his kicks, he was so pissed at me. But I thought I'd just hang out with him there for a bit this morning, no pressure, see if I can get him to trust us a bit more."

"You'll talk him into it, man. You always do."

The older man smiled at the praise. "Well, sometimes I do and sometimes I don't." He looked at Jack with a gleam in his eye and he pushed open the cab door, jumping down with a spryness that didn't reflect seventy years of hard living. He fixed Jack with an impish grin. "Now, I may be old, and my vision failing me, but I saw you sitting up on this fence, staring down the hill at the old Rylant ranch below, and I gotta ask myself, what could make you sit there like that? Especially when you have a horse to deliver this afternoon? You've got a mile-long list of stuff to do today, thanks to your spending so much time chasing after wild horses on that fool charity project for Todd."

"I wasn't staring, Walt," Jack fibbed. "Must be that failing vision you mentioned, old-timer."

Walt was indignant. "My eyesight's better than yours has ever been, and I know what I saw!"

"And you think that it's your business?" Jack asked. Walt was glaring at him like a peeved chicken and Jack couldn't keep from laughing.

Walt chuckled along with him. But Jack knew all too well that once the old man got an idea in his head he was like a mosquito—wouldn't let up until he got what he wanted. "I know what's got you sitting here, pondering. It's Ruth's granddaughter you're mooning after, isn't it?"

Jack looked at Walt, not fooled by the innocent expression on the weathered face.

"What are you getting at, Walt?"

"Nothing much. Just seems like you've been holed up here feelin' sorry for yourself for three years now, ever since Amy took off on you. Seems like it might be time for you to start living your life instead of spending it on the porch with your dogs every night, drinking beers."

Jack stared at the man in shock. "Well, I appreciate your advice, Walt. I guess. But I haven't heard you complaining when I drink beers on the porch with *you* at night."

Walt grinned. "Who's gonna complain about that? You buy good beer." He leaned against the truck and started to pull another cigarette from the pack in his pocket. Seeing Jack's face he put the smoke back in the pack and pulled his hat off. He turned it over, staring into it with a philosophical look on his face. Jack waited, amused by his friend's sudden interest in his love life.

"Look," Walt finally said, looking up. "All I'm saying is that there's no shame in a divorce. Hell, I've had a couple myself. But you can't let one filly, who was half crazy and hell-bent on causing you trouble anyway, knock you out of the saddle forever."

"Walt, what the hell are you talking about?" Jack

countered. "One minute you're talking divorce, then we're back onto horse training."

Walt looked annoyed, his glance flinty in the gathering light. He poked his hat into Jack's chest. "Look, boy. I'm the closest thing you got to family in these parts and I owe you a lot. So I'm gonna tell it to you straight. You let that divorce of yours knock you flat and you've been hiding from folks ever since. So I'm just thinking that if Ruth's granddaughter is spending time next door, and if she's as pretty as Dan down at the store told me she was, that she just might be the reason you've been so absentminded all week. And I say that's a damn good thing!" Walt spluttered to a halt and stopped, staring down at his hat again, as if he'd run out of steam.

Jack just watched his old friend, amazed by this turn of events. Usually Walt's topics of conversation were limited to horses, cattle, rodeos and saddles...in that order.

"Er, Walt...thanks for trying to look out for me." Jack thought for a moment, looking out over the hillsides to the distant desert below. Walt's words stung, which probably meant there was some truth to them. "You may be right, Walt. Maybe it's time for me to get out more." Jack clapped Walt's shoulder absentmindedly and then gave him a cuff on the upper arm. "Now get to work and stop getting all Dr. Phil on me."

"Dr. who?" Walt asked, as he opened the door and got back into his truck. He paused. "Just one more thing, boss. Have you asked about her plans for the ranch?"

He hadn't. Though he should have. He stared back down the hill in shock at his own idiocy. He'd been so drawn to her last weekend, so focused on just being near her, it hadn't really occurred to him to look too far ahead into the future.

Walt interpreted his silence as a need for more advice. "Maybe you should ask her about buying the place? It's pretty obvious she's not gonna stay, and you need that land to make this ranch work."

"Yeah, I guess you're right, Walt." He looked at his old friend, thinking hard. "But it seems a little awkward right now, with her grandmother just laid to rest and her trying to get things sorted out here."

"Well, I'm not trying to tell you how to run your business, but it seems like you don't want to wait too long. You need that land too much to miss out. I saw her out on her porch as I drove up the hill. Maybe you should head down there and be neighborly. Kill two birds with one stone, if you get my meaning."

Jack shook his head in disbelief as Walt slammed the door of his truck and started the engine. He'd never seen Walt so fired up before. Smiling, he walked over to gather his buckets and head back down to the barn.

He figured his friend was right, about the land, at least. But Walt had it all wrong about getting involved with Samantha. It was plain as day that she was not going to be the one to rescue him from his postdivorce exile. He was undeniably attracted to her. The sparks he'd felt on the porch the other day, the weight of her body against his when he'd supported her in his arms, it was all seared into him like a brand. He couldn't remember being drawn to anyone like that before, not even Amy. But he'd sworn off women like her long ago.

He'd met Amy in another life, when he was fresh out of college in New York City, a bold kid with a mathematical brain and a talent for making money. Amy's parents were high society and she'd loved that world, and loved bringing her successful boyfriend to all her big-name events. She'd loved him, or at least she'd loved what she thought he could and should be. Looking back, it was clear she'd never loved who he really was—an Oklahoma farm boy with a head for business, who'd managed to land a job at one of the most prestigious investment banking firms in New York.

For Jack, New York was a way to make the money he needed to live his dreams. For Amy, New York was a way of life. She hadn't wanted him to go West, hadn't wanted him to train horses, but he'd talked her into it, and into marriage, too. That union had died a quick death in the freezing winter amongst the quiet of the mountains. She'd fled as soon as the first snow melted, sending him divorce papers in the mail shortly after. She didn't recognize this new Jack Baron, she'd told him, but he'd never felt more like himself, and who he was meant to be.

Well, whatever Amy's reasons for leaving, there just hadn't been enough for her out here, and there definitely wasn't going to be enough for Samantha. She had "just passing through" all but tattooed on her elegant forehead and this time he was going to be smart enough to heed that warning.

The truth of Walt's words echoed in his head. Jack needed the Rylant land to make his operation a success. Leasing it had worked out well so far, but if Samantha sold the land to someone else he could lose everything he'd worked so hard for here. He'd have his house and barn and training facility, but not much acreage for pasture.

Jack called the dogs and threw his buckets into the back of his truck. Walt was right about another thing. His to-do list. And it wasn't going to get any shorter with him just sitting here worrying.

Thinking of his list, inspiration struck. Maybe it was too soon to ask Samantha if she'd sell him her grandmother's ranch, but he could certainly nudge her in that direction. Being the helpful neighbor that he was, he'd offer her a tour of her long-neglected property. He couldn't think of anything more effective than an infinite list of chores and repairs to turn a city girl's thoughts in the direction of a quick sale. And in the process, if he got to spend a little more time in the company of such a beautiful woman, well, he could live with that.

Jack grabbed a halter out of the cab and went to get Larry. He wasn't sure that he had enough charm to entice Samantha into a stroll around her ranch, but he'd bet good money that enormous, gentle and highly unusual Larry did.

CHAPTER SIX

SAMANTHA HAD BEEN trying to avoid thinking about Baron all morning. Which was hard since if she looked uphill she could see the side of his barn, and the edge of his driveway. And she didn't even have to turn her head to hear his truck engine revving. She turned the music up loud.

Of course, when she wasn't thinking about Jack, she was thinking about coffee. She was having visions of cappuccinos right now. Double cappuccinos and those amazing pumpkin muffins they made at the coffee shop down the hill from her apartment—her usual Saturday-morning treat. But this Saturday, she'd have to settle for some cold cereal and the instant stuff—she couldn't bring herself to call it coffee. How did modern people survive out here? she wondered.

She was taking on the second floor today. There were four bedrooms, two bathrooms, several closets and the stairs. But there were also work emails and a conference call and three different meetings to plan. It was a little too overwhelming to think about. Best just to pull on the gloves and start cleaning, and maybe at some point, either this weekend or some time in the future, it might feel like her life was somewhat under control again.

With a sigh, Samantha went out to the car to grab more cleaning supplies. As she straightened up out of the trunk and turned to face the house she noticed that the white siding and green trim were weather-beaten and peeling. She tried to look at it objectively. Would a prospective buyer care that the paint was coming off? Or maybe that would just add to its charm.

She loved the wide, wraparound porch, the bay windows off the living room and the high dormer windows of the attic. It was a huge old house. Someone could purchase it for a big family and still have room left over. Or they could turn it into a bed-and-breakfast. With some redecorating and landscaping, it would be a great retreat for vacationers.

Samantha wondered briefly if she'd ever want to be an innkeeper. Not likely, but she could easily imagine how she'd do it. She'd plant old roses by the gates outside, decorate the rooms in country chic, and hire someone to make an amazing breakfast every morning, complete with cappuccinos, of course. She'd offer hiking trips, horseback riding— a complete escape from city life.

Lost in the dream of it, Samantha didn't hear a sound until the hoofbeats were right behind her.

Turning with a gasp, she instinctively took two steps back from the large horse. Dark, liquid eyes regarded her with friendly interest. A homely white head with brown spots and flecks ended in a pink-and-black-speckled nose that nudged forward and sniffed at her hand. Laughing at the velvet touch of the horse's nibbling lips, Samantha looked up into Jack Baron's face. He was watching her with an oddly serious expression. Her breath caught—she hoped he hadn't heard it.

"Morning." He tipped his hat to her and leaned over the saddle horn, letting the reins go slack. "Larry and I thought we'd come down and pay you a little visit."

She couldn't help but smile. It was too absurd, being visited by a man on a horse at eight in the morning. "Isn't it a little early to be out riding?"

"Well, Frisco," he teased gently, "us country folk have been out of bed for hours, and Larry here has been raring to go since dawn."

"This is Larry."

"Yes, it is. Say hello, Larry."

"I think he already said hello. He startled me." She looked up at Jack suspiciously, squinting into the rising sun. "Do you always sneak up on people?"

He laughed. "Only people who don't seem to notice much around them."

"Hey! I was busy. Thinking. I notice things all

the time…just not you…or Larry, apparently." It had been so long since she'd been near a horse, but Larry's velvet nose, now searching her pockets, combined with the smell of sun and horse and dust, all brought memories of summer rides flooding back.

Larry shifted a few steps and Samantha could see his neck and flank. "He's polka-dotted!" she exclaimed, taking in the amazing, almost absurd coat. Larry was pure white with dark brown, perfectly oval spots scattered all over. "He's a Dalmatian! Only way bigger."

"He's a leopard Appaloosa. Have you ever seen one before?"

"No! It's startling, for sure! And also adorable."

Jack gave Larry a pat on the neck. "Hear that, fella? You're adorable." He was teasing again but there was pride in his voice. He obviously loved his horse. "You don't seem too scared around him. Do you ride, Samantha?"

"I used to, but it's been a really long time." Her last ride with her grandparents seemed like a lifetime ago, but the precious memory of it was still there.

"Why don't you hop on Larry here? We'll take you for a stroll."

"Larry can't hold both of us, Jack!"

"Larry is sixteen hands high and as strong as an

ox, and I'm sure you just hurt his feelings to suggest otherwise."

"Sorry, Larry." She stroked his soft nose and broad forehead. There was no way she'd ride double with Jack. Being plastered against him on a moving horse definitely did not fit into her plan to keep her distance.

"Come on, Samantha. Look." Jack swung a long blue-jeaned leg over Larry's back and stepped down lightly. "If it seems too cozy with two of us up there, I can walk."

The guy could read her mind and that was disconcerting. "It's not just that...I have so much to do!"

"Have you even seen this ranch of yours yet? Besides the house and the creek, I mean?"

"Well, not really," she admitted.

"Let Larry and I show it to you. You might as well know what you're working so hard for."

Samantha could feel her resolve disintegrating. She had a million things to do and not much time to do them in. Plus, after the way he'd made her feel on the porch last weekend, the last thing she should do is go anywhere near her gorgeous neighbor. But the early sun was lighting up the landscape, a breeze from the peaks above was filling the air with the scent and sound of pines, *and* she really should take a look around the ranch. Her ranch.

"Let me lock the house."

"You don't need to lock your doors around here, Samantha!"

"Force of habit." She glared at him as she closed the car doors and ran up the steps to lock the front door. "Do you always make fun of people so much?"

"Maybe it's something about you, Frisco."

She shook her head. There was no use even replying to that without digging herself in deeper. She walked to the edge of the porch.

"Hang on, I'll bring him over." Jack drew on the reins, leaned slightly on Larry's shoulder and the Appaloosa walked sideways right up to the edge of the porch.

"That's a neat trick." Samantha reached her right hand up to grip the pommel and put her foot in the stirrup.

"Larry and I are full of good tricks. We'd be happy to teach you some if you're interested." She chose to ignore that invitation for now and slung her leg over Larry's back to settle in the saddle. Larry stirred at the unfamiliar weight but settled at a word from Jack.

Jack shortened the stirrups for her. "Is that your phone in your pocket?" he inquired.

Samantha instinctively felt the back pocket of her jeans. "Yes."

"Maybe while we were exploring, I could help you make a list of the repairs and maintenance that

the ranch needs. You can take notes on your phone."
Jack pulled down to tighten the last stirrup adjustment and took Larry's reins.

"No, Jack, that's okay. I can hire someone for that."

"Well, you could, but it would be dumb when you have me right here." He grinned up at her and clicked to Larry, who promptly moved forward. "I'll let you steer eventually if you want. But he's not used to having such a light rider on his back. I want to make sure he doesn't get goofy while he's trying to figure out what's changed."

"I'm going to take that as a compliment, I guess," Samantha replied, adjusting her seat in the saddle to accommodate Larry's long gait. "And, since I don't want to appear dumb, as you put it, I'd appreciate anything you can tell me about what the ranch needs."

An hour later she was regretting she'd said those words. Seated on Larry while Jack poked around in the barn, she added "replace rotted siding on north wall" and "rehang doors" to a list that already included at least forty tasks. And they hadn't even made it to the rear of the house yet, where she could see, even from a distance, that a few elderly sheds were sagging earthward and a large portion of the kitchen garden fence had come down.

This, Samantha decided, was enough. It was really nice of Jack to offer to do this, but she had a lot to do today and if she added many more things to this list she'd be so overwhelmed she'd never get started. The key would be prioritizing the most crucial repairs. Luckily she was really good at that. "Jack!" she called.

His voice echoed from the back of the cavernous barn. "You're going to need to replace all the stalls in here if you plan to have cattle. They're outdated—they don't meet the minimum size."

"Jack!" she called again. "Can you come out here please?"

A moment later he emerged, wiping a streak of dust off his face with a bandana. *Yum,* Samantha thought involuntarily, watching the muscles of his arm ripple when he moved.

"Add this to your list. Remove and recycle outdated metal…"

"Jack!" She cut him off.

He looked surprised. "What's wrong?"

"Nothing's wrong. It's just a lot of information and I don't know if I'm going to have cattle, so as much as I appreciate it, I think maybe I don't need to know all of this right now."

"Sure. I just thought…"

"You've been so helpful. I'm really grateful. But I can't fix everything right away. How about this? Taking into account that I have no cows right now and won't need to use the barn or fences anytime soon, what are the top five problems you've seen today?"

JACK GROANED INWARDLY. He'd forgotten she was some high-powered executive who probably handled huge projects every day. Instead of looking overwhelmed and rattled, as he'd hoped, she looked calm and at home. Excited, even. He tried again.

"You know, some of these repairs are gonna cost you a fair amount."

She smiled at him and her green eyes sparkled, distracting him. "Yes, I figured that. So what do you see as the most important tasks?"

He could see why she was so successful. She was beautiful, unfazed, even smiling in the face of so much bad news. He thought about her question before he answered. "The cracked chimney, the roof, the rot in the porch supports, clearing the brush that's grown near the house and having the septic system checked out."

Her hands flashed as she recorded the list on her phone. Then she tucked the phone into her back pocket. "Okay, got it. Thanks again for giving me so much of your time and all this great information! If you don't mind, once I get these repairs done, would it be okay if we discussed this list again? I'd compensate you for your time. Kind of like a consultant. An old, dilapidated ranch consultant, that is!"

Jack couldn't help but laugh at her choice of words. "Are you calling me old and dilapidated?"

"No, the ranch!" Her cheeks flushed. "Those aren't exactly the words I'd use to describe you, Jack."

Heat flashed through him at that. He felt like a teenager who'd just been noticed by the homecoming queen. "Sure, I'd be happy to help," he answered her question. "But you don't need to pay me. I keep explaining to you, Frisco, it's called being neighborly."

"Oh yeah." Her glance was pure mischief. "I'd forgotten about the Boy Scout values around here."

"And I keep forgetting that you come from the cutthroat, dog-eat-dog world of San Francisco."

She matched his sarcasm with her own. "Yeah, it's a jungle for sure. But with really good food and frequent peace rallies."

Jack grinned, loving her humor and the way her laugh created a dimple in the flawless skin of her cheeks.

He knew he should get back to his work. He'd come down here on a mission to overwhelm and discourage her, and as far as he could tell, it had been a complete failure. But instead of heading back to his ranch, he handed her Larry's reins. "You've got a good seat, Samantha. Why don't you try being in charge of Larry for a bit? We can walk out through the lower pastures and you can have a look at the rest of your ranch, at least from a distance. And I promise, I won't say anything more about what needs to be fixed."

Samantha looked pointedly to her right, where an old water trough was upside down with a rusted roll of wire fencing leaning against it.

"I see nothing," he promised her.

"Okay, then, let's go. Lead the way and we'll go check out this ranch of mine."

Jack nodded and started down the faint path that led past the old kitchen gardens and out to the first pasture. He could feel Larry thudding behind him and looked back. Samantha sat straight and graceful, as if she'd been riding Larry forever. In that instant, she looked like she belonged here. And Jack felt the pull, like a gravitational force, to the thing he wanted and couldn't possibly have. He pictured that dead-end road again. The one he'd been down with Amy. But all he could think of was how good it would feel to walk down it with Samantha, despite whatever heartache might be waiting for them when they ran out of pavement.

SAMANTHA LOOKED DOWN at Jack from her high perch on Larry's broad back. Even covered in dust from the barn he was incredibly handsome. Golden stubble lined his jaw, and his skin was tanned and just a bit weathered. The old leather cowboy hat might be obscuring his eyes a bit, but she'd felt her stomach flip with desire every time he trained them on her. But today something felt different. It didn't seem like he wanted anything more from her than a neighborly friendship. Maybe she'd imagined all that heat between them last weekend. The thought brought with it a strange mix of disappointment and relief.

Well, a good thing about his complete lack of flirtation today was that it meant she could have more time on Larry, and she was so enjoying riding again. She'd had no idea how much she'd missed it until she'd settled into the saddle and her muscle memory had taken over: heels down, toes in, elbows at her sides. Everything her grandparents had taught her was still right there for her to access. Ignoring the voice in her head that was chiding her about all the work and housework she still had to get done today, she took up the reins a bit and urged Larry down the path that Jack was taking.

He glanced back at her. "You doing okay up there?"

"Yes," she answered. She watched the way his shoulders straightened when he turned forward again. They were broad, their strength obvious under his shirt, and for a traitorous moment she compared them to Mark's, which, despite all his time at the gym, just didn't look quite as attractive as Jack's.

"Are you English, originally?" Jack asked.

"No." She was surprised by the question. "But I spent a lot of time in the UK growing up."

"I can hear it in your voice sometimes," Jack said. "Not much, just phrases like *all right, then* and the way you always say *yes* instead of *yeah*."

"No one's ever mentioned that before." Samantha guided Larry around an old gate lying on the ground.

"And I'm not mentioning that downed gate."

She giggled. "Thanks for not *mentioning* it, Jack."

The back of the ranch narrowed into a steep valley and the acreage within made up what had always been called the lower pastures. The falling fences and weed-choked fields looked very different from the neat green fields of grass Samantha remembered. She glanced down at Jack. "You don't need to say it. I can see there's lots more for my list here."

"I've gotten my orders. I'm not saying anything more unless my consulting services are requested. But I was going to point out that despite its many needs, you have a beautiful ranch. Have you even stopped to take in all that you own?"

She hadn't. She halted Larry as they reached the middle of the lower fields and slid off, giving him a pat and holding his reins. He whuffled her cheek and then bent his head to start on the rich grass that poked through the weeds and brambles.

Samantha handed the reins to Jack and walked a few paces away, turning slowly in a circle and trying to take it all in.

The ranch house was behind her, at the entrance to the high valley. On the hill above it was Jack's barn, and presumably, his house beyond that. Turning east she saw sagebrush and granite-specked hills that rolled all the way down to the Owens Valley floor. "That's all mine, too, isn't it?"

"Yep. Your grandfather had so much land he never even developed that portion. Didn't need it because he had this whole high valley, and then the higher pastures."

"Which you lease now."

"Yep." Jack pointed up the hill, beyond his barn. "My barn and house are situated right at the edge of my land, bordering yours. I own all the acreage that goes back down south toward our driveways. And I own a bunch of acres straight up the hill from my house. But your grandparents, I mean, you, own all of the best, developed pasture that's to the northwest of me. There's good water there and it's where I graze my horses most of the time."

Samantha squinted up the hill where she could see grassy hillsides unfolding until, far up in the distance, they began to blend with granite crags. "It's beautiful," she marveled. "I cannot get my head around the idea that I own this."

"I imagine it'll take some getting used to." Jack

moved to stand next to her, pointing up into the mountains. "And you know you have a lot more than pasture up there. See all those peaks after the pasture ends? A bunch of them are yours. You've even got your own lake up there."

"I remember it," Samantha replied. "We used to ride up there and I'd swim. It's Stone Lake, right? Such a boring name. Grandpa didn't like it. He always said he was going to rename it Lake Beautiful Ruth after my grandmother."

Jack looked down at her in surprise. "Sounds like he was quite the romantic."

"Oh, they had a great love," Samantha told him. "Watching them together made me understand what true love really was. They laughed and played and worked hard and were always there for each other. I was lucky to witness it. I think that type of love is rare." She thought of Mark, and how he seemed so busy lately, or so tired from being so busy. Very rare indeed.

"It is rare," Jack agreed, echoing her thoughts. "And I guess if it ever shows up, you've got to just take a chance and grab it."

Samantha could hear a somber note in his voice. She looked up and his eyes met hers. She searched them, trying to read his mood. There was a depth to him she hadn't anticipated and she realized that it wasn't just lust she was feeling for this cowboy. It was worse. She wanted to get to know him better, and that wasn't good news. She took a step away and looked back at the mountains.

"We should go there," he said softly.

"Where?"

"Lake Beautiful Ruth. Don't you want to see it again?"

"Well, yes, of course," Samantha answered. But not, she reminded herself, a smart thing to do with Jack when she was so drawn to him. "Unfortunately I don't have a lot of time."

Jack's voice held a teasing note. The sadness or regret she'd detected had vanished. "I've been hearing you say that a lot, Frisco, especially when there's the possibility of doing something nice for yourself—something fun."

Jack's tall frame was lit by the eastern sunshine. With his hat tipped down over his face and his long denim-clad legs ending in worn cowboy boots, he looked like the hero from one of the Western movies her grandfather had loved. She *wanted* to say yes, to the ride, and to anything else he asked.... Their eyes met again and this time she had no more willpower left to look away. His hand reached out and picked up one of the ringlets that curled on her shoulders. He pulled it gently and watched it spring back.

"I like these, by the way."

He had her flustered. She prided herself on never

being flustered. "Oh, er…yes, I didn't get out the blow dryer today."

"I'm glad." The intensity was back in his look and suddenly she knew she hadn't imagined what had passed between them last weekend. She felt the heat from his gaze on her skin. He bent down until she could feel his breath on her lips, and her own quickened and caught as he brushed her mouth in a slight caress, just a gentle ghost of a kiss that left the taste of him on her lips. He stepped back and she stared at him in shock, the back of one hand involuntarily pressed to her lips as if to hold the kiss in place.

This was crazy. This was a black hole of danger and complication.

"I have a boyfriend." The four words seemed to ring out over the quiet pasture as Jack looked at her in silence, his expression fading from wanting to surprise.

"Mark." She stumbled on. "We work together. We've been together a long time. It's pretty serious."

Finally he spoke. "I think I read you wrong then, Samantha. I apologize."

"No, you didn't. I mean, yes, well, it's complicated. I'm sorry, too." This was not going well. Her cheeks were hot and, very likely, beet red, and she'd just kissed someone who was definitely not Mark. It was time to go.

"Where is he?" Jack asked abruptly.

"Mark? He's in San Francisco."

"Why isn't he here? Helping you out with all of this?" His arm waved to take in the vast land around them.

Samantha remembered the disappointment she'd felt when Mark couldn't come to the funeral, and when he'd been unable to join her this weekend. "He's busy. He works a lot. And the fact is, I don't need his help."

"It's a big challenge, trying to straighten up this place. Just seems like the guy who loves you would want to come out here and lend a hand."

That stung. "Jack, I'm not sure which century you're living in out here, but I don't need my boy-friend, who does love me, by the way, to help me out with every little thing. I can take care of most things on my own! I'm used to it and I like it that way."

"Oh, believe me, I know you can. I saw you almost break your neck last weekend taking care of things on your own!" He chuckled and leaned back on Larry, arms crossed across his chest, watching her from underneath the brim of his hat. Samantha glowered at him and he stopped. "Look, I didn't mean to step on your toes. I was just surprised that he isn't by your side, taking all this on."

"I guess every relationship is different. We don't all want or need what my grandparents had, for example. It's wonderful that they were so romantic, and always together, but I'm not sure I inherited that particular gene." Why was she standing out here, justifying her relationship to a guy whose views on love stemmed from the dark ages? A guy whose unwanted kiss was making her wish for things she absolutely couldn't have.... This was all just way too uncomfortable to deal with any longer.

"Anyway, Jack, this has all been very enlightening but I have a conference call at eleven." She glanced at her wrist and realized she'd forgotten to put her watch on this morning. There was a line of paler skin where the band usually was. She looked up.

Jack was smiling at her, the friendly mischief back in his eyes. "Forget something?"

A sigh escaped her. "Yes, my watch, as a matter of fact."

"Stick around here long enough and you'll realize you don't even need it."

"Sounds nice," Samantha retorted. "And impossible. I've really got to get back. But thanks for your help with the ranch today, and for letting me ride Larry. And for this." She waved her hand vaguely at the gorgeous scenery around them. She gave Larry a farewell pat and turned to go back the way they'd come.

"Samantha!" His voice sent a thrill through her as she turned.

"Yes?"

"We should take that ride. If not this weekend, then sometime soon."

After everything he'd made her feel today, Samantha was pretty sure it was best to never get within twenty feet of Jack Baron again. "Maybe, but I'm going to be very busy. Thanks for the offer, though. Goodbye, Jack."

She had a long walk across the pasture, and when she glanced back, Jack was still leaning against Larry, watching her go. Needing something to distract herself from his eyes on her, she pulled out her phone, punching in numbers to set up the call. It took a moment to realize that, of course, she had no reception in the middle of a pasture, in the middle of the mountains, in the middle of nowhere. She hurried toward the ranch house, thinking that maybe Jack was right. Owning a ranch was going to be a whole lot of trouble. But it wasn't the long list of repairs that worried her—it was the trouble she had keeping her distance from Jack Baron that concerned her most.

CHAPTER SEVEN

Right now Samantha missed her beautiful apartment. She missed her clean, tiled shower. She missed the heater that turned her bathroom into a cozy retreat on even the coldest, foggiest days. She was filthy, and it was late in the day, and thanks to her misguided decision to see the ranch with Jack, and several work phone calls, she'd lost cleaning time and the upstairs bathrooms were still unusable. The downstairs bathroom had a tiny sink and no shower. So she stood in the kitchen, hunched over the farmhouse sink, trying to wash her hair under the old iron faucet.

She wrung out her hair and reached for a towel and comb, wandering out to the front porch to attack the tangles. She sat down on the worn front steps. Staring down the driveway, pulling idly on the curls and knots, she thought back to the morning, and Jack's unexpected kiss. She knew it was wrong—was that why it was haunting her? Or was it because she'd never had a kiss like that. So slight, but so searing?

She had to keep in mind that this was all some

sort of fantasy, a distraction because Mark had been so busy lately. She knew very little about Jack, besides the basic facts—he was handsome, funny and liked horses. Why was he alone, single and living in the middle of nowhere? He had to be in his mid-thirties, and years of big city dating had taught her that if a beautiful man was alone at that age, there was usually a good reason why. Her friend Tess called it the fatal flaw: commitment phobia, an addiction to the chase, an addiction to drugs, alcohol, infidelity... Which flaw was his? And why did she care anyway? She'd be going back to her extremely busy, fulfilling life in San Francisco tomorrow evening.

She was so involved in pondering these questions that she didn't notice the car making its way up the drive until it was practically on top of her. It was a Porsche—sleek, gray and reeking of wealth. Wondering why anyone would come out to her ranch, especially someone in this type of car, Samantha jumped to her feet. The engine stopped and out sprung Robert Morgan, the lawyer who'd handled Grandma Ruth's will, looking clean and professional in a tailored gray suit and tie. He tugged mirrored sunglasses off of his face and strode toward her with a hand outstretched.

"Samantha!" He was beaming like a long-lost friend rather than her lawyer whom she'd met for the first time a few days ago. "How are you?"

Samantha tried to wipe the surprise off her face. She didn't think they had any more business to take care of, and she certainly hadn't expected him out here. But maybe he was a much-needed dose of reality. From his expensive suit to his leather loafers he was a reminder of her real life among professional people, far away from this ranch tucked up against the wilderness.

"Robert, what a surprise!" She took his hand in a firm shake. "I didn't expect to see you here."

"I had an appointment with a client over in Mammoth," he said. "I was hoping I could talk you into having dinner with me. Thought I'd drop by and see how the city slicker was doing with ranch life. So what do you say, can I take you for an early meal?"

Samantha took a long look at him. His face was earnest and betrayed nothing. If this was a date it didn't show in his professional demeanor and easy smile. He probably just wanted to go over some last minute stuff about the ranch. And why was she worried, anyway? She'd just been kissed by a cowboy. Having dinner with her lawyer seemed tame in comparison.

She looked down at her old jeans and T-shirt. "Can I get changed?"

His demeanor was warm and reassuring. "No problem. I've got to make some calls. How about if I hang out here on the porch while you get ready?"

Samantha took a hasty sponge bath in the bathroom and rummaged around for some decent cloth-ing, deciding on slim black jeans and a fitted red sweater. She pulled the comb through her tangled hair and grabbed the blow dryer. In ten minutes her hair was transformed into a sleek, straight wedge and she was dabbing on some makeup. She picked up her purse, grabbed her keys and was out onto the porch moments later, locking the door.

Rob stood and eyed her appreciatively. "That was quite a transformation. When I arrived here I wasn't sure that it was you under those clothes and curls."

"Oh, yes, it was me," she answered crisply. "I guess I have many sides."

"You?" Robert laughed. "I have a feeling you're a city slicker just like me. A lot more at home in a good restaurant or a nice car than we are in a tiny town like this."

She was quiet. Why did his comment bother her? He was right, wasn't he? She certainly didn't fit in around here. But it was one thing to think it about herself, and another to have someone she barely knew point it out.

They cruised the downtown, all seven blocks of it, until Rob pulled up at the Sierra Grill, which he said had the only remotely edible food in town. Samantha tried to ignore the stuffed elk and deer heads staring from the walls with empty glass eyes. As they settled into their booth and ordered wine and an appetizer, Samantha asked, "So, tell me about Mammoth. That's where you were today wasn't it?"

Rob's expression lit up. "You haven't been up there? It's awesome! They have some of the best skiing around, incredible scenery, beautiful shops and good food. A lot of people from L.A. go up there to vacation. You'd love it."

"And you were there for…"

"Business this time. I'm working on a little real estate transaction. Some clients of mine are setting up a new resort there."

Samantha was surprised to learn this. She'd judged Rob as a small-time lawyer, sliding easily into his daddy's practice. "I didn't know you were in real estate development, Rob."

"Well, I deal with more of the legal side of it, but yes, I've been getting more involved lately. You see, Samantha, this area is booming. Lake Tahoe is so crowded and the economy in such a bad state that people are staying close to home. They want more local vacation destinations. That's one of the reasons I wanted to talk to you tonight."

"Oh?" Samantha echoed. "Why me?"

"About your land. The ranch. I imagine you're considering selling it and I wanted you to know that my business partners and I might be interested in buying."

"Really? Selling it has crossed my mind, but I

haven't thought anything through. Why do you and your partners want it?"

"Well, Benson has never been really developed as a vacation destination the way that Mammoth has. The potential here is enormous! Your property, with the lake, and the direct access to the mountains and the highway, could really transform this town."

Samantha sipped her wine quietly, absorbing his words for a few seconds, looking at Rob's eager face. The timing of this was amazing. Just this morning she'd realized she should put as much distance as possible between her and Jack. And this afternoon she'd been so torn between the demands of her job and what she wanted to accomplish around the ranch that she was starting to accept reality. She needed to sell the ranch soon. And now, magically, Rob was here and wanted to make an offer. But the ranch as a vacation destination? It was one thing to imagine it as a bed-and-breakfast, but as a resort?

"Rob, I'm not sure what I want for the ranch yet. But I do know that I will likely have to sell it at some point," she told him. "It's the practical thing to do."

His smile was understanding. "Well, yes, it is. I can only imagine how overwhelming it must be to take on such a huge property. Especially when you already have a full-time career in San Francisco.

"But a resort, Rob? I'm just not sure." The waitress brought her wine and Samantha took a grateful sip of the crisp white.

"Well, I suppose you could call it a resort. But certainly in this area we would do something on a much smaller scale than Mammoth. The point is, we're interested in buying at a very competitive price."

There was a knot in her stomach that she didn't understand. This could be a great opportunity for her. Why did it feel so stressful? "I'd need to consider my decision carefully," she reminded him.

"Of course you would, Samantha. Your grandma liked to tell me how smart you were, and I trust you won't make any moves without being certain. I just want you to know that even though I am representing a group of buyers, I'm still your lawyer first and foremost, and I will keep your best interests in the forefront of all our dealings."

"Thanks, Rob."

"And on that note, just keep in mind that you should do what's best for you. Your grandmother loved you like a daughter. And she knew you well, right? She couldn't have expected someone like you to want to live out in the middle of nowhere on a ranch."

Samantha nodded in reluctant agreement. She'd already broken three fingernails today and had not been happy about it. She'd fallen off a ladder on her first attempt to do real work around the place and she was lucky she hadn't broken her neck. "No." She sighed. "I don't see how she could have expected me to run a ranch."

"Well, I'll tell you what. I'll put a proposal together and send it to you." He paused as their meal was served. "No pressure. You can look it over, see what you think. Then we can talk again after you've had a chance to consider it."

Samantha felt the tug in her stomach again, and a small flutter of panic. Things were moving awfully fast. But she was too practical to walk away from what could be an extraordinary opportunity. "Sure," she answered. "It's just difficult to think about letting it go."

Without warning, Rob leaned across the table and covered her hand with his. His hand was cool and soft, the nails manicured and neat, and she instantly contrasted it with how Jack's hand had felt earlier: work-roughened and strong. "I want you to know how much I respected your grandmother, Samantha. What she left you will give you security for the rest of your life. I believe that's what your grandmother would've wanted for you."

"Samantha, I hope I'm not interrupting." Samantha jumped at the sound of Jack's voice above her. The cowboy hat was gone. His hair was stylishly mussed with a bit of gel, and his face was clean-shaven. He looked ridiculously handsome in clean jeans and a blue linen shirt. His eyes were the same deep, intense blue, but with a harder edge as he glanced meaningfully down at her hand, lying frozen under Rob's.

Wrenching her hand back, Samantha straightened up and tried to control the blush flooding her cheeks. What must he be thinking of her? Earlier today she'd told him she couldn't kiss him because she had a boyfriend, and now, a few hours later, he found her holding her lawyer's hand in the local restaurant? She summoned her confidence, drawing on that cool strength that served her so well in tough meetings at work. "Why, Jack Baron. You do clean up well."

"Why, Samantha Rylant, I can say the same about you." He gave her a questioning look and turned to Rob. His smile disappeared completely. "Robert Morgan, it's been awhile."

"You know each other?" Samantha forgot her manners in her surprise. Then she realized. "Oh, of course, the lease on the ranch."

"Yes, the ranch," Jack confirmed, but Samantha was sure she heard hostility drip from his voice when he continued. "The whole east side of these mountains is like one small town. We're all bound to cross paths eventually. Robert and I have met a few times now."

"You might say that," Rob confirmed, but he looked so uncomfortable that Samantha wondered what the real story was. Clearly these two men weren't fond of each other.

Jack smoothly changed the subject by turning to a couple that had just walked up to the table. "Samantha, meet Jed and Betty Watkins. They own the ranch just to the south of us. They're old friends of mine and kindly agreed to come out on the town with me tonight."

Jed was a large man, gray-haired and portly, in a plaid shirt, dark jeans and shiny dress cowboy boots. "Pleased to meet you, Samantha," he said, holding out a hand the size of a dinner plate. He shook hers warmly and moved aside as his wife stepped up. She was all smiles and plump dimples as she reached out and kissed Samantha on the cheek.

"It's so nice to meet you, Samantha! I knew your grandmother and she used to love to tell stories about you. And Jack's talked so much about you already this evening that I feel like we're old friends." Silence fell over the group as they digested this information. Jack looked down at the floor, then away out the window—anywhere but at Samantha.

Samantha decided that she liked Betty very much, if only for the reason that finally it was Jack who was blushing and not her. "Well, it's been interesting to make Jack's acquaintance and it's very nice to make yours," she said. "My grandmother mentioned your name many times, Betty.

I know she valued your friendship. But I suppose we should let you all get on with your meal. I hope we meet again soon."

"Oh, I'd like that," Betty replied effusively. "Why don't you come on up to the ranch for a visit next weekend? We're having a barbecue that Sunday. A few friends are coming, so you could meet some of the folks that live around here."

"Be careful," Jack warned. "When she says a few people she really means the whole town."

Betty giggled and gave Jack a little punch in the ribs. "Don't listen to this one. Just come on over around one o'clock. The Hidden Mountain Ranch out on Aspen Creek Road. Jack can bring you if he behaves well enough tonight to be invited."

Samantha flashed a conspiratorial grin at Betty. "Well, I won't count on his company then. I'll just have to find my way over without him."

Betty hooted with laughter and Jed let out a guffaw, clapping Jack firmly on the back.

"Samantha, I like you already!" Betty exclaimed. "You make sure and come on over. I'll leave you to your meal then." She turned to go and the men followed, Jack shooting one more questioning look at her as he walked away. It was only then that Samantha realized that neither Betty nor Jed had even acknowledged her lawyer, who'd been sitting quietly at the table during this exchange.

"Well, I see you're getting to know the locals," Rob said as she sat back down.

"Just a little." She sipped her wine, trying not to think about Jack, and what he must be thinking of her right now. "They seem nice enough."

"Sure they are, if you like talking cows and weather."

The note of resentment in his voice had Samantha glancing up at him, studying his face for a moment. Behind the charming demeanor she thought she caught a glimpse of something hard. Anger?

He interrupted her thoughts with an engaging smile. "Tell me about this amazing job you have in the big city."

She wasn't sure she wanted to think too much about her job right now, especially considering the amount of work left to do by Monday. "Well, it keeps me pretty busy," he answered.

She couldn't help it. She glanced over to where Jack was sitting. He was watching her over the rim of his glass of red wine. His gaze was steady on her and she swore she could feel it like a heat on her skin. She shifted in her chair. Jack's brows were drawn together. Was he concerned, or maybe a little angry?

She turned her attention back to Rob and somehow managed to keep it there for the rest of their meal. As they paid their bill and got up to leave, she kept her head high and gave Jack a casual wave across the restaurant, making sure to laugh at a comment Rob made. That would show Jack, she thought—though she wasn't sure what *exactly* she hoped to show him.

AT THIS MOMENT, one of the things Samantha appreciated the most about San Francisco was that she could be certain there were no pine trees lying in the driveway of her apartment building. And if a tree ever did have the audacity to fall down within city limits, there was a crew of people in orange vests and white hard hats who miraculously appeared to chop it up and carry it away before it could really inconvenience anyone. Samantha looked around her driveway hopefully, but it was just her, and it was Sunday evening and a pine tree was blocking her way home.

She got out of her car and pulled on her wool coat against the wind that was racing down the mountains and was most likely responsible for the demise of the poor tree in her driveway. Her hair whipped in every direction and she tried to tuck it into her collar.

Samantha walked to the tree and tugged at one of the branches, hoping to slide the trunk to the side of the road. She pulled harder, throwing her weight backward. The tree wouldn't budge.

She turned to the broken limbs scattered across the gravel drive. At least she could take care of those. She pulled them over to the grassy verge between her driveway and the pastures that bordered it. Stacking the branches neatly against the fence, she went back for more, a little dismayed to find pine sap stuck all over her fingers. So much for the nail polish she'd carefully applied a few hours before.

She checked the time on her watch. Earlier, Mark had called and asked her to meet him for late-night drinks at the San Francisco airport, before he caught the red-eye to New York. She wasn't going to make it on time unless she thought of a way to move this tree.

Maybe it could be rolled. Samantha stood in the driveway with her back to the wind, scraping sap off her wrist and trying to think. Inspiration struck and she ran to her car and opened the trunk, taking out the jack. Running back as best she could while heading downhill on gravel in four-inch heels, she wrestled the jack under the tree. Inserting the handle, she cranked hard and was thrilled to see that the heavy pine was lifting. She stopped when the tree was several inches off the ground and grabbed it by some of the thicker branches, lifting and pushing until it rolled off the jack and slid about a foot down the hill.

Samantha was triumphant. She was not helpless on this ranch. With a few tools, she was absolutely capable on her own. Picking up her jack, she lowered it, slid it under the tree trunk again, cranked, and shoved. But this time, as she heaved the tree forward, the jack slid backward, hit the ground and broke into several pieces.

Why was this happening? Samantha picked up a broken bit and threw it out of sheer frustration. It landed against the pasture fence with a sound that the afternoon winds quickly tore away. She needed to see Mark. She missed him. She needed to kiss him, to remind herself that she had a boyfriend, to wipe away the memory of Jack's lips on hers. A glance at her watch showed her she only had a few more minutes until it would be impossible to keep her date. She had to think hard and move quickly.

A few years ago, she'd bought a preassembled emergency backpack for her car. She'd never actually opened it, but this felt like an emergency of sorts. She unzipped it and rummaged through and was rewarded by a length of rope. Peering at the rear bumper of her car, she saw a spot where she could thread the rope through and tie it.

Hopeful once more, she got into the sporty BMW, reversed up the driveway to the house, turned around and reversed back down. Jumping out of the car, she tied one end of the rope to her bumper and the other to the tree trunk. Running back to the driver's seat, she slammed the door, put the car into gear and accelerated up the driveway. The wheels spun on the gravel and the engine groaned and suddenly there was a sound, sort of a metallic, tearing, crashing noise that boded no good.

Samantha slammed on her brakes, stopped the engine and jumped out, heart pounding. What she saw brought tears to her eyes. The tree had moved. A little. But her bumper was tethered to it, lying in the gravel. The only good news was that the tree was now at an angle across the drive. There might be enough room to maneuver the car around it if she was careful.

Cursing everything about the ranch, Samantha stomped over to her bumper and yanked at the knot until it was free. She moved her luggage to the backseat and heaved the battered bumper into the trunk. It didn't fit well so she tied it in and used more rope to tie the trunk down as much as it would close. The slam of the car door as she pulled it shut behind her echoed through the hills but she didn't care. She was angry.

Her foot hit the accelerator hard and she gunned the car up the driveway again, turned around one last time, and drove slowly down to where the tree was angled across the road. She steered right, aiming for the narrow spot she'd created between the tree and the hillside, while trying to avoid the drainage ditch that ran along the edge of the drive-way. She rolled down her window and peered out.

Trying to keep the tree from scratching the BMW's paint, she inched down the driveway.

Samantha knew it was silly to worry about scratches when she'd already decapitated her bumper, but so much had gone wrong, and she wanted to get this one thing right. And she almost did. The front wheels got past the tree. She was peering behind her, trying to keep an eye on the back end, when the car gave a jolt and the back right corner dipped suddenly down. As she slammed on the brakes she heard a scraping noise that could only be the bottom of her beautiful car on the rocks that lined the drainage ditch. Shutting the engine off, she rested her head on the steering wheel. It was clear that she wasn't going to make it to her date with Mark. She grimaced with bitter humor. At least she could honestly say she'd made every effort to be there.

Grabbing her phone she sent him a text to cancel, citing car trouble, which seemed too mild a phrase for the mess she'd made in her driveway. She sat in her tilted car, cursing the drainage ditch. She wanted so much to be on the road right now, headed back to the city where she knew how to handle any problems that came her way.

Finally, out of words and energy, Samantha opened her car door and heaved herself out of the driver's seat. She turned around to look at her once-beautiful car, now battered and pathetic, with one corner down in the ditch and the bumper sticking out of the trunk like a flag of surrender.

And she really did have to surrender. She'd tried to improve things with Mark and now she was missing their date. She'd tried to handle the tree by herself and ended up half destroying her car. There was only one thing left to do and she really didn't want to do it. With angry tears welling in her eyes, she turned and walked back to the house and up the path to Jack's property. It was time to ask for help.

As she approached the top of the hill, a border collie appeared and peeked over the rise at her, barked twice and disappeared. When she got to the top Jack had arrived to meet her, a leather tool belt slung around his hips and a pair of pliers in his hand. It was obvious Samantha was interrupting a project.

"I'm sorry to bother you," she started, shoving windblown hair out of her face for the millionth time in the past hour.

"Don't worry about it," he answered shortly. He looked at her face more closely and concern sharpened his features. "What happened? Are you all right?" He had no hat on, and the wind was blowing his hair on end. His eyes were a fierce blue as he waited for her answer.

"I'm okay. Sort of. I...I need your help. There's a tree down in my driveway, and I hate to admit it, but when I tried to deal with it I made a bit of a mess." That was a triumph of understatement.

Jack grimaced. "I bet I know which one. It's been dying for a while. I thought about taking it down last fall, but it's not on my land."

"I wish you had. In the future you have my permission to chop down anything that looks like it might block my driveway."

His answering smile was warm and eased Samantha's anxiety and frustration a bit. Jack stepped forward and reached for her hair and Samantha wondered for an instant if he was going to kiss her again, but he instead he removed a twig. And then some loose pine needles. And what looked to be a small piece of pinecone.

"Thanks," she said, too tired and disheartened even to blush.

"Hey, it's going to be fine." He was too close. When he was serious his eyes became slate blue and she could see perfectly the dark brown lashes that rimmed them. She shouldn't want so badly for him to kiss her again.

A sudden strong gust of wind hit them and sent her hair flying everywhere. Jack grinned and stepped back and Samantha looked up at the sky. The afternoon was turning to evening and dark gray clouds were appearing over the mountains.

Jack followed her gaze. "We better get you out of

here or you might hit that storm when you're trying to get home over the summit."

"I really appreciate your help." She glanced at his toolbelt. "I'm sorry I interrupted your work." Now that the asking for help part was over, she noticed how good the belt looked on him, and then flushed, realizing that she'd let her eyes linger there.

"Like I said, don't worry about it. I'll just go get my chain saw."

"That would be great. And…um…does your truck have a winch?"

Jack looked at her and the humor was back, that lopsided grin familiar, though maybe not welcome at the moment. "A winch? What exactly happened down there?"

Samantha sighed. "It's a long, sad story. It might be best not to ask."

There were plenty of questions in his eyes, but he didn't voice them. Instead, his eyes roved over her outfit, chosen for her late night drinks with Mark. At the sight of her stiletto boots, he grinned. "My old friends from the side of the road?"

Samantha smiled, despite her frustration with the tree, and the missed date with Mark and her guilt over Jack and his toolbelt and the way there'd been this unwanted hope that flashed through her when she thought he might kiss her again. "My amazing shoe repair guy resuscitated them last week."

"I gotta admit, I'm kind of glad to hear it. It would have been a loss to this world had they been ruined."

She laughed and shook her head. "Okay, Cowboy, enough with the boot fetish. Can you help me with the tree? Please?"

"Samantha Rylant asking me for help? It's music to my ears."

She rolled her eyes, thinking he might not feel quite that enthusiastic once he saw the carnage in her driveway.

"Look, I'll need to bring the truck," Jack said. "Why don't you go wait for me in the cab and we'll drive together?"

The last thing she needed was to be in any confined space with Jack right now. Especially Jack in low-slung jeans and a toolbelt. "I need to make a quick phone call," she lied. "I'll just walk back down and meet you there."

"Are you sure?" He glanced down briefly, obviously thinking that she was going to break her neck going down the steep trail in her boots.

"I'm good," she said. Good as long as she kept her distance from Jack Baron. Samantha started down the path, trying not to think about the teasing she was going to get when he saw the state of her car.

She arrived at the tree just as Jack pulled up the driveway. He got out of his truck and stopped in his tracks, eyebrows raised in amazement as he took in the half-moved tree, the pieces of jack still scattered alongside, and the car in the ditch with the bumper sticking out the back. The wind tousled his hair and he ran his fingers through it a few times, as if searching his brain for words.

"Did you…" he started, and then paused, and stepped over the tree to look more closely at her car trunk and the bumper. "How…" And then comprehension dawned and the smile slowly spread. Samantha could actually see unshed tears of laughter building in his eyes.

In what must have been a colossal feat of self-control, he didn't quite laugh. He just shook his head and looked at her in astonishment. "I am in awe, Frisco. Speechless and in awe."

He turned toward his truck and his shoulders shook with silent laughter as he went to grab the chain saw.

Samantha was glad that the furious noise of the saw prevented conversation. While Jack sliced up the pine tree, she busied herself with dragging parts of it over to her pile near the pasture fence. Less than an hour later they had the driveway clear. Jack put the saw back in the truck and came over to where she was adding the last pieces of tree to the now-enormous stack.

"I can haul all this up to the house if you want,

cut it up and stack it for you. With time, you'll have pretty good firewood."

"Jack, you don't have to do that," she protested.

"Samantha." He gestured to the scene around them. "I think we have the proof right here, that it really is okay to ask for help occasionally." His grin was back. "You don't need to do stuff on your own out here. Like move pine trees."

Her former bleak mood faded. This situation she'd gotten herself in with her stubborn independence was pretty ridiculous. Funny even. She smiled back. "All right, I see your point. But at least let me pay you for your time."

"How about, the next time you come, bring me some really good coffee. Whole beans, organic, from one of those local roasting places in the city."

"What?" Jack Baron, resident cowboy, was a coffee connoisseur? She realized she was staring at him in surprise.

"You think that just because I live out here and train horses I want to drink bad coffee? Come on, Samantha. Good coffee beans are like gold out here. It's a fair trade."

Laughter was dancing in his eyes and she had no idea if he was just teasing her, but it seemed like a good deal for her. And then she was laughing. She couldn't help it. Her car was mangled and in a ditch and she'd missed her date with her boyfriend, but Jack's offbeat humor was infectious.

He joined in the laughter, with a light in his eyes that she shouldn't want to see again. Their laughter slowed and their eyes caught and Samantha forgot for a minute that she wasn't supposed to be encouraging this. She simply didn't want to look away from him.

Thunder rumbled from high up in the mountains and they both jumped, startled by how much the clouds had traveled.

"We'd better get you out of here," Jack said. "Assuming I can get your car out of that ditch without pulling the other bumper off." His wink was so quick she almost missed it, and then he'd turned and was heading for his truck, to unwind the cable on the winch.

With quick and confident skill he freed her car in moments and then they stood there, on the gravel and sawdust driveway, cars facing each other, and Samantha wasn't quite sure how to say goodbye.

"I can't thank you enough," she finally said.

He was looking down at her with an expression she couldn't read and the lines of his face creased into a smile. She wanted to trace them with her fingertip. "Coffee." He reminded her. "Really good coffee."

"Right. Coffee." Her thoughts were scrambled up with a compelling urge to touch him—throw her arms around him and show him her gratitude. Instead she fished her car keys out of her pocket. "I guess if my car runs well enough to get me to San Francisco. Thank you again, Jack. Really, I can't say it enough."

"Anytime, Samantha. Anytime at all."

She turned to go.

"I like having you here." He blurted it out as she was walking away.

If she answered him, there might be another kiss. *She wished she didn't want that kiss so much.*

"Thanks again," she called over her shoulder, and got into her car, locking the door as if it offered safety from the way she felt when she was near Jack. She started the engine and sat, listening thankfully to its steady hum, waiting for Jack to move his truck out of the driveway. Waiting for a clear road home.

CHAPTER EIGHT

SAMANTHA'S OFFICE CHAIR had a squeak in it. Since she didn't usually spend much time at her desk, she'd never noticed it before. But today she'd discovered that if she propped her feet on the windowsill, she could turn her chair back and forth and give herself a nice panorama of the San Francisco skyline, accompanied by an occasional squeak. She'd had this office for years, but today was the first day in a long time that she'd really looked out the window and appreciated her view.

Watching all the busy people on the sidewalks below reminded her that she needed to get busy herself. It was a few hours before one of the most important presentations in her career and she was having a hard time focusing on work.

Even though she'd been back in San Francisco for three days, she felt like she was in limbo. Half of her was still back at the ranch, surrounded by ethereal granite peaks and breathing the spicy scent of the sagebrush. It seemed so strange to miss the mountains after spending just a few days there. Especially after her disastrous encounter with the fallen pine tree. Her poor car had been in the shop all week.

"Are you all right in there, Samantha?" She spun around, feeling her cheeks heat with embarrassment at being caught in such an undignified position. Mark leaned on the door frame, his deep brown eyes regarding her with concern and a slight wariness.

"Welcome back, boss." She smiled at him. He looked tired. His brown hair just a little mussed. "How was the flight from New York? Did you just get in? Cutting it a little close, aren't you?"

Humor flickered at her teasing. "Always. Speaking of which, we need to meet with the team in ten minutes. Our last run-through. I though I'd find you in the conference room, setting up."

"I took care of that a while ago." Samantha tried to keep the frustration out of her voice, but sometimes his random acts of micromanagement grated.

Mark closed the door behind him and took a few steps toward her desk. "Hey, Kiddo, I'm sorry I didn't call. You know how it is when you're on one of these work trips. Late meetings, dinners…"

"No, Mark, please." Samantha felt something inside of her recoil at his need to make excuses. "It's not that. I'm just having an off day, that's all."

"Did everything go okay at the ranch? Sorry I couldn't be there to help."

Mark looked so uncomfortable that Samantha took pity on him. "Thanks. It was fine."

"Listen, Samantha, I came in here to talk to you about something, and it's kind of urgent, but maybe now's not the time. Could we grab a drink after work tonight?"

A sharp knock made them both jump and Eileen, Samantha's assistant, popped her head around the door. "Skinny latte as ordered…oh, hello, Mark! I was coming to find you next. Everyone's ready for the final prep meeting. Is there anything I can do before it starts?"

Samantha took the latte appreciatively, inhaling the steamy scent. "Thanks so much, Eileen. I think we're good. Ready to get started. Let's all head in there." She grabbed her papers and followed Mark and Eileen out the door, wondering what it was Mark needed to talk to her about. Maybe he wanted to schedule time together before they both got too busy? Or maybe it was to talk about her promotion?

Giving herself a mental kick, she pushed open the door of the conference room. The only thing she should be thinking about now is Peter Claude Beauty. If all went well today, the international skincare company would become Taylor Advertising's newest client.

Her colleagues were sitting around the table, looking expectantly at her. Samantha looked at Mark. Now that he was back, she wasn't clear who was running this meeting. "Mark, would you like to start?"

"No, you go ahead." He was busy fumbling in his briefcase. "Do you have a pen, Samantha?"

Mark was rarely prepared for meetings, so Samantha always brought extra supplies. Samantha handed him a meeting agenda and a pen and turned to the group. "Before we go into this, I want to thank all of you for the incredible amount of work you've put into this pitch. I know we're going to blow the competition out of the water. If you all do as well today as you did on our run-through yesterday, I have no doubt we will soon be representing Peter Claude Beauty!"

Everyone started clapping. Mark clapped the hardest and Samantha felt herself forgiving him for his inattentiveness the past few days. As the applause died down, Samantha continued. "Just glancing around this room I can see all the hard work you've put into making everything perfect. Let's just go over our final checklists and we'll be done."

They went through the list of what was needed—easels, the storyboards, the samples, the packets to accompany the video presentation. Samantha reviewed who was going to speak at different points. Her team was generally amazing and today was no exception. Everyone was ready.

Drawing the meeting to a close, Samantha asked,

"Are there any questions about what's going to happen in the next couple hours?"

Her request was met with silence. People were shifting in their seats, some of them nervous, everyone ready to just get on with it. She continued. "Does anyone have anything else to add?"

Eileen's hand shot up. "Dana has some good news to share." Dana, Mark's assistant, was currently leaning over her notepad on the table, voluminous cleavage on display as per usual. At Eileen's introduction, her face brightened and she opened her mouth to speak.

Mark's voice interrupted sharply. "Eileen, I really don't think this is the time…"

"But Mark, it's the perfect time for good news," Eileen enthused. "Everyone loves to hear about this kind of stuff. Come on, Dana, didn't you say you wanted to make your announcement today?"

Dana looked around the group, joy illuminating her face. "Okay, well, I thought that good news, you know, really perks people up, and I thought it would be great to share this before we go into this huge presentation, to kind of pump us all up, right? So, really quick because I know we have to get going. I'm pregnant! Mark and I are having a baby!"

There was a ringing in Samantha's ears that seemed to muffle the sound in the room. Mark was accepting the handshakes and backslaps with a strained smile attached to his troubled face, which was a curious pasty color. Dana was busy being hugged and congratulated. Samantha felt rooted to her chair, unable to move.

"Samantha." Mark appeared in front of her, looking terrified and apologetic. "I never meant… I mean, this is why I asked if we could meet after…"

She held a hand up to stop him. If she spoke right now she had no idea what would come out of her mouth. She put her head down and pretended to be very busy with the pile of papers in front of her. When Dana came toward her, she stood up quickly and walked to a table at the far end of the room, flipping through the storyboards, as if to double-check them.

Staring blindly at the logo in front of her, she forced her mind away from what had just happened. She'd faced so many challenges in her life alone, without her parents or anyone else there to support her. She was alone now, in this pain and anger and shame, but she was good at overcoming things and she *would* overcome this. Not just overcome it, but give the best damn presentation this company had ever seen, and never, ever let Mark see how much his hideous betrayal had hurt her.

The room grew quieter behind her, as everyone finished their congratulations and cleared out. She turned around to go and Mark was still there, approaching her with a pathetic expression on his reddened face. "Don't!" she commanded.

She walked past him and into her office to collect what she needed for the pitch. It was showtime. But when the curtain went down, and the crowds went home, she was going to call her best friends and go find the strongest glass of scotch this fair city had to offer. And then, only then, would she let herself think about the fact that her boyfriend was having a baby with another woman.

"HE WHAT? WITH who?" Tess's face was a picture of horror, surprise, and a just a touch of guilty delight. Despite her poised, businesslike exterior, she loved gossip in all its forms.

Samantha took another sip of her scotch and looked around the crowded bar, making sure there were no familiar faces nearby. She leaned toward her two best friends, huddled around the small table in the corner. "Mark is having a baby with Dana, his assistant."

Jenna's Kewpie Doll lips were pursed together in horror as she stared at Samantha, her glass halfway to her mouth. Today she was dressed like a 1940s bombshell: pale make up, red lips and her auburn hair swept into a smooth chignon. "Dana? Not the one with the cleavage?"

Samantha buried her head in her arms on the table. She didn't know if she should laugh or cry or both. "Yes, Jenna. Thank you for reminding me. The one with the cleavage."

"Sorry. That was a bad thing to say." Jenna put her hand on Samantha's shoulder. "Sam, I'm so sorry."

Samantha felt the tears she'd kept in check all day swim to the surface. Wiping her eyes on her sleeve she sat up and took another long swallow, hoping that the alcohol would have a much-needed, mood-altering effect. She set her glass down and looked at her friends' expectant faces. "I've been a fool. I feel like such an idiot."

"No, Sam…" Her friends jumped in, always quick to protect her, but she wouldn't let them.

"No, I'm just *so* stupid. First of all, no one, absolutely *no one,* dates their boss. Isn't it, like, the number-one rule that we're all taught when we get our first job out of college? But I did it anyway! And then when he stopped calling as much, I just assumed he was working really hard. Now, looking back, I guess I was the only one working really hard."

"Oh, he was working hard all right!" Tess cut in.

Jenna giggled and Tess motioned to a passing waiter. "Another round, please. No, wait. Just bring the whole bottle. It'll save trouble later on."

Jenna was still giggling. "I'm sorry, Sam!" She dabbed at her eyes. "It's not funny, it really isn't, it's just, it's just…"

"Pathetic?" Samantha offered. "Disgusting? Trust me, I know."

"Disgusting?" Tess looked at Sam shrewdly. "Exactly how pregnant is she?"

Samantha took a deep breath. This was the worst part. "A little over three months, apparently."

Tess slammed her drink on the table, sloshing single malt over the lacquered surface. "And the last time you slept with him?"

Samantha felt herself flush. She didn't have Tess's boldness, couldn't talk about sex with her incredible candor. She took a deep breath. "A few weeks ago."

"Ouch. And yuck," said Jenna, completely serious now.

"I'll kill him." Tess's eyes took on a savage gleam. "What do you think, Jenna? Should we wait for him in a dark alley somewhere? Castrate him? Break his kneecaps?"

"No, he's not worth it," Samantha answered quietly. "I mean, he's horrible to have done that, really horrible. If I think about it in any detail I feel like I'll throw up. I just want to put it behind me. And to not care!"

"Well, of course you care, though," Jenna said gently. "You were with him a long time."

"Yes, but I'm trying to remind myself that in the grand scheme of things, this is nothing. Honestly, I just lost Grandma Ruth. In light of that, this Mark thing can't count as a total heartbreak. My heart hurts, and my ego *really* hurts. But I know the hurt's not permanent. Not like losing Ruth."

Samantha sipped her drink and looked around. It was six o'clock and the after-work crowd filled the Edinburgh Castle, a dive bar where Samantha and her friends held all their emergency meetings. They'd discovered the pub years ago, charmed by its massive wall of single malt scotch and the bagpiper who wandered through each evening. Right now it was filled with a younger, very hip-looking crowd, all jostling, talking and drinking. She wished she were one of them. They looked so carefree.

"I never liked Mark anyway." Tess broke the silence and reached for Samantha's hand across the table. "I can be honest about that now, can't I? He was too boring for you, Sam. Cute, smart and successful, it's true, but boring. And admit it, you were never madly in love with him."

"Maybe I'm just not the type to fall madly in love," Samantha mused. "We seemed so perfect for each other. We both work a lot, we got along fine and we made each other laugh and, well…" She paused, trying to remember what, exactly, she and Mark had shared.

"Exactly. You had nothing in common but work!" Tess paused as the waiter arrived with a tray and set down a brand new bottle of Macallan, eyeing Tess with a sort of awe as she took the bottle and promptly cracked the label, pulled the cork out and started pouring. "And maybe he made you laugh, Samantha, but did you *want* him?"

With a groan, Samantha buried her face in her hands. "Okay, maybe it wasn't totally passionate all the time but… Ugh! Who am I kidding! Obviously it wasn't that passionate if he was cheating on me!"

"So, there's your answer," Tess told her. "Look, I know you feel terrible right now, but the bright side is that you are now free to go find the guy who you want more than anything. And guess what? When you find him, you can have him, because you are now a free woman!"

"I'll drink to that!" Jenna exclaimed and they clinked glasses.

Samantha pondered Tess's words and swore she could taste Jack's kiss on her lips along with her scotch. Tess was right. She was free. And at least she didn't have to feel so guilty about the way she felt around Jack anymore. Maybe that was a tiny bright spot in this horror of a day.

Jenna interrupted her thoughts. "Now, the first thing you need to do is take some significant time off. Spa day, tropical vacation, shopping sprees, the works."

"Absolutely," Tess agreed. "If I'm not mistaken, not only did Mark drop this baby bombshell on you at work today, but you nailed your pitch to Peter Claude a few hours later, right? Not much Mark can say at this point if you want to spend the next month lying on the beach in Hawaii, Sam."

"It's not that simple. I have other accounts to worry about."

"Samantha, it's time for a change. All you ever do is work! You need to get a life, honey. And coming from me, who spends way too much time at the office, that's saying something."

"I guess you're right." Samantha sighed. She set the empty glass down and picked up the bottle, sloshing more into her glass. She took a swallow. She didn't drink that often, but she appreciated good scotch, and the bar certainly had a nicer glow to it than it had when she arrived. "But a tropical vacation on my own? Just this morning I thought I'd be taking one with Mark! Going alone sounds depressing!"

"Well, maybe you could find a nice cabana boy." Tess grinned at her.

"Not really my style," Samantha retorted. "But I do have the ranch. It feels really far away from everything. And right now I want to be far way."

"Any sexy cowboys out there?" Tess purred.

"Well, I have met one," Samantha answered, smiling a little. "He lives next door, so it's complicated. He's also my tenant."

"Uh-oh. Not good." Jenna shook her head. "I think if we've learned one thing from your terrible experience today, it's that we *all* need to avoid dating anyone we will ever have to see on a regular basis if and when things fall apart. Neighbor and tenant equal two strikes against him!"

"My thoughts exactly," Samantha agreed. "But it's a bit hard to stay away when he's gorgeous and funny and actually seems pretty smart. And he's got this hat and boots and jeans…"

"Say no more." Tess cut her off. "I disagree with Jenna. Go for it. Sexy cowboys trump all dating rules."

Samantha started to laugh again. It amazed her how even when she felt so awful, her friends could get her smiling. "Well, I've never actually had a fling. I wouldn't even know how to start one. I'll just lust from afar."

"Samantha!" Jenna exclaimed. "You are always so practical! And cautious! Tess is right. If there was ever a time to break all the rules and have a fling, it's now. I second the motion for wild sex with the cowboy. Just go tell him you want him!"

Samantha giggled incredulously. "You mean, just show up on his doorstep?"

"In a beautiful trench coat with nothing on underneath. Works every time," Tess informed her casually.

"What?" Jenna and Samantha shrieked in unison.

"And you've done this?" Samantha asked, looking at her friend with newfound awe.

"What, and you haven't? Ladies, what kind of dull lives have you been living?" Tess gave them a salacious wink and refilled their glasses with more scotch while Jenna leaned on Samantha and giggled.

Samantha took another sip from her glass. The room was starting to look kind of hazy and suddenly, with a dull thud in her heart, the reality of the day caught up with her. It was fun to joke about affairs and cowboys, but it was just a momentary distraction from what had happened. Mark had been cheating. For a while. Which meant that everything she'd believed about him, everything he'd told her for the past few months, had been a lie.

She tried to put on some kind of smile for her friends. "You two are incredible. I can't believe you've managed to cheer me up on one of the worst days of my life. But it's getting late. I should go home." She was done. Done with this horrible day. Done with relationships. Maybe forever.

Jenna sat up, sobering. "I'm sorry, I'm sitting here cracking up at our friend Tess's wild ways, while you are suffering from major heartbreak. You are amazing and strong to come out with us tonight, but if I were you I'd want to get home, too."

"You're my hero, Sam." Tess raised her glass in a salute. "I can't believe you kicked butt on that pitch right after you found out. You are tough."

Jenna set her drink down and put her forehead in her hand. "Is it just me or is this room spinning?"

"Definitely spinning," Samantha agreed. "Let's go find a way home. I swear, if I can't find a cab, or a bus, I'll grab a cable car. Any mode of transport that will get me into my bed as quickly as possible."

They walked up to busy Van Ness Avenue and looked for taxis. "See? Miracles happen!" Jenna said as a cab pulled up to the curb next to them. "You get the first one, Samantha. You need to rest up for your big affair with the cowboy!"

"Stop!" Samantha giggled, opening the door and getting in. "I'm not doing anything with the cowboy!"

"Of course you're not." Tess grinned. She shut the cab door behind Samantha and leaned down to speak to her through the open window, her long blond hair hanging in a curtain to one side. "Sure you don't want to borrow my trench coat, just in case?" she asked.

"Pacific Heights!" Samantha called to the driver, and she was laughing, though it felt a lot like crying, as he peeled out from the curb and sped her home through the dark city streets.

CHAPTER NINE

THE SOUND OF the old barn door squeaking startled Jack out of his thoughts. Familiar footsteps shuffled down the center aisle and Sugar, recognizing the slow rhythm, pulled her foot from his grip and stuck her head out the door with a nicker welcome. A weatherworn hand, gnarled and scarred, came up to stroke the inquisitive nose.

"Afternoon, Jack." The voice was low and gruff as gravel.

"Hey, Walt." Jack leaned an arm on Sugar's back.

Walt leaned against the door. "Our new neighbor is back."

A jolt hit Jack's stomach but he kept his voice neutral. "You don't say."

"I do say. Saw her pull up in that fancy car of hers just as I turned in from the main road. Must've had the day off to get here on a Friday afternoon."

"Must've," replied Jack, trying not to care.

Walter stood watching him, his old eyes a watery blue beneath the bristling gray brows. He broke off a piece of hay from Sugar's manger and chewed the stalk thoughtfully. "I can watch the place tomorrow if you want to ask her."

"Ask her what?" Jack watched Walt carefully, knowing his friend had something he was after.

"To go riding."

"She doesn't want to go riding, Walt." Jack knew his voice sounded as frustrated as he'd been feeling all week. "She wants to talk on her cell phone and work on her computer and…"

Walt cut him off. "She just needs you to convince her otherwise."

Jack stopped and stared. "Walt, what are you getting at?"

"Trying to convince you to get off your lazy ass and ask the lady out."

"Why do you care who I go out with?" Jack was trying to be patient, but Walt's newfound career in matchmaking was getting tiresome.

Walt's voice was suddenly serious. "I care because you've been storming around this place ever since you saw her out to dinner with that weasel lawyer last week."

"Hey, she's a grown woman. She can have dinner with whoever she wants." He wished he actually felt that way. Walt was right, though he'd never admit it. Jack hated that Samantha had gone out to dinner with Rob Morgan. He hated it that Samantha had a boyfriend. It wasn't his business, Samantha wasn't for him, but it did not stop him from wanting her, and from thinking about her way, way too often. Even another week of Todd's stubborn, feral mustangs hadn't been able to keep his mind off his beautiful neighbor.

"Well, good. If you don't care for her, then it shouldn't be a problem talking business with her. Rumor has it she's thinking of selling soon."

Jack felt it like a kick to the spine. "You're kidding."

"Nope."

"That can't be true," Jack protested. "She just inherited it…there can't be anything set yet." He paused, considering last weekend, how savvy Samantha was about handling the huge repair list, how adamant she was that she could handle things on her own. Well, with the exception of downed trees. He grinned at the memory of her bumperless car in the ditch, bits of jack scattered in the gravel as if blown to bits. "She doesn't strike me as the type to take the first offer out there without weighing her options."

"Well, I still think you should take her riding tomorrow. Check it out. You might learn something about what she's thinking, and if not, well, you still get to spend time with a mighty pretty lady."

Jack looked at his old friend, considering all the things Walt didn't know, like Samantha's reaction when he'd been an idiot and kissed her. "I'm not sure she'll go with me, Walt. I may not be her favorite person right now."

"Well, get down there and become her favorite person, son. Or at least the person she's gonna want to sell to. You sit around here much longer and you're gonna find yourself without your best grazing land."

"I'll go down and see what I can do. If—" Jack shoved open the stall door and passed the shovel to his friend "—you finish cleaning out this stall and rubbing down Sugar's leg."

Jack strolled casually out of the barn, pretending that he didn't want to race down to see her again. Walter was onto him though; his creaky laughter following him out of the barn and into the warm afternoon air.

SAMANTHA WAS KNEELING on the porch when Jack arrived, a scarf holding back her hair and a paintbrush in her hand. She looked up and stood, watching him come with a wary expression he didn't recognize.

"Hey, neighbor. How was your week?" Her voice seemed artificially bright. She gave him a smile but it was hesitant, and there was something on her cheek. A tearstain?

He took the porch steps two at a time, sudden dread hollowing his stomach. "What's wrong?"

"Nothing's wrong." She took a few steps toward him.

"Something's wrong." He looked down at her face, pale in the evening light. She looked up at him defiantly, and he met her wide, green eyes, then looked beyond at where she'd been working. Outrage welled up and he took her by the shoulders and firmly moved her out of the way so he could see the porch behind her more clearly. Scrawled on the floor of the porch in black spray paint were the words *Go Home!*

He turned to face her, taking the paint can and brush from her shaking hands. "Who did this?"

"I don't know. When I got here a few minutes ago it was here." She was trying to keep her voice firm, but it wavered, and she looked away.

"Did you call the sheriff?"

"No!" Noticing his incredulous look she continued. "Jack, it's probably just kids. I found some of this old porch paint in the shed and I can cover it up. It's fine."

"You may be used to this kind of thing in the city but it doesn't usually happen out here." A slow burn of anger rose as he imagined what kind of person would drive all the way out here to vandalize her porch. And what he'd like to do to that person. "You shouldn't be dealing with this on your own, Samantha. Why didn't you come get me?"

She looked away and her chin tilted up at a stubborn angle. "I think I've bothered you enough. I'm perfectly capable of fixing this problem myself."

He couldn't stop the worry that was flooding him. "Did they go inside? Did they take anything?" His voice was urgent. "You need to call the sheriff!"

"Jack, I'm fine!" Frustration took the worry out of her voice and straightened her spine. "I don't need you coming here telling me what to do! The doors were locked and it doesn't look like they tried to get in. It's just bored teenagers. I'm not calling the sheriff and having news of this spread all over town." She grabbed the paint back and strode over to the words, kneeling down to slather the thick gray over the sprawling letters.

Jack watched her bemusedly for a moment, trying to calm down. She was right, he had no business barking orders at her, but he didn't like the feel of this. He'd be quiet for now, but he was going to have a talk with the sheriff this week, whether she liked it—or knew about it—or not.

He walked toward her and knelt down, so he could see her face. Her jaw was set, and she looked away.

"Hey, Samantha…I'm sorry. I shouldn't have tried to take charge." She kept painting with fierce, determined strokes. "Samantha, wait. Let me finish this." For all her brave words, she was shaken and furious, and there were tears still threatening to spill over.

"No, thank you. I've got it under control." Her voice was coiled with tension.

"Samantha." He made his voice gentle, putting a hand on her shoulder. "Yes, you *can* do this yourself. I know that. But please, let me do it for you. It's not a bother. I *want* to."

She paused for a moment, then shoved the rusty paint can and brush in the direction of his voice and stood, turning away from him without a word. He picked up the paint and started slathering it on the boards, giving her the space she needed. Eventually she spoke.

"I'm sorry, I know I'm overreacting. It's just that I had a really, really rough week. And this is my grandma's house, and she entrusted it to me and…" Her voice trailed off and he could hear her taking a shaky breath. "I guess I feel like I failed her. In just a few weeks I've already messed it up."

He stood in shock at her words. "*You* messed it up? *You?* Jeez, Samantha, do you really think that you have control over everything? You were out of town, for Pete's sake. You weren't even here. How did *you* mess it up?"

She turned and shrugged, pointing to the remnants of the graffiti. "Well, it is a little personal, isn't it?" Her lip quivered and she brushed her wrist across her face. "I don't know why this has me so upset!" She turned away again but he caught her arm and pulled her back toward him. Her face registered surprise, then anger at his rough handling but he didn't care.

"Samantha, listen to me. I don't know you very well, but I know you had nothing to do with this." He could taste her breath he was so close. See the wet shimmer of her lip where she'd licked it, the unshed tears that her pride held back glittering in her eyes. The urge to pull her close and give her comfort was overwhelming. He quickly set her away from him.

"Come riding with me tomorrow." It was a demand, more than a question.

Her voice was breathy and he realized that she'd felt it too, the pull that was between them. "I can't."

"Why not?" He watched her battle to put that mask of composure back on her troubled face.

"I just have a lot to do here." She gestured around the house. "You should know, you made my to-do list for me!" She gave a halfhearted smile.

Jack tried to ignore the disappointment and just stood, watching her. She looked miserable. Tired and worn and more in need of a day in the mountains than anyone he'd ever seen. He paused, wondering how to say what he needed to without offending her.

"What's going to happen to the house if you

don't get it all cleaned up this weekend?" he finally asked.

"What do you mean?"

"Just what I said. This house has been closed up for years. So what if you don't get the whole thing clean now? The house doesn't care, and the dirt sure as hell doesn't care."

Samantha gave him a surprised look. "But I care," she blurted out.

"Why?" *Here it comes,* he thought. *She's going to tell me that she's found a buyer.*

She looked at the house, obviously searching for an answer. Her voice was shaky when she spoke. "I know it's stupid." She reached up and swiped at her eyes. "I know it won't bring her back. It just feels like if I take care of what she loved, if I tend to it, she'll be okay, she'll be at peace."

That wasn't at all what he'd expected to hear. Jack felt a lump rise in his throat at the heartache in Samantha's voice. He came up behind her, wanting to put his hands on her shoulders and lean her against him. Instead he stopped and clenched his hands to keep them from reaching out. "Ruth's gone, Samantha. You're not going to make all the sadness go away by cleaning everything."

Her laugh was part sob. He went on, trying to say what might comfort. What might allow her to give herself a break.

"The day I met Ruth, she spent most of our time

together talking about you. She loved you, Samantha, a lot more than she loved this ranch. So why don't you tend to *you* for once? Look at yourself. I'm not trying to be rude, but there are some pretty big shadows under your eyes and you're really pale, I'll bet you've barely slept all week." He lost the battle with his self-control and his hands went to her shoulders, automatically rubbing the knots of tension that he found there. "Come riding with me. Come take care of yourself for a day. Let the house be."

She turned toward him suddenly, buried her face in his T-shirt and clung. He paused in surprise for just a moment, then wrapped his arms around and held her while she shook, her tears soaking into his shirt. He pulled her closer and found himself murmuring words into her dark hair, aimless words to comfort and reassure. The tenderness he felt astounded him, her usual strength and composure making this moment of weakness all the more precious.

When she stopped shaking she was still for a few moments, as if startled to find herself in his arms. When she pulled away he silently handed her the faded orange bandana from his pocket. Her face was pink and flushed as she took it from him.

"I'm so sorry. I don't know what came over me." She dabbed at her eyes. He wanted her to look at him, but she didn't, so he wrapped one arm

around her shoulder and gave what he hoped was
a friendly, lopsided hug.

"I guess you needed that." His arm felt her absence as she pulled away.

"Yes, I guess I did. Sorry you were caught in the
flood." He smiled at that. He was getting to like the
dry humor that lurked under her polished exterior.

"No problem. I'm a really good swimmer."

Her face warmed and she touched his shirt, wet
on the shoulder. "Well, it's a good thing, because
you got soaked."

Jack glanced at his watch. It was growing dark
and he needed to get back to help Walter finish the
feeding. He walked over to finish painting, surprised that she didn't protest. She watched him, silently, leaning on the porch railing, obviously lost
in thought in the violet shadows of the dusk. He
put down the last stroke and stood up to face her,
trying one last time.

"So, how about it? Can we take a ride to the lake
tomorrow? Let the house and the work wait a day?"

Samantha gave him a long look, and he looked
right back, challenging her to say no.

"Okay," she finally answered. She took the paint
can from his hands and gave him a wan smile. "I've
had the worst week and I deserve some time off.
What time do we saddle up?"

"How about nine o'clock? And bring a bathing
suit. It's supposed to be warm tomorrow. Maybe

we can get in one final swim before the real fall weather shows up."

He went down the porch steps and took one last look at her, a pale wraith in the gathering dark. "Are you all right, Samantha?"

Her voice was firm and resolute in the dark. All traces of tears had been brought under her fierce control. "I'm fine. Jack. Thanks for everything."

He turned and started up the path toward home, squinting in the darkness to see the twists and turns. *This path is kind of like life,* he mused as he picked his way over rocks and roots. *You never know what's around the corner, you just kind of peer ahead and try your best not to trip when the bumps come.*

An hour ago he'd come down this trail all pumped up to talk about selling the ranch, expecting to find the strong and poised Samantha he'd been butting heads with since they met. Instead he'd found her sad and lonely and trying so hard to be brave. And now he didn't want to talk real estate. All he wanted to do was comfort her and put a smile back on her face.

Hopefully a trip to Lake Beautiful Ruth tomorrow would bring her some happy memories and take away the pain he'd seen in her eyes tonight on the porch. And once she was feeling better, well, maybe then he'd feel better about asking to buy the ranch.

CHAPTER TEN

SAMANTHA EXAMINED THE bags under her eyes in the mirror—suitcases, more like it. There'd been way too much crying last night. Here she was planning to ride the range with a gorgeous cowboy and she had eye luggage.

She rinsed the washcloth in cold water again and wrung it out, holding it against her puffy eyelids, trying to get the swelling down. The cool cloth was momentarily soothing but her unruly thoughts betrayed her as the endless questions filled her mind. What did Dana have that she didn't? Why had Mark cheated? Why had he lied for so long? Tears welled up, ruining whatever de-puffing she'd accomplished and Samantha threw the cloth into the sink.

The third day since "Babygeddon," as Jenna had dubbed it, had been the worst so far. Two days ago Samantha had been too hungover from the previous night's scotch to care much about anything. She'd curled up on her couch with a blanket over her and stared blindly at daytime TV, slept, and watched the comings and goings on the street below her window. Mercifully, her mind had taken that day off. Yesterday had been about getting out of town. Packing, closing up her apartment, getting some groceries and driving with the music blasting had distracted her from most of her unruly or painful thoughts.

The trouble started when she'd seen the graffiti. Once she'd started crying she couldn't stop. As soon as Jack had left, she'd gone inside for another huge cry and this morning the tears just kept coming.

Maybe the initial shock about Mark had worn off, because now she just felt dumped. She'd opened her eyes this morning and it had hit her like a wave to the face, crashing all over her, leaving her stranded on some depressing shore. She'd been cheated on and dumped and there was no escaping it.

Samantha wiped the tears off her face with her sleeve and ordered herself to stop crying. She thought of Tess, the strongest, most independent woman she knew. Tess never let a man get under her skin. Maybe her advice the other night was a good idea. Maybe having a fling with Jack would get this thing with Mark out of her system. Jack might be from a different world, and there was no hope for a future with him, but he was gorgeous and he was nice....

Samantha tried one more time with the cold water. She layered on sunscreen and some makeup, though no amount of concealer could truly disguise her puffy eyes. She rummaged through the duffel of clothes she'd brought and pulled out a tiny bikini that she rarely had the courage to wear. It wasn't Tess's trench coat, but it just might do the trick, assuming she could gather up enough shreds of her self-confidence to make a move.

Shoving it in her pocket, she tore down the stairs to the front door before she lost her nerve. Grabbing the big bag of coffee she'd brought Jack from San Francisco, she started up the path to his ranch.

Outside in the brilliant sunny morning, Samantha was glad she'd found the strength to pull it together. She climbed up the path feeling like every step took her farther away from San Francisco and Mark.

When she got to the top of the hill, Jack was nowhere to be seen. She'd only been here once before, that windy evening last weekend when she'd had to ask for Jack's help with the pine tree and her stuck car. But she'd been so upset, and so embarrassed that she hadn't looked around at all.

The path had brought her to the edge of Jack's driveway, covered in the same crushed gray gravel as hers. To her right was Jack's barn. The old wood, weathered gray in most places, with some faded red patches here and there, made the vast building picturesque. Despite its age, it was obviously well maintained. The huge, wide doors were open and she could see that it was light and airy inside, with stalls on either side of a central walkway of packed earth.

About fifty yards ahead of her, and off to the left, was Jack's house. She could only see part of the back and one side, but what she saw amazed her. She'd been expecting an old clapboard farmhouse like her grandparents'. Or maybe a more suburban, low-slung ranch house. Whatever she'd imagined, it certainly wasn't this.

The house was modern, but built from the bounty of the mountains. The stone foundation and river rock chimney contrasted with the deep honeyed browns of the logs used for solid walls. It looked like it had grown from the timber and rock of the mountains it nestled against. Arched windows ran from floor to ceiling adding grace to the design. The windows faced away from the mountains on this side, allowing a view across the valley floor to the hills and high desert beyond. It looked like something out of a magazine.

"What do you think?" Jack was standing beside her, a couple of halters over his arm.

"It's lovely. Really." How did you feel someone else's skin, apparently radiating electricity, six inches away from yours? She took a step away. "It's unexpected. Did you build it?"

Jack smiled. "I wish I could say I did. I *had* it built. Though, I did have a lot of input into the design."

Samantha studied him for moment trying to

reconcile this new Jack who'd helped design a beautiful, modern house, with the cowboy she'd thought he was. "You're not much like I imagined you to be when I first met you," she told him.

"I'm going to take that as a compliment, since I'm not sure you had a great opinion of me when we first met."

Samantha laughed. "Well, you did give me a bit of a hard time."

"And I think you judged me a bit, right, Frisco? Your hick neighbor rancher?"

"Oh, maybe, just a little," she confessed with a grin. "And speaking of going against stereotypes, here's your coffee, as requested. San Francisco's finest."

Jack took the bag from her and bringing it toward his face, inhaled. He put an expression of stunned ecstasy on his face and staggered around as if in a daze of delight.

"You're silly!" Samantha said, laughing. His goofiness was endearing.

"It's great coffee and I will think of you, and that poor old pine tree, every time I savor it."

"Yes, I saw all the wood stacked in the shed. Thank you. I still think I got the best side of that deal."

"I think we're even." Jack pulled out one of the coffee sacks and pointed to the label. "See? It says it right here. Fair trade."

Samantha laughed again. "I don't think that's quite what they meant when they put that on the label, Cowboy!"

Jack grinned and tucked the bag of coffee under his arm. "Hey, it's my mission to make you smile today, however I can."

Her cheeks flushed at the memory. "I'm really sorry I cried all over you last night."

"I'm glad you felt like you could." He handed her a halter, lightening the mood. "Ready to go riding?"

"I think so." Samantha took the halter and started walking up the driveway by Jack's side. She hoped she wouldn't fall off the horse, or do anything else humiliating as she usually did when in Jack's presence. But today felt different. Maybe it was because she'd cried all over him yesterday, or because he'd been so kind about her pine-tree-versus-car smackdown, but she felt so much more at ease with him this morning.

Jack led her up to the higher pastures, and it was beautiful. Pure air filled her lungs and the grass rolled gently upward, always upward, dotted with granite boulders, until, in the distance, it became a tumble of rocks and aspen trees. The grass was almost knee-deep and was dotted with a few wildflowers, lingering since summer.

Near the far edge, horses were grazing, their muscles rippling under shining summer coats as they foraged. The vast landscape around her pushed Mark's betrayal into perspective.

Jack let out a shrill whistle and heads came up. A chestnut broke away from the group, white socks and a white blaze down the center of her face giving her a jaunty air as she trotted toward them. She stopped a few yards away and tossed her head as Jack approached her. He murmured a few quiet words to her and she settled, allowing him to run his hands over her coat, ruffle her forehead and put the halter on. He turned back to Samantha, and caught her watching him.

"Do they all come when you call?" she asked, though she'd been concentrating on the way his hands looked so capable slipping the halter on.

"Just Apple, so far. And Larry sometimes, when he suspects I have a treat." Jack walked Apple toward Samantha and handed her the lead rope. She held her hand out for the pretty, young mare to snuffle. Apple stepped right up to her, rubbing her face against Samantha's arm, sending her off balance until she braced herself.

"See, she likes you already. My horses have good taste." Jack walked over to Larry and put his halter on. As they started for the gate, Samantha felt a hint of contentment, tinged with excitement. It was like she was a girl again, with the pretty horse walking by her side, the early sun warming her skin and the scent of pine and sage all around.

They took the horses to the barn and brushed them. The simple work was soothing, Samantha watched Jack furtively. He moved with such an easy grace and confidence around the horses. He was always gentle with them, but very much in charge at the same time. He'd been gentle with her, too, last night on the porch, when she'd needed it.

She realized that he'd caught her staring. He didn't look away, just held her gaze for a long moment while Samantha tried to keep breathing. So this was what it was like to want someone this much.

He took a few steps toward her and she wondered if her legs would hold up when he kissed her. But he paused by the fence instead and picked up the pad and saddle that were balanced there. He carried them over to Apple and Samantha moved out of his way, a little disappointed. The saddle smelled like leather and he smelled like salt. The combination made her dizzy.

Jack set the pad carefully on Apple's back, then the saddle. When he reached under Apple's belly to tighten the cinch, she had an amazing view of him in his faded jeans. She wondered what was underneath then quickly turned away. She looked down the hill toward her ranch, focusing on the view, trying to stop this crazy rush of hormones or whatever it was that had her aware of Jack every single moment.

"You ready, Frisco?" She forced herself to calm down and turned back to face him. He had the bridle on Apple and he handed her the reins. "Remember, no worrying, no working and no feeling guilty about not working. Today is just for enjoying the mountains."

If the butterflies in her stomach and the hurt in her heart would go away, she might be able to follow his rules. Samantha took the reins, put her foot in the stirrup and swung up onto Apple's back, hoping that whatever happened in the mountains today, it would wash away the murky residue of Mark's betrayal.

ASPEN LEAVES RATTLED like gold coins in the warming breeze. Larry's long strides ate up the rocky terrain underfoot and Jack let the contentment he always felt up here wash over him. There was nothing like a lungful of pine-scented air and the flat, mineral smell of granite baked by the sun. And every time he looked back and saw Samantha behind him, riding Apple so well, it was like an added bonus to an already damn near perfect day.

A small stream tumbled down the hillside and across his path. He looked down to make sure Larry found his footing and quickly pulled him to a halt. "Look, Samantha. Bear tracks. Do you see them?" She brought Apple close and followed his gaze to the far bank where huge paw prints had dried into the clay. "Old though." His smile was reassuring. "Nothing to worry about today."

She studied the tracks carefully. "Oh, that's comforting."

"Just wanted to make sure you weren't scared."

She narrowed her eyes at him, but took the bait. "I'm not scared. I spent my summers here, remember? And when I wasn't here, I was living in some pretty wild places. Your bear doesn't scare me."

Or if it did, she wasn't the type to let him know it. He admired her attitude. Last night's tears had definitely been a rarity.

Once they got past the stream, there was room for them to ride side by side so he moved Larry over. Samantha brought Apple up beside him and Jack turned to her, asking quietly, "What was that like?"

"What, growing up?" She looked troubled. He'd never seen her at such a loss for words. A few moments passed, then she answered, "I don't know, different from most people's childhood, I guess. My parents are filmmakers. They make documentaries. So we moved a lot, usually two or three times a year. We lived in some pretty exotic places. Asia, the Middle East, Ecuador, India, Kenya."

Jack hadn't imagined this, not in a million years. Her manners, her slight accent, her composed beauty had misled him. He'd pictured her growing up in a mansion somewhere, punctuated by a few rustic summers on the ranch. "Really? Did you have a favorite place?"

Her face was serious, brows momentarily furrowed, her eyes deep green and far away. He liked watching her think. Her answer was hesitant. "I loved Kenya. My parents were filming in one of the wildlife preserves there. We saw every kind of animal imaginable. We had to be really careful of the lions."

"Well, I guess I won't worry about you and a few black bears then." He wanted to keep her talking, to learn more. "Did you like all that moving around?"

"No." She answered emphatically and looked down the hill at the view, obviously done with that topic. He wondered what had made her shut that door into the past so quickly.

"What about you?" she asked him. "Where did you grow up?"

"Oklahoma," he said. "My dad worked as a ranch foreman on a cattle ranch. He still does. I can't get him to retire." Jack paused for a moment, and then went on. "My mom left, when I was pretty young, and moved to the city. Ranching just wasn't for her. My dad pretty much raised me on his own, so I learned most of what I know from him."

"He must be quite a man, to have taken care of you like that," she said quietly.

Jack pictured his father's face—the craggy features, the graying hair, the kindness and humor in his eyes. "He didn't have a lot of choice, I guess. But he's a good guy, a character. I've tried to get him to move out here with me, but he says I'll have to get some cows first."

She laughed at that and her smile lit her pale face and he felt like he'd won the lottery. She was that beautiful. But something was different about her this weekend. He sensed an underlying sadness, or bitterness, and he didn't really understand where it came from. He hadn't been exaggerating yesterday evening when he'd told her she looked tired.

The landscape changed as they climbed higher. The aspen gave way to pine trees growing sparse and twisted among the granite boulders that jutted up through steep hillsides. It occurred to Jack that, tired or not, she was here with him and he was missing an opportunity. If Walt's rumors were true, and she was already considering selling the ranch, he had to plead his case sooner than later.

Maybe her heartbreak last night made it difficult to talk business today, but he could at least show her how well he'd taken care of the land all these years. Then, when the right time came for him to make an offer, she'd know how much work he'd invested in the property already.

Up ahead was a small bridge crossing a gully. He'd completed the project a few weeks ago and the logs were still fresh. "What do you think of my handiwork?" he asked, turning in the saddle to motion to it as he crossed.

"You did this?" she asked, examining the bridge as Apple walked calmly over.

"A few months ago. The one your grandpa built had rotted through." He gave her a cocky smile, motioning to the bridge. "How am I doing, landlady? Am I taking good care of your ranch?"

"Looks like it to me. Seems like I'm lucky to have a tenant who's so good with his hands."

It was exactly the answer he'd been hoping for, but her look was pure mischief and it made it hard to think straight.

Samantha went on, minus the flirtation. "Grandpa used to complain about the time it took him to maintain these trails, but he loved it. Sometimes he'd come out here with his pickaxe and stay the night, just to work on them."

"Your grandpa understood something that a lot of people don't."

"What do you mean?"

"I didn't know him, he was gone by the time I moved here. But I saw the work he did, the years of care that he put into this property." Jack halted Larry and looked around at the mountains he'd come to love so much. Samantha stopped Apple as well and let her put her head down to nibble at a tuft of grass.

Maybe he was preaching, but she was listening.

"It's not just about owning land like this. How do you own all this, anyway?" His arm circled, encompassing the ravine they were climbing out of, the tall pines on the ledge above them, the huge sky. "This land's been here for millions of years. It's going to be here for millions more when we're gone. I think your grandpa understood that there's an obligation to do what's right for the land, not just what's right for the rancher."

She looked surprised. "I didn't know you could be so poetic. Does everyone around here share your views?"

"Not always." He nudged Larry and they moved forward again. "But I think a lot of people, especially people who work the land, or ranch on it, have a healthy respect for it. They're not going to trash it when they're making their livelihood running cattle or horses on it."

Her voice was serious now. "I'm glad my grandmother found you to take such great care of her land. Thank you, Jack."

This was the perfect opening to ask her to sell to him. He could almost hear Walt's voice urging him on. Then he remembered her tears last night. The way she'd been so sad about her grandmother, so anxious to do right by her in taking care of her house. She'd been so conflicted then, so upset, and he didn't want to put that sorrow back on her face. Not right now when her eyes sparkled green fire at him and the smile she'd flashed a few times already had lit up the landscape. Not right now when he'd promised to give her exactly what she needed—a relaxing sunny day at the lake.

They wound their way up the trail until they reached the pass. Surrounding them on all sides were bright blue sky and panoramic views back the way they'd come. The mountains tumbled out into the distance, chaotic bands of peaks and valleys.

"Gorgeous!" Samantha exclaimed. "It's amazing to see how big it all is."

They turned the horses the other direction and there was the lake—the azure water a sharp contrast to the granite boulders surrounding it.

"There it is, Rock Lake. Now known as Lake Beautiful Ruth. You ready for a swim?"

"It's so good to see it again!" Samantha looked happy, like she was returning home, and Jack knew he'd done the right thing bringing her here.

Jack nudged Larry forward and led the way toward his favorite swimming spot, a place where flat granite boulders lined the shore, perfect for lying in the sun. He dismounted in a meadow that surrounded the lake and pulled off Larry's saddle, replacing his bridle with a rope halter.

"They can graze here," he explained.

Samantha slid off Apple, then stretched and groaned. "I won't be able to walk for a week after this!"

"You'll be all right. You're tough, Frisco," he reassured her and moved over to unsaddle Apple. He pulled a couple towels out of one of the saddlebags and tossed them to her. "Why don't you go find us a spot over on those rocks by the shore? I'll let you heat up a bit before I toss you in that water."

Her eyes widened in alarm. "You wouldn't dare!" She headed to the rocks, calling over her shoulder, "Don't make me have to hurt you, Jack Baron!"

Jack shook his head in amusement as he pulled off the mare's saddle and bridle. He slid the halter on and sent her off to graze beside Larry. Turning toward shore he stopped in his tracks. He'd felt like this before, after a bad fall from a horse, gasping for breath when the impact knocked the wind out of him.

Samantha was standing on the granite that sloped gently toward the water's edge. Her back was to him as she looked out over the mountain lake. She'd removed her jeans and boots, revealing slender, muscled legs that ended in a tiny black scrap of bikini bottom. Unaware of her audience, she pulled off her T-shirt and unhooked her bra, unveiling elegant shoulders that tapered into a long thin waist that flared into rounded hips—hips that called for a man to put his hands on them. He swallowed hard as she tossed the clothing aside and tied a bikini top across her smooth back.

He turned away quickly, rummaging through the saddlebags for the shorts he'd packed and giving himself a few crucial minutes to compose himself and get used to this new vision of her. *She has a boyfriend,* he reminded himself. And she'd gone out on some kind of dinner date with Rob Morgan, the one man he could truly say he hated. He liked her, he wanted her, but she was not for him. He had to keep his eye on his goal: to make sure she sold him her ranch.

Shorts in hand, he went back up the trail to change behind a rock, then brought the saddlebags with lunch over to where she lay on her back, eyes closed, lips in a half smile of feline pleasure as she basked in the sun.

"Hey," he said as he spread his towel out next to hers and sat down.

She put a hand up to shade her brow, and cracked a sleepy eye open. "Mmm?" It was more of a purr than a question.

"You ready for that swim now?"

"No." She shook her head and closed her eye again.

"You seem pretty warm. I think you are…"

"I think you're wrong, Cowboy!" She gave up on her attempt at napping and sat up. "I think I'm pretty happy right here soaking in this warm sun. You can go jump in that icy puddle. I'll even cheer you on."

He couldn't help it. He knew he should keep his distance, but she was challenging him with a saucy smile and her beauty went to his head like a drug.

"Not swim!" he cried in mock dismay. "I brought you all the way up here, Frisco, and you're not going to swim? You've been living in the city way too long." He knew he was acting like a teenager, but he scooped her up anyway and carried her to the water's edge while she wriggled in his arms and laughingly smacked at his chest, halfheartedly trying to escape. It felt great and he wouldn't have minded hanging on to her like this forever. But the water beckoned. He paused for a moment with her suspended over the blue depths. "You can swim, right?"

"Of course I can, you hick…"

He cut off her insult by tossing her in with a satisfying splash, promptly diving in alongside her.

"Argh!" She surfaced from the icy water spluttering and shaking off droplets. "It's freezing!"

"Snowmelt," he answered.

"Not nice." She glared at him, treading water and shivering. He saw the idea when it hit her, and the evil gleam that appeared in her eye as a result. He dove under. When he came up she was there and a wall of water splashed into his face.

He inhaled it, sputtered and splashed back. Water was flying and they were shrieking and laughing like two kids. Her grin was a sight to behold, but as he was contemplating it she dove under and grabbed his ankle, startling him enough to send him under and give him a mouthful of water.

Coughing, he turned around and saw her surface at the shore, pulling herself up out of the water and onto the sunbaked rock.

"Don't mess with a city girl," she called as he swam toward her, still coughing. "We know how to defend ourselves, or get revenge as needed!"

He reached for her ankle but she danced back, smiling triumphantly at him as she sat down on her towel, shaking out her wet curls.

"Okay…truce. I've got to get out of this water. Crazy that it's so cold after a whole summer of sitting in the sun." His skin felt raw as he pulled himself up onto the rock and made his way over to his towel, only to find it gone, with Samantha looking innocently up at him. "Towel comes back on one condition, Cowboy."

Her eyes sparkled and he realized he'd done what he planned. She was happy.

"I'm at your mercy."

"No more dumping innocent women into the lake."

"But you're smiling! Admit it Samantha, you're having fun. That's a big change from the woman I saw last night. Maybe you should be thanking me."

She shook her head in mock disbelief. "For dropping me in subzero water? Probably not. Come on, Cowboy, you're shivering. No promise, no towel."

He gave her his promise and lay down gratefully on the towel she pulled from her bag and returned to him. He let the sun thaw his frozen bones. He listened to the peaceful sound of the water lapping against the shore and thought about all the reasons she was not for him.

CHAPTER ELEVEN

IT WASN'T FAIR that Jack looked so gorgeous when asleep. No snoring, no drool, just a quiet breathing and a bronzed body that looked like a dream in cut-off Levi's shorts. His chest was hairless except for a small golden patch in the center. His legs were pale compared to the rest of his body, but strong and more gilded by the sun than she would have expected from someone who wore jeans every day.

She realized his eyes were open, watching her watch him. Her cheeks went hot and she quickly looked out toward the lake. "You're beautiful," he said in a low voice. "You're incredibly beautiful."

"Really?" she asked.

"Really," he answered.

She turned to look at him, trying to read his face. "How beautiful?"

He obviously wasn't expecting that. "Um…very." He sat up, a look of concern replacing the admiration.

Samantha's heart was pounding through her chest with nerves. She could do this. She needed to do this. He wanted her, she could tell, and his desire was a balm, already soothing the blow her ego had taken from Mark. "Beautiful enough that you still want to kiss me?" She leaned toward him then, and brought one hand up to touch the angles of his face, the lines around his eyes. She brought her mouth to his. He didn't kiss her back, just looked at her warily. She kissed him again.

Tess had been right. This was just what she needed. Mark had blindsided her with his betrayal and left her feeling discarded, undesirable. This kiss was her salvation. She kissed him again and heard the sharp intake of his breath. A rush of want lit her down to her chilled soul.

And finally he kissed her back. His firm mouth going soft for her was almost her undoing. She wanted more from him and pushed her mouth against his, relieved when he answered her demand with his own, coiling a hand in her hair and pulling her hard into his arms. His next kiss opened her mouth and she slid her hands down his bare torso, molding the hard muscles of his back, clinging to his strength for support as she rose to her knees with one fleeting thought: that this is what she'd always knew kissing should be like.

"Samantha, wait." He stopped kissing her so suddenly that she felt disoriented for a moment. He pulled back and she sat down abruptly on the towel, alone.

Jack moved back to put a few more inches of

space between them. His voice was hoarse. "There are so many reasons this can't happen." He looked down at her with eyes that had turned almost black with wanting. "Number-one reason being that you have a boyfriend."

His words hit her like a dash of the icy lake water. She'd been hoping he'd somehow have forgotten about Mark, the way she'd miraculously forgotten about him for the past few minutes. The last thing she wanted was to explain to this beautiful man, who probably had women fighting for his attention, that she'd been found so completely lacking in sex appeal by her boyfriend that he'd been sleeping with someone else for the past three months. Jack was looking at her expectantly, his breathing still a little ragged.

Samantha couldn't meet his eyes. "When I told you that last weekend, I really did have a boyfriend. But I don't have him anymore."

"What?" Jack looked at her in surprise. "When were you going to tell me?"

"I don't know." She looked past him, out over the lake. "Soon, I guess."

"What happened?"

She didn't want to go into this now. Didn't want to think about it now. She just wanted to lose herself again, as she had a few moments ago. She leaned over, brushed a damp lock of blond hair off Jack's forehead, and kissed his cheek. "Do you think we could maybe not talk about this?" She gently turned his head and kissed his mouth, trying to silence his questions. "Or maybe just talk about it later?"

Her efforts at distraction paid off. He turned toward her and with a sudden hunger, deepened the kiss. She lay back, pulling him with her, wanting to drown out all memory, all emotion except the passion she felt for this man.

His kisses were bruising and her blood was racing as he leaned over her. Jack's hand felt enormous as it brushed past her breast and wrapped around her rib cage. His fingers travelled to her waist, her stomach, and grazed her hip at the edge of her bikini. She heard a low sound and realized with a shock that it was from her. It hit her that this was going to be sex in about thirty seconds and maybe when it was it would burn away all memories of Mark—all the discomfort, all the worry.

Her hands seemed to have a mind of their own as she reached up over his broad chest and trailed her fingers over his muscled shoulder, his upper arm and back down toward his belly until he stopped her hand with his. It took a moment for her to realize that he was moving her hand away from him, but then his voice, saying her name, penetrated her disordered mind, and she realized he was pulling back again, and gently helping her to sit back up.

"This isn't right." His voice shook. He ran a hand

through his hair and turned away to face the lake. "I want to, I really do, but it's not okay."

"But we can, Jack." She wanted this so much she was almost begging. "I'm a free woman. We can do anything we want."

"But I don't want this, Samantha. I mean, I don't want you like this."

Ouch, was all she could think. Rejected by two men in one week. She must be setting some new kind of record. She couldn't look at him, and she knew her cheeks were on fire. Tears were threatening. This was mortifying.

His voice was kind. "Samantha, listen to me." He reached over, and trailed his knuckles down her elbow to her wrist. Her skin rippled under his touch and she yanked her betraying arm away. "I want you, Samantha. I've wanted you since I met you. But I learned a long time ago that wanting's not enough."

She couldn't answer, with the lump that was in her throat right now, the tears of shame threatening to fall. How could she do this to herself? How could she let herself lose control like this, especially when she was already so bruised from Mark?

Jack went on. "I don't want to be the guy you have sex with just because you can. I'd want it to mean a lot more than that."

Samantha kept watching the lake, trying to will herself to listen to his words, to understand what he was saying, rather than just lose it because of the voice in her head that kept reminding her that Mark hadn't wanted her and now Jack didn't, either.

When she didn't answer he went on. "But that can't happen if you're confused about what you want. And you seem a little confused right now, Samantha. You just got out of a big relationship and you just inherited a ranch. And then there's whatever is going on between you and Rob Morgan. It seems like you need to take some time to figure out what you want, and who you want to be with."

His words were so unexpected, it took a moment for them to sink in. When they did, her laugh was sharp and mirthless. He thought *she* was the one playing the field? Outrage cooled her blood and doused the fire she'd felt just a moment before. "Wow, you have quite an opinion of me, Jack. Rob Morgan? You think I went on a date with Rob Morgan while I was still in a relationship with Mark?"

"Well, I don't know, Samantha. You kissed me, and you were in a relationship. And a few hours later you were out to dinner with Rob."

"No, *you* kissed me, and I told you it couldn't happen again!" Anger helped to bury the embarrassment and the rejection. "And it wouldn't have happened again except that I am now free to kiss whoever I want."

"Like Rob…"

"Who, for your information, is the lawyer for

my grandmother's will, and not someone I want to date. Or kiss."

"I saw you holding hands in the restaurant," he reminded her quietly.

"He put his hand on mine for one brief moment! I think he was trying to be sympathetic about my grandmother or something. You just had the fine timing to walk in at that instant! And obviously you have a very low opinion of me if you judged me so quickly!"

She just wanted to get back to the ranch. So much for trying to be like Tess. She'd finally worked up the nerve to have a fling, and Jack didn't even want her. Worse than that, he saw her as some sort of confused nymphomaniac.

"I'd like to go back now," she told him.

"Samantha, please don't take this the wrong way. I'm trying to be a gentleman here. I just want to be sure your motives are clear. I was wrong about Rob, I apologize. But sleeping with me a couple days after a breakup just doesn't make sense."

She could hear the logic in his words but all she could feel was the rejection. "Thank you for trying to be the gentleman. I appreciate the effort. Can we just not talk about this anymore? Ever? In fact, can we just not talk at all right now?" He gave her a long look, his eyes dark and unreadable. She turned away and silently pulled on her jeans and shirt. She pulled on her boots and gathered up her things. Jack did the same and they walked over to saddle the horses.

It was a long, long ride home. Samantha kept Apple on a tight rein and made sure she walked slowly enough to keep a good distance between her and Jack. He made no attempt at conversation, which was fine because she was pretty busy talking to herself. Well, more like lecturing herself about taking such a stupid risk today and trying to be someone she wasn't. About letting herself be talked into going riding when she should've kept her focus on the ranch and her work.

It won't happen again, she promised silently. I let my guard down with Mark, and now with Jack— and the results have been disastrous. Live and learn, the saying goes, and I'm learning, once again, that it's best just to keep things simple and safe.

Samantha listened to the soothing rhythm of Apple's hooves on the trail and resolved to focus on the tangible things in life—her work, the promotion she'd been striving for, seeing friends and, of course, selling the ranch.

By the time they reached Jack's barn, she was composed, at least outwardly. *Work, promotion, friends, ranch.* She repeated it in her head like a mantra as she helped pull Apple's saddle off. She repeated it as she thanked Jack politely and said goodbye. And she repeated it again as she worked late into the night, scrubbing the old farmhouse until her arms ached and fatigue had dried up the last of her tears.

THE KNOCKING NOISE seemed to be coming from a long way away. Lifting her head, Samantha looked around the sunlit living room, then buried her head back into the couch pillow trying to remember why she was sleeping here. She'd cleaned into the early hours of the morning, and she must have just tipped over onto the couch and fallen asleep at some point. She peered over the edge of the couch and there were her broom and dustpan, lying just below.

The knock came again and she sat up, glancing at the clock in annoyance. Who was bothering her at this early hour of... She blinked. Noon? She'd slept until noon? The expletive she muttered under her breath was uncharacteristic of her, but so was oversleeping.

She jumped up to answer the door, trying not to think about how she'd look, rumpled and half asleep, when she yanked it open. When she saw Jack on the doorstep, she closed it again. Leaning against the old wood, she tried to come to terms with the fact that her day was starting with more embarrassment—it was becoming her most common state of mind.

She pulled the door open again silently and watched Jack looking her over in surprise, taking in the bare feet, the disheveled hair and the throw pillow she just realized she was inexplicably cradling in her arms. Jack reached over and took something off her shoulder and handed it to her. It was a feather from the couch.

"Sleep well?" he asked.

"Yeah…no…sort of." All the memories from yesterday came flooding back, humiliating her, angering her, flustering her. She tried to ignore them and press on. "I fell asleep on the couch…what are you doing here?"

"Betty's party is today. Did you forget that I was going to take you?"

She'd completely forgotten. Another first for her, right up there with oversleeping. But after yesterday, the last thing she wanted was to spend the day with Jack. "Look, why don't you just go without me? I don't want to make you late, and I don't really need to go. I mean, it was really sweet of Betty to invite me, but I'm sure she was just being polite."

"Samantha, Betty loved your grandmother like the mom she never had. She listened to Ruth tell stories about you for years. So yeah, you could skip it, but she hasn't talked of much else all week. She wants to get to know you. Not to guilt you into going or anything." He leaned on the door frame and he was gorgeous and he didn't want her and Samantha knew she had to come up with some reason not to go.

"It's just, after yesterday, it just seems like we

shouldn't be around each other, Jack. It's awkward and embarrassing, and honestly, I have several different dates with several different men lined up for this afternoon and…"

"Okay, I get it. I was a jerk yesterday." Jack gave her a wry smile. "I was hoping we could talk about that for a few minutes, actually."

A feeling of dread started in her stomach—she'd be much happier if they never talked again. "No, let's not talk about it anymore. I think everything was made really clear yesterday."

"I was up all night, thinking about what happened. Can you please give me a chance to apologize?"

She took a closer look at him. An edge of stubble framed his usually clean-shaven face. Shadows gathered under the piercing blue of his eyes. He looked genuinely tired. She nodded reluctantly. "I can't face it without coffee, though. Come into the kitchen and I'll make some. It's instant, would you like some?"

He grimaced. "I guess I can survive instant, but I think you'll need a coffeemaker if you're going to spend any amount of time out here."

"Believe me, I know." She put the kettle on and spooned the black crystals into two mugs. Then she leaned against the counter waiting for the water to boil. "Okay, Jack, let's get this over with."

He shook his head at her dark humor. "All right,

I'll make it quick. I'm sorry I offended you, Samantha, with my comment about Rob. Maybe I was a little jealous of him the other night and that might have made me speak a little too harshly."

Samantha raised an eyebrow at him and he looked sheepish.

"Okay, way too harshly. So I'm really sorry about that. And I'm sorry about whatever happened with Mark. No matter what the circumstances, breakups suck."

She smiled at his blunt term. "Yes, they do."

"I guess I wanted to tell you that I was there myself, a couple years ago. I was married, actually, briefly. She hated it here and so she left."

"Where is she now?" Samantha asked.

"New York. Where she found true love with a *Forbes*-list billionaire and is living very happily ever after." He paused, then took a breath and went on. "I was pretty broken up about it for a while. It took a long time for me to feel like myself again. Everyone is different when things end, but I just wanted you to know that I sympathize. And that's why I couldn't let things get out of hand with you yesterday. I don't want to end up feeling like I took advantage of you while you were in a bad place. That's not who I am and that's not how I want things to be between us." He leaned forward and took the steaming cup she offered him.

"Well, thanks for looking out for me," Samantha

said wryly, wishing he wasn't quite so chivalrous. Wishing she'd never made a pass at him.

"Anytime."

It was her turn. "I'm really sorry if I made you uncomfortable at the lake." This was no fun, but she knew it was the right thing. "I don't usually do things like that."

"I don't usually have beautiful women making passes at me. I'm not complaining, believe me."

She wanted to believe him, wanted to believe that he was holding himself back for her own good, but it still smacked of rejection and it still stung. She reminded herself to be practical. Jack was right. It would be a bad idea to jump into something with him. She had to keep her mind on yesterday's mantra—work, promotion, friends, sell the ranch. But his story had somehow opened the door to her own.

"Mark was having an affair," she blurted out. "With his assistant. It's been going on for months, evidently. I only found out because she's pregnant."

Jack let out a low whistle. "Wow. That's bad." He was silent for a few moments, but not still. His foot tapped and he shoved his hands into the front pockets of his jeans, as if to keep from hitting someone. When he spoke his voice was low with fury. "What an idiot. I'd like to meet him, you know. Tell him to his face what he threw away. Then kick his ass from here to San Francisco."

The image made her smile and she didn't usually

go in for violence. "That's the nicest thing anyone has said since it happened," Samantha told him. "But you'll have to get in line because my girlfriends have already planned his demise, or at least the demise of his kneecaps."

"Well then, I like your girlfriends. Maybe we can all take him on together." Jack picked up his cup and rinsed it in the sink. Then he turned and looked at her with that clear gaze, the one that seemed to see into her. "You know, I doubt there's anyone in this town who needs to go to a party more than you. So go get ready?"

She hesitated, wondering if it would be kind of depressing to spend time with this man when there was so much between them that couldn't happen. But she really did enjoy his company. As long as she blocked out the memories of what it had been like to kiss him yesterday, and how his touch had made her feel, and how mortifying it had all been, she might be okay.

And what he'd mentioned about Betty stuck with her. After her grandfather had died, Samantha had felt so guilty about being in San Francisco when Ruth was out here on the ranch by herself. She'd comforted herself with the knowledge that Ruth had so many close friends nearby who looked after her. She owed Betty a debt of gratitude, and if she could repay a bit of it by showing up at a barbecue, then she'd go.

"Why not?" she said, keeping her words light. "A barbecue full of cowboys, might be just my thing."

He laughed at that. "I like you, Samantha Rylant. I really do."

Samantha sighed. "I like you, too, Jack Baron," she answered. She swallowed the rest of her terrible coffee and headed upstairs to get dressed.

CHAPTER TWELVE

"JACK!" BETTY BUSTLED toward them like a cheerful locomotive as they climbed out of the pickup. "You brought Samantha!" She pulled Samantha into a welcoming hug, planting a loud kiss on her cheek. "I'm so glad you could join us! What a treat!"

Betty reached out and took Jack by the other arm and walked them both toward the crowd, chattering all the way. "Dan's here, Samantha. Do you remember him? He owns the Blue Water Grocery, down by the highway? He says he knew you as a little girl. And he told me some story about Jack scaring the pants off you in the store? I tell you, I try to keep this boy in check but he's just impossible!" She gave Samantha a conspiratorial smile, seemingly unaware of the embarrassed flush that was creeping over her cheeks.

"Thanks, Betty. But I know you love me just the way I am." Jack planted a smacking kiss on the top of Betty's head, caught Samantha's eye and gave her a wink. "You'll get used to it," he said. "News definitely travels fast around here."

They reached the barbecue area on the other

side of the driveway from Betty and Jed's old ranch house. There were several picnic tables, an enormous brick barbecue and a horseshoe pit surrounded by a few pine trees. About forty people crowded around the picnic tables, while children, chasing each other with water balloons, wove through the crowd, shrieking and laughing. It was just another scene from this western movie she'd landed in, Samantha thought, smiling to herself. If Jenna and Tess could see her now, surrounded by folks in cowboy hats, they would not believe it.

"Jack, you go get this one a beer, or a soda or some of that wine you brought by earlier and I'll introduce Samantha around." Betty took Samantha's arm proprietarily.

Jack turned to Samantha. "What'll it be, Samantha?"

"Just water, thanks."

"Sticking to the hard stuff, are you?"

Before she could reply to his teasing, Betty swept her off into the crowd. By the picnic tables there were Betty's sisters, sons, daughters, nieces and a few grandchildren to meet. Next they went to the barbecue area where Jed was grilling what looked to be about five different kinds of beef, surrounded by three rather portly men who Betty introduced as Jed's brothers. And then they were off again and Betty kept up a steady stream of introductions until Sam was certain she must have met the entire town of Benson, from the local fishing guide to the high school English teacher.

When Jack found her she was sitting on a blanket in the shade of a pine tree and Andrew the teacher had her laughing at stories of his various mishaps in the classroom.

"You enjoying yourself?" he asked as he handed her a bottle of water.

"I'm having a wonderful time. Thank you for bringing me. Everyone is so friendly." And she meant it. This was fun, surprisingly fun.

"Yeah." Jack shot Andrew a meaningful glance. "Folks are very friendly around here. You know, Andrew, I'm pretty sure I saw your wife looking for you a few minutes ago."

Andrew looked flustered and excused himself, hurrying off. Samantha turned to Jack, amazed. "Are you doing what I think you're doing?"

Jack was all innocence. "What do you think I'm doing?"

"Scaring that man away."

"I wasn't scaring him." Blue eyes teased over her face. "I was just reminding him of his familial duties." Jack sat down next to her on the blanket.

"So let me get this straight. You don't want me, but no one else is allowed to be interested?" She was only half teasing. She didn't want him, or anyone, messing with her head, or her heart, ever again.

He looked at her seriously. His voice was low.

"You know I want you, Samantha. I don't think you have any idea how much." He took a long drink of his beer. A smile crinkled the corner of his eye as Samantha watched his profile. A grin started and he turned to her with a challenge in his eye. "Maybe I'm just not the fling guy. Maybe I'm the next guy. The one you keep."

Samantha studied him, her heart pounding hard against the wall of her chest. She couldn't figure out if he was serious, so she deliberately misunderstood him. "So you're saying I should go have a fling with someone else then?"

Jack looked at her steadily for a moment. She tried not to squirm under his gaze. "Well, here's the thing, Frisco. I don't think you really want to have that fling. I don't think you're really the fling type, either. So how about you just take some time for yourself, get over that bozo you were just dating, and then we'll talk?"

She was stunned. Did he really want her like that? Thinking about it felt as if a light had gone on inside her, illuminating all the dark corners where so much doubt and angst had been hidden. She looked over at him. He was smiling at her, and she wondered if he was just teasing her one more time.

Samantha looked down at the ground, trying to remind herself that even if he was serious, nothing long-distance could possibly work out. He'd be snowed in half the winter up there on the ranch.

Plus, he'd have to be there every day to take care of the horses, so she'd be the one driving out here all the time, which would eventually make her resentful and then they'd be miserable.

"You just lived through our whole relationship, didn't you?" Jack was leaning back against the tree. He had one knee up and was trying, and failing, to balance his beer bottle on it. "Right here, under this tree, our entire relationship, start to finish, in less than thirty seconds."

"I'm just organized," she quipped. "I like to figure things out beforehand." She tried to keep it light between them but regret had her sitting in silence. Her run-through of their possible future relationship made it clear that there was no happily ever after in sight. She could enjoy the fact that he might want her, let it be flattering and fun, but that's all it could be.

"Well, Frisco." Jack looked over at her, his expression relaxed and lazy, betraying nothing. "I knew you were an amazing woman, but I didn't know predicting the future was on your lengthy list of talents."

She leaned back on the tree trunk next to him, trying to get back to just enjoying the party, despite her nonfuture with Jack. In front of her a few older folks were sitting in lawn chairs watching kids blow bubbles. Off to the right, a young couple was throwing a ball across the grass for a puppy.

Maybe everything about her love life was disastrous, but it was nice to just sit here quietly for a moment, watching people be happy.

JACK MADE HIS way through the crowd, stopping to talk with his friends and neighbors as he went, occasionally glancing over to make sure that Samantha was entertained. Every time he looked over she was in conversation with someone new, obviously enjoying herself. He tried not to notice that many of them were men, who seemed to be finding reasons to end up in her vicinity and introduce themselves.

He couldn't keep his mind off the conversation they'd just had. He knew he'd said too much, probably scared her off forever with his mention of being the guy she kept. Where had that come from anyway? Of course a big part of him wanted to be with her, but he knew it could never work out. He'd seen firsthand what went wrong when you tried to bring two worlds together. They clashed, blew up, and the aftermath wasn't pretty. Maybe a part of him had been hoping that by bringing her to this barbecue, and introducing her to people out here, he would somehow convince her to stay in Benson.

He meandered over to the barbecue pit to see Jed and find some food. Jed's brothers, Dan and a few other locals were lounging around the fire, beers in hand, shooting the breeze. They looked up as he approached and he saw that they were cracking up over some story Dan was telling. He raised his beer bottle to them and said, "I can guess what he's saying, and none of it's true."

Jed looked up and slapped him on the back, his eyes streaming with tears. "I wish I could have seen the look on your face when she started giving you the cold shoulder right there in the grocery store!" He erupted with humor again and threw an arm across Jack's shoulders. "You always did have a way with the ladies, eh, fellas?" Laughter redoubled until Jack broke in.

"Okay, okay! I acted like a jerk and got what I deserved. Oh, and by the way, thanks, Dan. Old friend."

Dan let out a whoop of laughter. "You're welcome, old friend! Couldn't resist telling that tale." He threw an arm around Jack's shoulder. "So Walt told me he thinks you got it bad. Could it be that the local bachelor is considering settling down?"

Jack shot him a look of disgust. "You and Walt are like a couple of old lady matchmakers. No, I'm not settling down and neither is she!" Even as he spoke those words he wished again that things could be different.

"You're a smart man, Jack." It was Jed's brother Hank who broke in with his deep voice. "I know a guy up in Reno, who knows that lawyer fellow, Robert Morgan. I talked to this guy last night. He says that Morgan's saying he's making an offer on that ranch. He's been bragging that it's pretty much in the bag…and that he'll finally be bringing us that big development project he's been trying to start for years."

Silence fell over the group as they all stared at Hank. "You sure about that?" Jed asked.

Hank looked smug, clearly enjoying the audience. "Sure he's trying to get that property. Sure he's offering her a hell of a lot of money for it. Whether she takes it or not, I dunno. But my guess is it will be a pretty tempting offer, especially for someone like her who's not gonna want to stay out here very much anyway."

Jack took a long pull of beer, trying to calm the disappointment and anger he felt churning his stomach. She was accepting an offer from Morgan and hadn't bothered to mention it to him? *Oh, sorry, Jack, I didn't think you'd need to know that I'm about to sell the land all around your ranch to a developer. Oh, by the way, Jack, here's an eviction notice for all your best pastures.* Jeez, she hadn't even asked him if he'd want to buy the damn land himself. Probably figured he couldn't afford her price. He suddenly became aware of the deafening silence that had built around him and looked up, mustering what he hoped was a relaxed smile.

"Well, fellas, I think I better be getting back home. Got a filly with a bad leg and another with a long drive ahead of her." The men chuckled in appreciation and Jed gave him one of his paralyz-ing swats on the back as Jack took his leave.

Jack walked through the crowd, blindly greeting people, frustration and worry building with each step. He found Samantha, sitting at a table with Betty and a few other local ladies, sipping a lem-onade and chatting. She caught sight of him and her smile widened, then dimmed when she saw the anger and strain that he knew he couldn't keep out of his expression.

"Ladies?" He tried to put what he hoped was at least a somewhat charming look on his face. "I think I've got to take Samantha home now. She's got a long drive to San Francisco tonight."

As Samantha said her goodbyes and made end-less promises to visit with Betty and several ladies whose names she was trying to remember, she could feel Jack glaring at her back. The ten-sion coming off him was coiling around her like an electric current. The flirtatious man from under the pine tree was gone, and she didn't like the look of this steel-eyed stranger who had stepped into his place.

Well, whatever his problem was, it wasn't her fault that he'd gotten himself into such a state, she thought as he marched briskly alongside her to the waiting truck. Anger flared. Who did he think she was? Some child to be ordered out of the party at his whim?

"Jack, I'm not sure why you're so upset, but why couldn't you have just waited until we were out of here before you made a scene?" she asked.

They'd reached the truck and he opened the door of the pickup for her.

"What is going on?" Samantha asked. "I don't really want to get in this truck with you until I know what's wrong!"

He looked away. She waited and when he finally turned back to her he was somewhat calm. "Can we just go somewhere quiet to talk? There's a lake a mile away, and a nice view from the roadside."

She got in and they rode in uncomfortable silence until Jack turned the truck onto a side road. After a couple twists and turns on the dirt track, blue water unfolded before them, ringed with pines and boulders. A few fishermen were scattered on the shoreline. Jack swung the truck into a small dirt lot that overlooked the water. Shoving the gears into Park he set the brake and turned toward her. His face was grim. "So, Samantha, do you want to tell me what's going on with Rob Morgan?"

She couldn't believe it. "Jack, all this drama is about Rob Morgan? It's none of your business if I have dinner with my lawyer!" Why was he so obsessed with Rob? Was this his fatal, relationship-destroying flaw making itself known? The psychotic, jealous flaw?

"Samantha, you're in Benson, and out here we're used to people being up-front and saying what they mean. So just say it. Are you selling the ranch to Rob Morgan?"

"Jack, that was a private conversation between Rob and I! How can you know about it?" She searched her mind, trying to figure out how word could have gotten around. Maybe someone had overheard them talking at dinner?

"So it's true then." His voice was heavy and he looked out over the lake.

A stab of guilt flashed through her. He was obviously upset. She should have said something yesterday, but her mind had, unfortunately, been on other things. And then, once she'd thoroughly embarrassed herself, she hadn't wanted to talk about anything.

Out the window, bright blue water danced and crested in the rising afternoon breeze. What could she say to Jack, when she didn't know herself what she was doing? She turned back to meet his burning glare.

"Rob says he's going to make an offer—I assume for a lot of money," she offered truthfully. "It's tempting, and it would certainly make things simple just to sell right away."

"Simple? Simple for who, Samantha? For you?"

He looked away, drumming his fingers restlessly on the steering wheel.

"Yes, I suppose." Somehow she felt as if she was betraying him, which wasn't fair since she hadn't done anything wrong.

"Have you thought about this, Samantha? This is a real decision, with real consequences."

"Of course I'm considering the consequences!" she blazed back. "Please don't patronize me!"

He rolled down his window and let the cooling air in. With obvious effort, he kept his voice calm. "All I'm saying is it's not a simple equation. Do you know what that bastard will do to your ranch if he gets his hands on it?"

"He mentioned something about a small resort. With a few rooms."

Jack's laugh was bitter, mirthless. "A few rooms. Try a few hundred, honey."

"That's impossible!" Samantha wondered who, at this point, she could trust. "Jack, Rob's my lawyer! He wouldn't lie to me! He was Grandma Ruth's lawyer, or, at least, his father was."

"Exactly. His father was, and his father is an honorable man." Jack turned in his seat and his eyes bored into hers, intent on convincing her. "Look, Samantha, trust me, I've been here before with Rob Morgan."

"What do you mean?" She looked at him in surprise.

"He's tried to get land around here before. He and his partners actually owned thousands of acres on the southern side of the valley a few years back. Luckily we found a few endangered species there before they could turn it into condos, hotels, a golf course, a shopping mall and a massive ski resort." Jack must have seen the shock on her face because his expression softened. "Is that what you want for the ranch your grandparents worked so hard to preserve, Samantha?"

Samantha was silent, trying to imagine the future Jack described, trying to reconcile it with the benign image Rob had painted for her. Jack was silent, too, watching her, waiting. Finally he spoke. "I know he's going to offer you a lot of money. I'm sure it will be hard for you to walk away from it. You could buy yourself a lot of great stuff with all the money he'll throw your way."

Did he not understand her at all? Anger and shame coursed through her. Anger at the idea that Rob had been lying to her, if what Jack said was true. And shame that Jack saw her as some bimbo who only cared about shopping. "It was my grandparent's ranch, Jack. I grew up here, as much as I grew up anywhere. You have no idea about me, or what any of this means to me."

He didn't answer and she looked out at the lake, wondering what to say next. Jack shifted in his seat and she could tell he was looking at her. "Samantha, we've never talked about this, but if you're selling the ranch, I'd really like to be the one who buys it."

She should have been happy. Two offers on the ranch and she hadn't even had to advertise. But instead, his words just left a sick feeling in her stomach. *He wanted to buy the ranch.* It all made sense now. No wonder he'd been spending so much time with her. And no wonder, after all his flirting, he'd pushed her away yesterday. He didn't really want her, he just wanted her to sell him the ranch.

She remembered all of his deliberately vague talk about relationships while they sat under the tree today. More flirtation. Empty talk. She should've seen it for what it was. She should be an expert on all that emptiness after Mark. All of yesterday's humiliation returned and quickly mixed in with the grand humiliation that was Mark's betrayal. "Is the ranch the real reason you've been spending time with me?"

She glared at him but he was looking straight ahead, a muscle twitching at his jaw. Finally he spoke and his voice came out in clipped syllables. "There just wasn't a good time to ask. Your grandmother had just died, and every time I saw you something else was going on. You were busy, or falling off a ladder, or hurt or sad and I felt bad for you. It just never felt like the right time to bring it up."

Great. He pitied her. He'd spent time with her

just so he could ask about buying her land, but then she'd been so pathetic that he hadn't been able to? This was too much to bear. This was too mortifying.

"You felt bad for me?" Her voice was shrill and she tried to get it under control. "You spent time with me because you felt sorry for me? And you thought somehow that would be helpful? Show your pathetic new neighbor a good time and maybe get a deal on some acreage?" She glared at him but he was silent. She could feel angry tears threatening. *Don't you dare cry in front of him,* she commanded herself.

He turned to face her, but she couldn't look at him. His voice was low and gentle now. "Samantha, I was trying to do the right thing."

Her heart dropped to her stomach and landed with a thud. He couldn't even deny the accusation? So he did want the land. And he was just one more guy who'd been lying to her. Only it was almost worse than Mark or Rob, though she didn't quite know why. A tear escaped and she brushed it off. No way would she fall apart with him watching.

"Fine, Jack. I get it. You want to buy the ranch. I'm glad I know that now. But I'm not making any decisions today, so please take me home."

He didn't answer, just gunned the engine. The truck rattled and bumped its way back to the highway. Samantha looked straight ahead at the unfolding scenery, paralyzed by the force of the silence between them.

Why was she so clueless about men? Even after all of Mark's lies it had never occurred to her that Rob might lie to her, too. And all that flattery and heat from Jack had come out of nowhere and yet she'd never once questioned that it might not be genuine on his part. And while she was angry with all of them, she was most furious at herself. She'd always tried so hard to be strong and independent. Lately she'd been failing miserably.

He drove up her driveway to the farmhouse porch. "Well, it's been enlightening, Jack." Her voice sounded like some squeakier version of her own as she reached for the door handle.

"Samantha, wait." His voice was urgent.

"Why? So you can make me feel even worse than I do now?" She stepped out the door and into the cool evening air and turned to face him one more time. "No, thank you, Jack. I've had enough of that for one weekend."

She ran into the house and grabbed her suitcase, racing upstairs to throw clothes and toiletries in, pull down shades and check that windows and doors were locked. It was five o'clock, which meant that she could be back in San Francisco by eleven tonight. She couldn't wait to be home, safe in her cozy apartment. And she couldn't wait to put as many miles between her and Jack Baron as she possibly could.

CHAPTER THIRTEEN

"I JUST CAN'T BELIEVE Rob Morgan is trying to get land around here again," Betty said. "After what you put him through last time, Jack, you'd think he'd at least choose another part of the mountains." She set a cup of steaming hot coffee in front of him, and a slice of the best blackberry pie known to mankind. Jack picked up his fork gratefully and took a bite. It tasted like pure summer.

"Well, Rob's a weasel and he sees an opportunity to take advantage of Samantha," Jed answered gruffly, tipping his chair back from the kitchen table. "He's just a money-grubbing kid with more plans than sense."

"Oh, Jed, you know it's not that simple." Betty poured herself a cup of coffee and sat down at her homey kitchen table. "I've told you before, Robby Morgan is up to his ears in debt, from what I've heard. His daddy has threatened to kick him out of the family law practice if he doesn't get himself together. And not only that, my friend Erma, who knows Rob's mother up in Reno, says that Rob's gotten involved with some pretty shady characters and his mother is worried sick."

"Well, all I know is he's going to offer Samantha a ton of money for Ruth's ranch and it's going to be hard for her to say no to that kind of cash." Jack knew he sounded gloomy. He took another bite of pie and a sip of scalding coffee.

"Samantha doesn't seem like the kind of person who only cares about money, Jack," Betty chided gently.

"Well, how would I know? Apparently she's been planning on selling the ranch right out from under me, and she didn't even see fit to mention it." Jack's frustration boiled again at the thought. The barbecue was two days ago and he still hadn't been able to calm down.

"Jack Baron, I'm surprised at you!" Betty waved her spoon at him. "Samantha has every right to consider her options. And so far that I know, Rob Morgan's offer is the only one she's been given to consider!"

Jed took a gulp of his coffee and set the cup on the table. "Jack, there's the thing that I don't understand. Why don't you just make an offer? I don't know the details, but it seems like you're pretty well set up financially. Couldn't you do it?"

Jack considered carefully before he answered. "I could. And if she's selling, I need to be the buyer.

The problem is, I should've offered to buy it a while ago, but I didn't."

"Why? I mean, we all know you're not shy about speaking your mind." Jed chuckled at his own joke.

Normally, Jack enjoyed Jed's ribbing, but today was different. This whole thing with Samantha had him off his game.

"I'm not sure why I didn't ask," he told them. "But I did tell her I wanted to buy it after the barbecue the other day, though I may not have used those exact words. And my credibility with her wasn't too strong by then."

"Jack Baron, what did you do to that woman?" Betty's hands were on her hips and she looked outraged. "She's a lovely person, and Ruth Rylant's granddaughter. You need to mind your manners with her!"

"I screwed up, Betty," Jack confessed. "I think I was wondering if she might keep the ranch for herself…and maybe stick around." It felt good to finally confess what had been haunting him since the barbecue.

"Oh, it's like that, is it?" Betty asked, her voice gentle now, as she brought over the coffee pot. "I thought so."

"Yeah…it is. Well, it was," Jack said regretfully. "Now it's just a big mess. She's positive I was trying to get close to her so that I could get a good price on her land. So I don't think she's going to be very receptive to any offer from me."

"Well, did you at least tell her what Rob Morgan is really like?" Jed asked.

"I tried to, Jed. But I don't know if she believes much that I say at this point. Plus, I'm sure he's painting her a pretty rosy picture of himself and his plans. All I know for certain is that Samantha Rylant is the most stubborn person I've ever met."

"You mean you've finally met your match?" Betty softened her words by refilling his coffee cup.

Jack shook his head and Jed let out a guffaw. "Give the guy a break, Betty. Can't you see he's all lovesick and conflicted?"

"Are you calling me stubborn, Betty?" Jack picked up his fork and grinned at her. "Can't imagine why."

"It's a good quality, Jack," she told him. "It certainly served us well the last time Robert Morgan tried to develop these mountains. I'll never forget how hard you worked to stop him and his cronies. Remember how you and that biologist practically lived in those ranges until you found those little toads?"

"I remember feeling cross-eyed for weeks afterward, I'd spent so much time staring at the ground hoping one would show up." Betty and Jed laughed with him.

"Well, if Rob gets his hands on the Rylant land, we'll just fight him again," Jed said, wearily. "But it would be a hell of a lot easier if you could work something out to buy the ranch."

"That's true, Jack," Betty chimed in. "Or, if you want to give Samantha a chance to spend some more time on her ranch, why not try talking to Rob? Maybe he just needs a little manly heart-to-heart to finally see some sense."

Jack wanted to laugh at that pipe dream. But he looked at Betty, with her good heart out there on her sleeve, and he couldn't say no. "I'll try," he promised her.

Jack knew too much was at stake to wallow in his misery over Samantha any longer. "Look, I made a mess of this and I'll figure it out. I'll talk to Samantha and try to make it right before she sells to Morgan just to piss me off."

Jack remembered again the dark hurt in her eyes as she stepped out of the car on Sunday evening. He'd let her think she'd been used. He'd let her feel betrayed. All because he didn't have the guts to tell her the truth about how he felt.

He knew it for sure at the barbecue, when they sat under that pine tree, but he'd had glimpses of it since the first time they'd met.

He wasn't after her land—buying her ranch was

his second choice. If he could have what he really wanted, she'd keep the ranch and stay right here in the mountains, with him.

CHAPTER FOURTEEN

THERE WAS DEFINITELY something good to be said for reality television. It was Wednesday night and Samantha was so tired she found herself curled on the couch at nine-thirty in the evening, surfing channels with the remote. Skipping the gym and getting some Chinese takeout had been the right thing to do after a thirteen-hour workday, she concluded as she watched a bunch of rugged-looking people waiting anxiously to see if they were voted off the island. She flipped the channel to another program, where ten nervous guys in tuxedos were hovering around a beautiful young woman who was passing out roses. "If it were only that easy," she murmured to her chow mein.

Her phone jangled and she almost dropped the noodles on her lap. She immediately thought of Jack, then wished she hadn't. She kept hoping he'd call to apologize, to say that it had all been a misunderstanding. She wasn't sure exactly what she wanted to hear. That he thought of her just as much as she was thinking of him? That he wasn't just trying to get his hands on her ranch? It was pretty clear that wasn't going to happen. But still, when she didn't recognize the number, a spark of hope shimmered. "Hello?" she answered cautiously.

It was Robert Morgan—the spark flickered out. Rob seemed friendly and helpful enough, definitely not at all the lying, scheming nature-destroyer that Jack had described. He asked her to meet for lunch tomorrow. "I'm really looking forward to seeing you again," he told her. "And I've got some great news for you about selling your ranch. You'll be thrilled to hear it."

She wasn't sure she'd be thrilled. Her mind had been filled with images of the ranch all day, the view over Owens Valley, the granite peaks behind, the rustling noise the wind made in the aspen trees. It was becoming very clear to her that selling the ranch wasn't going to be *thrilling* in any way. It was a necessity, but it was also a sad ending. She made the arrangements for their lunch date, and as she said goodbye and hung up, she wondered how much money was enough money for her grandma's ranch.

ROB LEANED OVER his appetizer. "Five million," he stated.

"Five million?" It was hard to keep her voice low when she contemplated that amount of money.

"Five million dollars. That's what my partners are prepared to offer you." Rob's bright, confident smile gleamed at her in the bright light of the patio

restaurant. Beyond him the bay rippled in blues
and grays under a surprisingly sunny San Francisco sky. It was one of those days that tourists
hoped for and rarely saw, where sailboats whisked
by on the light breeze, and the clear sky made all
the grand bridges and picturesque buildings stand
out in sharp relief.

Samantha thought about five million dollars,
took a sip of her iced tea and studied Rob's face.
He didn't look dishonest. He looked handsome,
clean-cut, and his expression was open and relaxed.
She wished she could just be attracted to someone
like him, who was from her own world. Someone who picked good restaurants and worked in
the business world and seemed so straightforward
and easygoing. He really was just her type. Except
he wasn't, she reminded herself. If Jack was correct, Rob wasn't honest at all, and after Mark, that
characteristic was now top on her list of what she
wanted in a boyfriend.

She realized she should have done her research.
The normal Samantha would have come prepared
with appraisals, figures and questions, but somehow despite all her attempts to keep as busy as possible lately, she hadn't found time to do anything
that related to selling the ranch.

Five million dollars certainly seemed like a lot
of money. Assuming Rob had no terrible plans, a
part of her was tempted to take the offer and run.

How incredible to be that wealthy! She could invest it, maybe even start her own company. And it would immediately get her far, far away from Jack Baron and all the uncomfortable feelings that went with him. With effort, she swallowed those dreams and put on what she hoped was a calm smile. The truth was, she had no idea if five million was a good offer or not.

"That's a lot of money, Rob," she stalled.

"It sure is, Samantha. I told you we'd make you an offer you couldn't refuse."

"I see." Samantha let out a long breath, trying to think through the emotion that was suddenly welling up inside. Ruth's ranch…gone forever if she agreed to this.

"We think we're offering a fair deal and well above market value."

Samantha tried to think of what to ask—what would she normally say if she weren't fighting the lump of panic rising in her throat at the thought of saying goodbye to the ranch? "It's a great deal of money, but you and your partners are obviously going to make a great deal *more* money on this or you wouldn't be offering me this price."

Rob fidgeted with his knife but gave an easy chuckle. "Well, of course, Samantha. But we'll be investing so much money and time into the property, and we all need to make financial gains. This is business, you know." He flashed his open, charming smile. "And as your lawyer and, I hope, your friend, I should advise you that an offer like this won't come around again."

He might be right. Samantha looked beyond him for a moment, at the busy restaurant entrance, and tried to say goodbye to the ranch in her head. The weatherworn house flashed into her mind, framed by tall mountains beyond. She pictured the front pasture in spring, with shorn grass, wildflowers, and roses blooming on the old picket fence. Jack's words echoed in her head, and the beloved house fell down before her eyes, bulldozed to make way for hotels, ski resorts, golf courses. She quickly tamped down the images and dragged her eyes back to Rob's face, wondering if there was a way to figure out if he was being honest.

"Can you tell me more about your plans?" she asked.

"Sure." He set his glass down and leaned forward. "Like I mentioned before, we're thinking a resort. A very small resort. You know, catering to an upscale clientele."

"So by a small resort you mean...?"

"Well, just a boutique hotel really. An upscale lodge with rooms and great dining, maybe a few cabins."

"And the farmhouse? The buildings?"

"If you want to stipulate that we keep them, we

will. Maybe they could become a small museum, or a gift shop selling local products."

That didn't sound too bad. Maybe Jack was over-reacting. "Would there be anything else planned?" she asked. "Any shops?"

"Probably not," Rob answered. "Our goal is to attract a discerning type of clientele to the area, while maintaining the integrity of the natural surroundings."

He was so calm, so sure, it was impossible that he was lying, Samantha thought. A knot formed in her stomach at the thought. Maybe Jack had it all wrong. Or, more likely, she thought cynically, maybe Jack had been trying to scare her into selling the ranch to him.

Rob's phone buzzed and, glancing at the screen, he excused himself and left the patio to take the call.

Samantha nibbled her salad and pondered starting her own advertising business. She tried to calculate how many of her team members would follow her if she went out on her own. A lot, she was pretty certain. And she had to admit that the idea of revenge against Mark was intoxicating. But she knew better than to make any decisions now.

"Sorry about that." Rob sat back down. "Work never stops, as I'm sure you know. So, what do you think of the offer? Are you excited?"

That was definitely not the word she'd use. Rob

was wearing a confident smile and obviously waiting for her yes. With a jolt in her stomach, she knew she couldn't give it. At least not now.

"It's a big decision. I really appreciate the offer, but I'll need some time to think about it."

She caught an expression flit across his face that she didn't recognize. Fear? Anger? But it was gone in an instant and he gave her a sympathetic smile, signaling the waiter to refill her water glass. "I get it, Samantha. It's a big decision. Just don't wait too long, okay? An offer like this won't come along twice."

"But no pressure, right?" she teased gently.

"No pressure." He reached into his briefcase and pulled out a manila envelope, handing it to her across the table. "Here's a write-up of what we're considering. When you have a little time, just take a look at it and give me a call."

CHAPTER FIFTEEN

IT WAS STILL too close to Babygeddon to spend a weekend on her own in San Francisco. Samantha discovered this when she woke up Saturday morning to the quiet of her apartment, and the loneliness of her day. There was a lot she could do, and should do, but normally Mark would have done it with her and she just didn't want to feel his absence.

Samantha had endured breakups before. She'd even been dumped before. But there was an unease that came with the knowledge that Mark had cheated on her for so long. A dirtiness to the memories of time spent with him, that left her feeling wretched and made her want to avoid any reminders that she could.

It felt much better to drive away. Every mile she put between herself and the city lifted weight off her shoulders until she arrived at the ranch, six hours later, singing happily along with Sheryl Crow, the sunroof open to let the brisk evening air pour in. She stepped out onto the gravel driveway with a lighter heart than she could have thought possible this morning and jogged up the steps to the porch.

As she crossed the old boards, something crunched under her feet. Startled, she jolted to a stop and looked around her. Glass was scattered in a thousand shards across the porch. Her front window had been broken, the gaping hole surround by jagged edges.

Her heart sped up until it was banging against her rib cage. She pulled in a deep breath, then another, trying to calm herself. She kept pepper spray in the glove compartment of her car, so she went there first, taking comfort in the fit of the cool metal cylinder in her palm as she approached the front door. It was still locked, so Samantha pulled out her key, opened it and went through.

Nothing looked different. The iPod dock she'd left here was still perched on the kitchen counter. Grandma Ruth's antiques were in place. If this were a robbery, wouldn't all of this be gone?

Samantha stepped quietly into the front parlor and saw the rock where it had landed among the broken glass littering the wood floor. A rock wrapped in paper. She grabbed it and stepped out onto the porch, not wanting to be in the violated house any longer than she had to be. The paper was tied with a red string that slid off easily. A note, scrawled in red ink, read "We don't want you here. Go back where you belong."

Another prank. That was her first thought. Another prank by the same teenagers who'd left the graffiti on her porch. But it was the second time and this was far worse than the first. She couldn't dismiss it this time. Grabbing her cell phone from her purse she called information and asked for the sheriff's number.

JACK STROLLED BACK toward the barn from the upper pasture, throwing an enormous stick for Zeke and enjoying the dog's antics. Zeke treated the stick as his mortal enemy, growling at it, wrestling it to the ground and then dragging it back to Jack so another battle could begin.

Almost to the barn door, Jack heard the wheels on the driveway below. He willed himself to keep moving toward the barn, rather than walk to the edge of the driveway where he could see down the hill to Samantha's house. He wasn't ready to face the hurt he'd put in her eyes last weekend. He wasn't ready to face the feelings he'd confessed to Betty and Jed a few days ago.

What was the point of those feelings anyway? It was futile to hope Samantha would stay. Her life was in San Francisco and the sooner he made his peace with that the happier he'd be. Amy had hated ranch life. His own mother had left his father, and him, because she hated ranch life. So why he thought Samantha might be any different was beyond him. "Hope springs eternal," he'd heard. Or maybe hope was just the idiot emotion.

Jack slid the big doors of the barn closed, latching them for the night. The day had gone to evening, sunlight fading to a gray-and-purple light that made the mountains above go soft. It was like one of those photographs where the person put a filter on the camera. He stopped to look and Zeke came bounding up and set his stick down at Jack's feet, smiling his crazy-dog smile, tongue lolling, waiting for the game to continue. Still watching the mountains, Jack threw the stick. It sailed past the hitching post, and landed at the top of the path that led to Samantha's house. The border collie sprang after it, a speeding arrow of black-and-white fur, but instead of pouncing on his prize he froze, staring over the hillside to the ranch below. He barked once and then stopped.

"Whatcha looking at, boy?" Jack asked, but Zeke didn't turn. He just stood there, one foreleg raised, peering down the hill. Jack called one more time and then walked over to where the dog was.

The sight of the sheriff's jeep pulled up in the driveway below had his heart hammering. He flung himself down the trail at a dead run, leaping the boulders and gullies with Zeke at his heels barking excitedly. He rounded the side of the farmhouse and skidded to a halt when he saw Samantha and

Mike Davidson, the local sheriff, conversing on the porch, surrounded by broken glass.

"Samantha? What happened?" He heard his voice come out loud, angry, hoarse, but he didn't care. He needed to know that she was all right.

They both looked up, and Samantha's eyes widened in surprise. The sheriff's face creased in a slow smile as comprehension dawned. Jack knew he must look like a desperate man. Mike stepped forward.

"Evenin', Jack. Ms. Rylant called me to come on out here…looks like there's been a little trouble."

Jack ignored him, his eyes on Samantha's face, taking in the pale skin, the worry that drew a faint line between her brows. He took a few steps closer. "Why the hell didn't you come get me? Did you stand around here by yourself waiting for Mike to get here?"

Samantha's usual reserve was back. "I am perfectly able to handle this myself, Jack. I didn't need to come find you because I had a broken window. I checked the house and called the sheriff. Everything is fine. Thank you for coming down here to see if I needed help, but I've got it under control." She turned back to Mike as if to continue their previous conversation. Her tone spoke volumes about the hurt he'd caused and the rift he'd created between them. Jack came up the stairs two at a time and took her hand.

"What do you mean you checked the house, Samantha? By yourself? Why? You could've been killed!"

"Oh, come on, Jack, I think that's a bit of an overstatement." She pulled her hand out of his and picked up a broom leaning against the railing, starting to sweep up the broken glass.

"Jack." Mike's hand was firm on his shoulder. "Look, she did the right thing calling me. You probably shouldn't have checked the house, though." He gave Samantha an admonishing glance before turning back to Jack, still keeping a firm grip on his arm. "But you need to settle down, Jack. Samantha has enough on her plate without you getting all upset at her. I'm here, I'm taking a report, and if you're so damn worried I don't know why you didn't call to let me know about the graffiti last weekend."

"She told me not to!" Jack glared at Samantha and then realized that he sounded like a little kid in a squabble. He tried to calm himself, to think clearly through the anger and worry. "Sorry. You did the right thing, calling him, Samantha. And we should have called you last week, Mike, but Samantha was sure it was just kids and I was half inclined to believe her. But now I'm not so sure. What broke the window…a rock?"

"A rock wrapped in this." Mike picked up the note and handed it to him. Jack read the cruel words through a haze of fury and then handed it back to Mike. He needed some air, needed a minute to calm down.

"I'm gonna go find some boards for this window," he muttered, and strode off to the barn, his shoulders tight and his hands clenched into fists.

Mike was right. Samantha had so much trouble coming her way right now. She didn't need him venting his anxiety about it on her. But if Jack could figure out who was doing this to her house, he'd relish the opportunity to show them just how angry he really was.

SAMANTHA WAS SILENT as she and the sheriff watched Jack stride away. She didn't know what to make of him. He seemed like a pretty modern guy a lot of the time, but right now he reminded her more of a Neanderthal, stomping through the overgrown grass, shoulders hunched, head down, throwing out curse words that got fainter as he wrenched open the door of the old barn and disappeared inside.

"Well, Ms. Rylant…" The sheriff's voice had a laugh hidden in it. "He's a little hotheaded this evening. But he's a good man…a great man, really."

Samantha felt herself flush, and looked away from the shed. Thankfully Mike went back to the crisis at hand.

"So, you got any enemies out there, Ms. Rylant?" He kept his voice light but his eyes were alert, scanning her face. "Any ex-husbands or boyfriends who could be holding a grudge?"

She scowled at the thought. "My ex-boyfriend is most definitely not the one holding the grudge, Sheriff. And I can't imagine anyone around here would care enough about me to write notes and throw rocks. I still think it was most likely some kids."

"Well, it could be teenagers who are used to having this old place for themselves and don't appreciate your arrival. I'll make some inquiries; see what the kids around here were up to this afternoon. That's one of the benefits of a small town, Ms. Rylant. It's not so easy to keep secrets around here." He shook her hand and started down the steps. He paused and turned, suddenly looking serious.

"Look, maybe you should go on over to the hotel. Stay there for a while until we get this whole thing sorted out." His broad face was etched in fatherly concern. "I don't like the idea of you up here all alone with this type of thing happening."

"She won't be alone." Jack came around the corner of the porch, laden with an armful of wood. "We'll just board this up to keep any local wildlife out and Samantha can come on up and stay with me."

"What?" Samantha asked. Annoyance crept into her voice. "Thanks for the offer, but the last time I checked, Jack, I was a grown-up, and very able to make these decisions on my own."

Jack set the boards down underneath the broken window. "I admire your independence, Samantha, I really do. But there's also a point where it's just foolish to try to handle everything by yourself."

"Jack! Why can't you understand? I don't need you, or anyone to hold my hand." Samantha turned to the sheriff. "Thank you for coming out here, Sheriff Davidson. You said yourself it's probably just vandalism. I'm sure I can handle a few teenagers with a rock. Just call me if you find out anything."

The sheriff enveloped her hand in his firm grasp. "You're a strong woman, Ms. Rylant, like your grandma. But even she knew when it was time to rely on the folks around her. You need to call me right away if you notice anything suspicious, anything at all. And if you can't reach me immediately, call this guy here." He nodded in Jack's general direction. Then he grinned at her. "Look, he may be a horse's ass at times, but he means well. Let him help you out a little."

Samantha's cheeks flushed in embarrassment but the sheriff had already turned away, hefting himself into his jeep and turning it back down the driveway.

When it was out of sight, she turned around. Jack was sitting on the steps behind her, his expression serious, the handsome planes of his face obscured by a streak of dirt. Her instinct was to reach out and wipe it off, but she reminded herself that her instincts these days were generally wrong. He looked tired and worried.

"He's right." Jack's voice was glum. "I can be a horse's ass. I've felt like one all week whenever I think about how I acted at the barbecue last weekend."

"Thanks." It didn't fix what had happened, but it was nice that he was trying.

"Stay with me tonight." His voice was quiet. "I really don't want you to be down here by yourself."

A part of Samantha wanted to say yes because despite her better judgment, she wanted an excuse to be near this man. The memories of his touch at the lake sent ripples over her skin, but she stilled them as much as she could, and tried to ignore the heat they created. She reminded herself that those were her feelings, not his. His feelings and his longing had a lot more to do with her acreage than with her. The last thing she needed was to get tangled up with another person who didn't truly want her.

"Jack, I don't know why you think I need your help. I'm fine on my own, always have been, always will be, so please quit worrying." She nodded toward the boards. "Look, you've already given me all the help I need."

He stood up and pulled a hammer out of his

back pocket and grabbed a bag of nails he'd thrown down with the boards.

"No." Samantha stepped up and gently took the hammer out of his hand. "It's my problem, I'll deal with it. Thank you, Jack."

He sighed. "Okay, Samantha, I give up. It's your problem and yours alone. Just take this." He handed her a business card from his wallet. It was cream, with copper embossed horses running across it. "My cell number is on there, and the office number is a landline in my house, so if there's anything suspicious, a noise, a rustle, anything at all, please call me."

His kindness was making it so hard to stay strong, and to stay away. She needed him to leave before she gave in to the desire she felt, the desire he didn't feel. Her voice was sharp. "Jack, this old-fashioned prince-charming-to-the-rescue thing is outdated. I'm not a damsel in distress. I don't need your guilt, or your pity, or whatever it is that has you showing up here trying to help me." She picked up a board and turned toward the window, calling back over her shoulder, "Good night, Jack."

He didn't answer but she heard his frustrated sigh before he called his dog and left, his footsteps striding purposefully away from her over the gravel. She didn't let herself watch him go. Instead she poured all her anger and frustration into hitting the nails. The window was boarded up in no time.

She went into the house, flipping on lights and checking all the locks and bolts on every window and door. Maybe it was just teenagers playing a prank, but somehow the house didn't feel like the same safe haven it had before.

SHE HATED TO admit that she was nervous. She'd left her computer in the car, but it was fully dark now and she was afraid to walk outside. For all of her bravado with Jack, the truth was that the rock through the window had shaken her up more than she was willing to admit. It felt so hostile, the note, the broken glass and the threat of an unknown person who seemed to hate her for no reason she could think of.

Steeling herself, Samantha grabbed her keys and a flashlight and went out the front door. The sky made her breath catch in wonder and for a moment she forgot to be nervous. Stars were hanging jewellike above the shadows of the mountains. Down toward the plains, they lit up the dark sky all the way to the horizon. There were so many stars here compared to the foggy San Francisco sky she'd grown used to.

This was the sky of her childhood summers, and she could almost hear her grandfather's voice, pointing out the constellations as he'd done so many times when she was young. Stepping down from the porch and onto the gravel of the driveway, she looked for the dipper, then found Orion in the east and searched for his dogs, who were supposed to be walking beside him. No sign of the dogs, but slowly the fear in her faded, leaving behind an odd sort of peace. It was almost as if her grandparents stood on either side of her, holding her hands, pointing to the sky.

If her grandparents were really here there'd be a blanket on the ground, a thermos of hot chocolate and some homemade cookies packed neatly into a tin, she remembered wistfully. If they were really here, they would remind her that all of this heartache would fade in time. She could almost hear their voices reassuring her. "I wish I could go back," she whispered to the stars. "I wish I could go back and stand here with them again—this time I'd cherish every second." The air was cold and there was no hot chocolate to warm her. Next time, she vowed, she'd carry on their tradition and make some herself. For now, the wide sky slathered in stars would have to be enough.

Samantha strode to her car and pulled her computer from the backseat. She slammed the door and turned in time to see a shadow, just a darker shape against the already dark landscape, disappear around one of the bushes in the lower pasture. Her scream echoed off the hills.

JACK HAD BEEN watching Samantha's house all evening while perched on the enormous boulder behind his barn, his back leaning on the rough wood wall. Not the most comfortable of accomodations. Although he'd worn his thickest parka, one of the wool hats his aunt periodically sent him, and he'd thrown a horse blanket over his legs to keep the rest of himself warm, he still felt the cold of an autumn night in the mountains. A thermos of Walt's blackest coffee and a sandwich helped a little.

He knew he couldn't do this forever, but tonight something didn't feel right to him. The rock through Samantha's window was one problem too many. Someone was out to scare her, or worse. He wouldn't be able to sleep from thinking about it, so he might as well make sure that no one attempted a return visit.

He wished again that she had just come home with him. He could have apologized again. Tried to atone for his idiocy last weekend with a good dinner. Maybe they'd be finishing off a bottle of wine in front of the fire right about now.

Jack took another gulp of coffee. Here he was, playing protector to a woman who'd probably smack him upside the face if she found out he was here. Here he was, thinking nonstop about a woman he couldn't have. Hadn't he learned anything from past hurts?

Then he heard Samantha scream and there was no thought, only his frantic reaction as he raced through the darkness toward the sound. The path flew by him in a blur of dark shapes that he leaped over in an attempt to get to her more quickly.

His voice sounded crazed, even to him. "Samantha!" he yelled as he rounded the back corner of the house, not caring who heard him, or what he might face when he got there. All he wanted was for her to be okay and the fact that no other sound had come after the scream had his feet moving faster and his heart beating in his ears.

He came onto the gravel drive and looked wildly around. At first glance all was quiet, and then he saw her, up on the front porch, pressed up against the wall of the house with a two-by-four in her hand. Relief flooded him and he vaulted the rail, then ducked as she swung the board within inches of his head.

"Jack!" Samantha dropped the board and grabbed his arm, panic in her voice. "Did I hit you? Are you okay?"

"You missed. Nice swing, though." He gasped, trying to get his breath. "Samantha, are you all right?"

"Sort of! What are you doing here?" Despite the fear that made her breathing audible she was staring at him in disbelief.

"I heard you scream. What happened?"

Her usual confidence was gone. Pale and shaken, she stared out at the driveway, her makeshift club again at the ready. "I came out here to get my computer and I stopped to look at the stars. And then I thought I saw something, a shape, over there." She pointed to some bushes on the other side of the front pasture fence."

"Stay here," Jack commanded. "And keep hold of that board. If you see or hear anyone, yell for me, and whack the crap out of them with that."

He started walking toward the bushes. He vaulted the pasture fence, but couldn't see anything behind them. He came back over to the fence to the driveway and started walking the edge of it, shoving bushes back, pulling the flashlight out of his pocket to scan the ground for footprints. Nothing. If someone had been there they were most likely long gone anyway. A crunch in the gravel behind him had him spinning around, torch raised to strike.

"Ouch! Jack! Stop shining that in my eyes!" It was Samantha, of course.

"I told you to wait over there for me!" Worry turned to anger. How was he supposed to protect her when she wouldn't listen to him for one minute?

"I didn't realize you were in charge. Plus, I figure if I'm supposed to whack people with this piece of wood, I might as well protect you while I'm at it." Her composure was back and she was smiling, damn it, and downplaying the whole situation, as usual.

"Samantha, it's not a joke. Something out here scared you and we need to figure out what it was.

If you won't listen to me, then at least help me." He started down the driveway, pushing aside bushes and shining the powerful torch through them, under them, and out into the pasture.

Thirty minutes later they'd covered the entire length of the drive and decided to give up. Walking side by side back toward the house, Jack was silent, thinking. If she'd really seen someone, it could have been the vandal who stuck around after throwing that rock. It seemed unlikely that someone would wait so many hours to make their next move, but it was possible. Tomorrow morning he'd get the sheriff out here and they'd take a better look at that front pasture. And he was going to do something about all this overgrown grass and brush, as well. There were too many places to hide on that hillside.

Samantha interrupted his train of thought. "Maybe it was an animal? A deer?"

"It's possible, but not likely. Did you hear it run away afterward? If animals are startled they often crash through the bushes."

"I don't think so." She sighed, wrapping her sweater more closely against the crisp chill of the mountain night. "But honestly, it startled me so badly that I screamed and ran for the house. It could have been jumping all over the bushes at that point and I wouldn't have heard."

Jack couldn't figure out who would want to scare her so badly that they'd hang around in the bushes half the night. It wasn't someone who wanted to really hurt her, because they'd certainly had the chance while she was getting her computer. The thought brought another wave of fear and anger and he glared out into the dark of the pasture, wanting so badly to wrap his hands around the neck of whoever was stalking Samantha.

She broke the silence again. "I wasn't that loud, Jack."

He knew what she meant but pretended otherwise. "What do you mean?"

"When I screamed. I wasn't *that* loud. I'm sure of it. There's no way it could have woken you up."

He could feel her watching him but kept his gaze straight ahead. "I'm a light sleeper."

"Oh come on, Jack. You know that's impossible. What's going on?"

He knew he'd have to come clean. He stopped walking and turned to face her. "Okay, I'll tell you, but don't get all upset at me. The truth is, I wasn't that far away."

She looked up at him sharply. "What do you mean?"

"I mean, I was worried, really worried, after that rock through the window stunt, and I decided to keep an eye on things. So I camped out on that boulder up there." He pointed up the hill to his perch, the huge mass of granite shining faintly in the light of the waning moon.

She blinked at him in disbelief. "You spent the evening on a rock? For me?"

"Look, Samantha, it's not a big deal. I've slept rough many nights in these mountains."

"Yes, but…"

He interrupted, not wanting to dig deeper into why he felt such a need to protect her. "If something happens to you here, with our houses being so close to each other, I'm going to feel responsible. I don't want that on my hands." He started walking toward the house again and she followed.

"You're not responsible for me. I can take care of myself. I always have."

Jack bit back his exasperation and faced her. "That's not the point, Samantha. I know you're used to doing things on your own. But you're not alone. You have me, and the sheriff, and I'm sure a whole bunch of friends in San Francisco who care what happens to you. No one wants to see you hurt. Maybe all this is nothing, but what if it's not? What if someone really is holding a grudge against you?"

Her green eyes flashed fire at him. "Why would they? It makes no sense! Jack, I'm sorry I screamed, and I'm sorry you heard it, but I think you're making way too big of a deal out of this whole thing. My grandmother lived out here on her own for years after Grandpa died, and never had a problem. It was probably a deer, like we said before."

It had been a very long day and it must be about

midnight, or past it by now. Jack's adrenaline was wearing off and fatigue was quickly setting in. "Samantha, I know you can take care of yourself." He gestured at the two-by-four she was still clutching in her hands. "It's the second time since I met you that you've threatened me with a stick and I have no doubt you could use it if needed."

He was gratified to see a corner of her mouth creep up to a smile. Progress. He knew he was begging and at this point he didn't care. "Think of it as a personal favor to me. It's freezing out here tonight and I'm stiff as a board from sitting on that rock. But for some reason, I'll never sleep knowing you're down here on your own tonight."

"That's not really my problem, Jack." But she didn't sound convinced and he knew he was reaching her.

"You don't want to be responsible for my early demise by sleep deprivation, right? I mean, that would be a terrible thing to have on your conscience."

"Maybe..." Her smile had grown now. "Or maybe I can exact my revenge for your poor behavior last weekend."

"I promise I will apologize for the rest of the weekend, and beyond, if you will please go inside, grab what you need and come up to sleep at my house. Trust me, all I want at this point is some food, a glass of whiskey, a roaring fire in my fireplace, and to not have to worry about you for a few hours. And just think, if you come with me, you'll be able to put that club down and relax a little, too."

Humor worked where begging had failed and she finally gave in. "Well, if you put it that way, let me get my things." Leaning her weapon neatly against the porch, she paused, and grinned up at him. "Okay, I'm ready for my first apology."

"I think it's actually your second, counting earlier today. But I'm a man of my word—I'm sorry I overreacted about Rob and the ranch."

"Very nice." She turned and ran into the house.

Jack watched the lights flicker on upstairs with gratitude, despite the weariness he felt to his bones. This definitely wasn't the way he'd imagined taking her home with him, but if it meant she was safe, he wasn't about to complain.

CHAPTER SIXTEEN

A SMOOTH SINGLE MALT was not at all what she'd expected when Jack had mentioned whiskey. Weren't cowboys supposed to drink Jack Daniel's or moonshine or something? Of course Jack's house wasn't at all what she'd expect from a cowboy, either. She looked around, realizing that nothing about this house fit the image she'd had of Jack Baron.

The downstairs was one great room, with an open kitchen and farther on a dining area. Some walls were made of pine logs, some of natural stone. The ceiling was high and supported with vast tree trunks for beams. Floor-to-ceiling windows, now dark with night, framed views of the mountains and valleys surrounding them. A massive river-rock fireplace dominated one wall. The floor was some kind of rock…slate maybe? And it was warm. He must have radiant heating under there.

Armchairs clustered on a Navajo rug in front of the fireplace. Samantha couldn't resist the thick sheepskin tossed on the floor directly in front of the hearth. She sat down on it and watched the flames in the fireplace, while slowly sipping her scotch. A huge yawn had her eyes watering and she realized how tired she was. She'd only left San Francisco this morning, but it felt like days ago.

It was hard to fathom this day with its charged emotions and events. Why would someone want her to go away from her grandmother's house? She stared at the fire, turning ideas over and over, but none made sense. Had she really seen someone ducking around those bushes tonight? Or was all this stress finally getting to her?

Plots from mysteries she'd read flitted through her tired mind. Had someone been using the property to manufacture drugs while it had stood empty? Had someone been squatting there and now they were upset that the owner was back? But Jack would have noticed anything suspicious going on next door.

The thought crept in slowly. What about Jack? He had more reason than anyone to want her gone. He'd already made it clear he wanted the land and he was willing to be dishonest to get it. Had he really been watching over her to protect her tonight? Or just watching? Had he written on her porch last week? Or thrown the rock earlier today? He'd come running from the opposite direction of the shadow tonight, so that couldn't have been him. Or at least not him working on his own....

Samantha shivered, and looked around the room,

hoping for clues about its owner. He obviously had money, and this house, in all its beauty, didn't seem like the property of someone who would take desperate measures to scare her off her ranch. Samantha noticed the signed landscape painting hanging by the stairs. Unless, she thought sarcastically, he's already spent all his money on decorating.

The man in question appeared by her side, setting a tray of crackers, cheese and olives on the rug next to her. Jack had showered and his hair curled around the nape of his neck. It was mussed, as if he'd carelessly pushed it back as he was preparing their food. He was barefoot, with a soft flannel shirt hanging untucked, and clean jeans, worn to a soft white in places. Samantha looked away, realizing that despite her suspicions, she still found him incredibly attractive. She wished she didn't.

Jack sat down on the other side of the tray and grabbed his own glass, holding it up to the fire and examining the color of the scotch inside. He took a long swallow and sighed. "It's not much." He gestured to the tray. "But I figured it's good enough for a midnight snack."

Samantha hadn't known she was hungry until she saw the food, but now she set down her glass and helped herself. She bit into a salty cracker and watched Jack furtively, while he watched the fire. He certainly didn't look like someone who'd vandalize her house. But what did she know? She'd certainly been wrong about men before, and very recently, too.

His voice broke into her thoughts. "You look like you're getting ready to throw that at me." He nodded his head at the half a cracker she was still holding.

Her own laughter surprised her. "I'm not always on the verge of attack, you know."

"Could have fooled me. What were you thinking about just now? If it's not me, is there someone else you wanted to decapitate with a saltine?"

The sign of a good sense of humor, Samantha decided, was someone who could crack you up even when you were thinking terrible things about him. Through her giggles she managed to assuage his fears. "No. I'm not decapitating anyone in the near future. I was thinking about men, however, and my really, really poor judgment about them lately."

Jack's voice was kind. "Aren't you being a little hard on yourself? So you missed the signs with one guy. It sounds like he was working pretty hard to make sure you missed them."

"But who's to say I'm not making other lapses, even as we speak?" Samantha watched him, waiting for a reaction.

Understanding lit his eyes and he turned to face her, sliding the tray out of the way. "Ah. So we're talking about me now, are we? And after I came to your rescue tonight?" He shook his head in mock disappointment. "You've got no sense of gratitude, Frisco."

She kept her tone light to match his. "Came to my rescue? Maybe. Or were you stalking me from your favorite rock? My new, skeptical self tells me that's another possibility."

"I guess it's one possibility." Jack sobered. "I hadn't thought how that might look. I don't know if you'll believe me, but I promise you I'm not your stalker." He was silent for a moment, staring at the fire. "Or your vandal."

Samantha studied his profile, and the way the fire cast warmth and shadow across the cheekbones and planes of his angular face. It was a lived-in face, she decided, and an honest one. She just wasn't ready to believe he was deceiving her, even if it meant she was only deceiving herself for a while longer.

His deep voice broke into her thoughts. "I honestly don't know why I feel like I need to keep an eye on you, Samantha. You certainly don't make it easy to. I can try to back off, though it seems like every time I do you're falling off a ladder or attacking a pine tree with your bare hands and a small car."

She laughed at the memory. "Well, I guess I should be grateful. I'm sure you've figured out how much I hate needing assistance with things, but even I can see that I've been lucky to have your help a few times now." She raised her glass in his direction. "Thanks."

"Anytime." He clinked his glass gently against hers in a silent toast.

She couldn't keep looking at the lopsided smile he was giving her. He wasn't for her, she reminded herself, and steered the conversation to safe ground. "So how did you—" Samantha gestured vaguely around the room "—end up here?"

"You mean, how did a hick guy like me end up in a nice place like this?"

"Those were *not* my words." She winced, though. He'd read her mind.

"Yeah, but I know you've had me pegged for a backwater cowpoke from the moment we met."

She gave in. "Maybe I'd stereotyped you a little. Okay, maybe a fair amount. But you've got to admit, you dress the part and there's that big old truck and the horses and the dogs, and I'm pretty sure I heard some kind of country music drifting down the hill the other day."

"Okay, you got me! Maybe I do fit the mold, a little. But I thought you San Franciscans were all supposed to be open-minded and nonjudgmental."

"I didn't judge you, I just stereotyped you. I'm pretty sure that's different. And since you constantly remind me that I'm from the city and therefore incapable of understanding the nuances of country life, I think we're probably even."

"Ah, but I am not guilty of stereotyping, since you consistently prove me correct in all my assumptions." He grinned. "I see you trying to navigate the terrain around here in those high-heeled boots you like so much. I see you checking your email and phone about a thousand times a day." He put up a hand to fend off the pillow she tossed in his direction. "Yup. There's a reason I call you Frisco, Samantha. You are city through and through."

"And what does a hick cowpoke like you know about the city anyway?"

Jack took a sip of scotch. "A fair amount, actually."

"Really?" Samantha had been trying to ignore all of her questions about him, but her curiosity was too much. "Jack, I have to know…you're like some kind of superhero, a man of mystery, swooping in to rescue me in your cowboy suit, but really hiding out in this mansion. Do you lead a double life?"

Jack flashed her a smile. "You are a whole lot funnier than you let on, Samantha, speaking of mysteries. I'll tell you my secrets, but honestly, they're not that exciting."

"I'll be the judge of that."

"Well, after high school I got involved in rodeo for a while. Did pretty good, made some money and got a few trophies. But it beat up my body pretty bad, and after a while it seemed clear that I needed a less dangerous way to make a living. So I went to college, and discovered I really liked numbers, and solving problems. So then I got my MBA and got a job in New York City, working in finance. Turned out, I was pretty good at it. I invested, made some good decisions and saved a fair amount of money.

"I liked New York, for a while, at least. And then I got sick of working all the time and being inside in an office all day, so I got out. And drove across the country until I found the spot that felt right—this land right here. After I bought it, I lived in a trailer while I fixed up the barn a bit and then I bought my first horses." He paused, his eyes burning shadows in the flickering firelight. "And then I got really sick of my trailer and built this house."

"I can see how it's definitely a few steps up from trailer living," Samantha said, looking around admiringly." Staring at the sparks and flames, she tried to digest what he'd told her. Jack Baron had worked in New York? In finance? He looked so natural here on the ranch she'd never imagined him anywhere else, with any other life.

He broke into her thoughts. "What about you, Samantha? Have you found a place that feels right?"

The answer to his question used to be a lot simpler. "A few weeks ago I would've told you yes. But now, I don't know. Work has always felt right. It's always what I've been best at." She paused, considering her words carefully as she sifted through her feelings. "And I still love San Francisco. But lately, things have just been *different*. It's a little hard to feel like I belong anywhere right now."

"I can see how that might be true," Jack said. "Considering that you've pretty much had your world turned upside down these past few weeks."

Samantha sipped her scotch, thinking about his words. Thinking about Jack and his gorgeous house and his history in New York City and trying to digest the fact that her hick cowboy neighbor was not a hick at all. Part of her wished she didn't have all this new information about him. It was a little easier to ignore the way she felt around him when she thought they were completely different. Her mind hurt from so much uncertainty, so much unknown. She yawned again. "Jack, thank you for all of this. The fire and the food and the scotch."

"You ready to hit the hay?"

She laughed. "Don't try all that cowboy lingo with me, Jack Baron. I'm onto your secret identity now!"

He grinned and stood up, offering a hand and pulling her to her feet. "Hey, I may have spent some time wearing a monkey suit in the city, but I'm still an Oklahoma boy through and through. Come on. I'll show you to the guest room."

They walked up the grand staircase to the landing above and then down a hallway. Jack opened a door into a room that belonged in an upscale bed-and-breakfast. An arched window showcased the night sky brilliant with stars. A bed with an aged iron headboard was covered in fluffy white duvets.

"There's a bathroom through there, and I put out some towels and stuff."

"This is perfect." Samantha turned around to face him. "Amazing. Unexpected. And as much as I hate to admit it, I do appreciate the rescue tonight."

Jack was leaning on the doorjamb, his face in shadow, but she could see his mouth curve into a smile. "You're welcome. I should be thanking you for staying here and giving me the rest of the night off from my superhero duties. I'll be glad of the sleep."

She didn't want him to sleep. She wanted him to stay and kiss her. It made no sense, her reaction to him. There was no future here, no stability, no safety, and those were the things she'd always craved. Yet she wanted him, wanted to feel the close strength of his body, his mouth on hers.

Her eyes were level with his chest, broad under faded flannel. Her hands came up, a whisper of movement, embodying her desire to unbutton his shirt, to lay her palms on his smooth skin, to feel his warmth, and his steady heartbeat there. She clenched her fists and willed them back down to her sides.

Then Jack stepped forward and his blue eyes

were on hers, mesmerizing in their intensity. "Good night, Samantha." He leaned down and she stood breathless, but his lips merely touched her cheek and then he was gone.

Samantha turned toward the window and stared blindly at the sky. Just a kiss on the cheek and she'd been standing there wishing for so much more. She had to stop this wanting. He'd already made it clear that he wasn't interested in her. Made it clear that he was mainly interested in her land.

There was a soft knock. "Yes?" she said, turning toward the sound.

Jack was there and on his face was written the desire she'd hoped for. He crossed the room in three steps and his mouth came down on hers and all her doubts receded in the wake of his need for her.

His strong hands wove into her hair and held her still. Samantha swore she could feel the power of his kiss flooding her entire body. Without thought, she kissed him back, over and over. He buried his face in her neck and his hands slid to her waist, gripping the curves there. She ran her hands over his shoulders and down his arms and the world narrowed to the feel of his skin, the iron muscles beneath his clothes, the thrill of his arms around her. They stayed there for a long moment, just holding on.

Jack straightened with a shuddering breath and looked into her face. "I've been wanting this for a long time," he told her and he slid his thumb gently over her bottom lip, tracing the full outline. His mouth followed, softly at first, and then deepening the kiss until his mouth was ravaging hers, and the heat of it blotted out all other sensations. Samantha slid blindly into pure desire, surfacing just long enough to think that kissing him was probably a huge mistake. And then his mouth found her neck and the only word her mind could shape for a very long time was *more*.

Somehow, through the wanting, through the ache of longing in her breasts as his hands caressed them, through the rough sound of their intermingled breath, other words formed. Words of fear and caution. Jack's angry words last weekend. His words of apology earlier today. He'd said he was sorry for being unkind, but he'd never told her what she truly needed to hear: that he wanted her, not her ranch. And now here she was, wrapped in his kisses and setting herself up for last weekend's hurt to happen all over again.

Samantha pulled away and looked at the darkness behind the window. She saw her reflection faintly in the glass, her lips parted, her hair wild, cradled against Jack's chest. She had to find some logical brain cells in her clouded mind to help her end this.

"Are you okay, Samantha?"

She turned to look up at him. "This is a bad idea."

"Are you sure?" Jack smiled down at her. "It feels pretty good to me."

"That's not what I meant."

He sighed. "I know." Pulling her in closer, he kissed the top of her head. "It's hard to let you go, but I understand." He stepped backward and the air of the bedroom felt suddenly cool without his warmth coiled around her.

"Good night, Jack." Samantha moved farther away, trying to end this before she went running back into his arms for more.

"Thanks again for coming here tonight. I know I'll sleep better than I would've up on that rock."

She wouldn't sleep better. She'd be tossing and turning, trying to figure out her hopeless, mixed-up feelings for him. "Just being neighborly." She threw the words he'd used so often back at him.

Jack smiled. "If this is neighborly, I sure do like having you in the neighborhood. Good night, Samantha." He shut the door behind him and she stood, staring at the wooden surface, wishing she'd had the courage to ask him to stay.

ROB MORGAN SHOWED up early. Jack had called him during the week and asked him to come by. He'd been dreading it, but he'd promised Betty he'd try to talk to the guy face-to-face. The problem was, Jack hadn't expected Samantha to stay the night. He knew she wouldn't appreciate this little meeting he was having if she found out about it. He glanced up at the window of the guest bedroom but the shade was still down. Hopefully she'd sleep in today.

Rob emerged from his Porsche and walked over to the barn where Jack was loading feed into the truck. He had mirrored sunglasses on and a coffee cup in his hand.

"You wanted to talk to me, Jack?"

He'd have to make this quick. "Rob, I appreciate you coming by. I'll just take a few minutes of your time."

"That would be great," Rob answered flatly. "I can't imagine we have much to talk about."

Jack took a deep breath. He'd need it for this exercise in futility. "I want to talk to you about the Rylant place. I want to ask you to withdraw your offer. Or at least modify your plans. Everyone in Benson is concerned about the negative impact your development project will have on the mountains."

"Geez, Jack," Rob drawled, taking a sip of his coffee. "It's sweet that you speak for the mountains. But this is business."

Jack bit back at least a hundred heated retorts and instead said, "There are a million real estate investment opportunities out there. Why don't you just sink your money into one of those?"

Rob leaned forward, looking at him intently. "You don't get it. You've made your money. But I haven't made mine. And I intend to."

"I do get that, Rob," Jack replied mildly. "And I think you *should* make your money. But there are other ways to do that, other projects that don't destroy what nature took millions of years to create."

Rob gave a derisive laugh. "You're a wealthy guy, aren't you? You're out here playing horse whisperer on your little ranch and you want to make sure you still have your pretty views to look at. You don't care if other people get their fair share or not. What about the jobs we'll be providing?"

"Our community doesn't want those jobs or your money, Rob."

"You'd be surprised, Jack. People think they don't want change, but once they've got money in their pockets, a new car in the driveway, home repairs done or a mortgage paid off, they're pretty darn happy."

"And you're doing all this for them due to your altruistic nature? Is that it, Rob?"

Rob actually looked earnest for once. "I think I'm on the right path, if that's what you're asking. But I'm also in a bind, Jack. You know it, and you know why."

"I'm sorry you lost money, Rob. That was never my purpose or aim with that lawsuit. We just wanted to protect the land around here."

"You ruined me." Rob's knuckles were white where he was gripping his coffee cup.

Something in Rob's voice was different. Jack

looked at him more carefully. There were new lines around his mouth, and his skin was drawn. He looked exhausted. The thought hit him like a punch to the gut and he had to ask, "Rob, do you know anything about the vandalism that's been happening at Samantha's?"

"Vandalism? What vandalism? Of course I don't know anything. Are you accusing me?"

"Not accusing, just asking the question."

"I don't know what…"

Samantha's voice cut through Rob's. "Stop it. Right now. Both of you." Samantha stood next to them in the driveway, a vision in long jeans, high heels and a whole lot of anger. "What are you doing here?" she asked Rob.

"Jack asked me to come. Didn't he mention it to you? He was hoping to talk me into withdrawing my offer on the ranch."

If she was angry before, she was furious now. Her eyes glittered like hard emeralds as she turned on Jack. "That is enough! I want you to stay out of my business!"

"Rob's not being honest with you, Samantha. He'll turn your grandparents' ranch into Disneyland by the time he's done with it."

"Jack, you know that's not true." Rob's voice was smooth and reassuring. It was eerie coming right after the strained desperation Jack had just seen. "Samantha and I have been through the details of the proposal a little already. She knows that's not the case."

"Samantha, I think Rob might know something about the vandalism."

"Jack Baron—out to destroy my reputation, once again." Rob looked bored and fiddled with his sunglasses.

"Rob? A vandal? Jack, he's my lawyer. He's not the one harming my house!"

"Samantha, I need you to trust me on this." The more Jack thought about it, the more he feared the intense resentment he'd heard in Rob's voice earlier.

"How do I know if I can believe you, Jack?" Samantha's delicate hands were clenched into fists. "You haven't been honest with me. If you were honest with me, you wouldn't be standing out here at the crack of dawn, pressuring Rob to withdraw his offer!"

Jack could see the disappointment and the hurt he'd put back in her eyes. He hated himself for it. He wished he could start this day all over again and do things very differently.

"I'm losing faith in you, Jack Baron." There was a coldness in Samantha's voice he hadn't heard before. "Are you sure you didn't write that graffiti and throw that rock? Because at this point I don't know what to believe." She took a few steps back, then looked at both of them sternly. "In case you'd forgotten, it's my ranch, and it's my decision what happens with it—and I'll let you both know when I make it. Until then, I don't want to hear another word about it."

She turned on her heel and stormed across the gravel to the trail between the ranches and was gone.

Rob was clapping. Slowly, appreciatively. Jack shoved his right hand, the one he usually hit with first, into his jacket pocket so he didn't punch the smirk off Rob's face. "Well done," Rob said, as he turned toward his car. "I am so glad you wanted to talk. I think you just did more to convince Samantha to accept my offer than I ever could."

He got into his Porsche and revved the engine, spraying gravel as he took off down the driveway in triumph.

Jack sat down on the tailgate of his truck. He took off his hat and ran his hand through his hair. He had no idea what to do next. He'd been apologizing to Samantha a lot lately, but he needed to find a way to do it again, and make it mean something, or he was pretty sure he'd be saying goodbye to his beloved ranch in the near future.

He loaded the rest of the hay into the truck and called Zeke and Hector to ride with him, hoping inspiration would strike during his morning chores.

CHAPTER SEVENTEEN

THANK GOODNESS THAT when men failed you there was always work. Samantha had her laptop open and her iPod on. The pure notes of opera always soothed her and she needed soothing right now.

She was so tired of men thinking they knew better than her. She was so tired of men lying. And she was bone weary of Jack, pretending to want her, kissing her senseless for half the night, when all his actions pointed to one indubitable fact. He'd do almost anything to get his hands on her land.

She was thankful now for the voice of reason that had told her to stop kissing Jack last night. It was one thing to kiss a man you didn't trust. It was quite another to sleep with him, and thank goodness she'd been smart enough to kick him out of the guest room before it had come to that.

One thing was for certain—she was not going to let Jack, or any other man, ruin another one of her precious days at the ranch.

She was furious, but at least now she knew where she stood with Jack. His kisses meant nothing. And if they were addictive, if they made her crazy with wanting more of them, well, that was a problem she was just going to have to get over. The last thing she needed was to get involved with one more guy she couldn't count on.

Samantha glanced at the clock. It was four o'clock on Sunday afternoon—time to get back to the city. And honestly, she was ready to go. She'd had enough unpredictability and excitement for one weekend. It would be nice to get back into her comfortable weekly routine of work, work and more work.

Then a commotion from the front of the house jolted her out of her thoughts. Samantha jogged down the stairs and then halted briefly, momentarily cautious. Whoever was vandalizing her property still hadn't been caught. But then she recognized the sounds and flung the front door open in shock.

Goats filled her driveway. There had to be at least three dozen of them, and they were bleating and shoving and eating the grass on what used to be the lawn as Jack's dogs barked excitedly and raced to keep the herd together.

Jack slammed the door of the big livestock trailer shut and turned toward her. He pulled off his hat and ran his fingers through his hair adding to his disheveled appearance. He was sweaty and dusty, rugged and handsome, and for the millionth time she wished he was different. Honest. Trustworthy.

Less interested in land acquisition. He took a few steps toward her, hat in hand.

"I told you that if you stayed over last night, I'd apologize all weekend. I didn't know then how much I'd have to apologize for."

"Jack, I don't really want to hear it." She was so tired of empty words. A goat came up on the porch and started nibbling her pant leg. She bent down and gently moved it away. "And what's with all the goats?"

"An apology gift—I should have told you I'd arranged to meet with Rob. I know it looked bad. It must have made you feel lousy."

Why did he have to be nice? It would be much easier to keep her distance from him if he would say more horrible things. She looked out over the swirling mass of goats around her porch. "An apology of goats," she mused. "Original, to be sure."

"Is there any way you'll forgive me?"

"I can try." She steeled herself to tell him the truth. He deserved that, if she was asking the same from him. "I don't trust you anymore, Jack. I'm tired of trying to figure out which of your words I can believe."

He was quiet, turning his hat in his hands. "I get it. I blew it. I'd like to try to earn your trust back."

"Look, the best way to have my trust? Be honest with me. You want my ranch and that's been your motivation for spending time with me all along. I get that. You don't have to pretend anymore."

"It's not. It wasn't." He stepped around a few goats to come closer, to the foot of the stairs. "It's never been my motivation. I promise you. Give me time to prove it."

Samantha had no idea what to say to that. She looked out over the goats. "What in the world do I do with these creatures?"

"This is how we help keep you safe. They're going in the front pasture and their mission is to eat down all that brush that makes a great hiding place for whoever's been giving you a hard time."

Unless the vandal is you, Samantha thought. *You wouldn't come through the front pasture.*

She walked down the steps to meet the herd. There'd been goats in a lot of the villages she'd lived in with her parents. And Grandpa had often kept them out front, calling them nature's lawn mowers. But she'd forgotten how cute and comical they looked. Most of them were pretty big, with long silky ears, but a couple of them were tiny. She looked at Jack and pointed to the little ones. "Are they babies? Can I pet them?"

"They're miniatures. Small but tough. But this isn't a petting zoo. These guys have to get to work!"

Nevertheless she knelt down to the smallest white goat and scratched it behind the ear. It reached up and nibbled at her hair. "I don't know what to do about you, Jack," she told him. "But I'll keep the goats." Jack was watching her when she looked up at him.

"Samantha, will you just do me a favor?"

She turned to face him, marveling at the way the afternoon sun turned his skin and hair golden. It would be a lot easier to hate him if he wasn't so gorgeous "What?"

"Be careful around Rob? Something about him doesn't feel right."

Disappointment flared. So all of this, the goats, the apology, was really about his feud with Rob? She stood up and forced the emotion out of her voice. "Of course, Jack. I will. And now I have to go pack."

"Samantha...wait."

"If you're thinking of making an offer on the ranch, you should probably do it soon," she told him. "As much as I love it here, I'm going to have to do something with it, sooner rather than later."

She turned on her heel and went back into the house, leaving him to wrangle the goats through the pasture gate on his own.

CHAPTER EIGHTEEN

WATERY LIGHT FILTERED in through the distorted glass of the ancient windowpane. This room had been hers as a child and Samantha had loved it. It was one of four bedrooms up on the third floor of the farmhouse. Through the window she could see over the back pastures and the old vegetable beds. Beyond that, the granite cliffs looked like the towers of a fortress. As a child they'd been the ramparts of an imaginary castle, complete with a dragon's cave and wicked witch. Samantha knew, from many summer nights' experience, that at night she'd be able to lean out this window and see a sky full of stars.

Samantha looked around the room and let the good memories drift over her for a moment. It was so nice to be back on the ranch again. It was strange, but all week she'd really missed it. She'd found herself thinking about this house and its graceful old lines. And the way the light hit the peaks around it at sunrise.

She'd even bought a copy of *Country Home* magazine, and sent Tess and Jenna into hysterical laughter when they'd found it in her bag during one of their lunch dates. Tess said she now lived in fear that Samantha would take up needlepoint and give them pillows stitched with verses on them for Christmas.

Samantha didn't think needlepoint was in her future, but she did find it odd that she was enjoying her magazine so much. And searching the internet with keywords like "eastern sierras" and "sierra ranches" when she was supposed to be writing slogans for one of her clients.

Though she was mainly here to clean, Samantha was happy. She knew she had to get the house ready to sell it, the tax bill that arrived this week was an unwelcome reminder of that. But as a reward for her hard work, she'd promised herself a couple of hikes around the property. She was looking forward to seeing the aspen trees, which were nearing their full fall color.

Grabbing a rag, Samantha started wiping the shelves. Surfaces began to gleam as she scrubbed at them, rinsing the dust out of the rag again and again. On the windowsill, behind the curtain, she found an old cardboard box. Flowers were drawn on it in a childish hand and it took a moment to realize that those were her drawings.

She'd given this box to Grandma Ruth years ago, when she was probably about eight or nine…for what? She paused, trying to remember. A birthday gift? No, it had been a thank-you gift, she was sure of that…with some kind of treasure within. She lifted the box as if it were porcelain, holding it underneath so the aging cardboard wouldn't crumble in her hands. The lid came off easily and Samantha set it aside.

She carefully lifted out the contents one by one and set them on the lid. There were rocks that she'd probably collected, though she couldn't see from their nondescript appearance what had made them so special. She took out a small pinecone that was losing its bristles, brittle and lacy. A pink ribbon was tied to a small model of a horse that she remembered begging her grandpa for at the local gift store.

Next was a pile of papers. There were childish drawings, a flyer for a local art fair, and postcards from local attractions: Reno, Carson City, Mono Lake and the old ghost town of Bodie. They had taken day trips to these places. She removed each item, studying it carefully, until she came to a fat packet of envelopes. Letters!

She lifted the paper, crisp with age, and looked at the shaky lettering on the front. Her letters to Grandma Ruth, sent diligently each month that she was away from the ranch as a child. The postmarks told their own story as she thumbed through Madagascar, Hungary, East Germany, Morocco, Turkey. There were a bunch from London, all the stamps as exotic as butterflies stuck forever onto the yellowing envelopes.

She took the top letter and gingerly opened it, sliding out the single sheet of paper inside. Her own adolescent writing, bold and flowery, crisscrossed the page. Going by the date at the top of the page, she'd been fifteen then, stuck at a boarding school in London while her parents were in Ethiopia. Samantha scanned the page. Most of it was news of school and her studies, deliberately cheerful and chatty. But the last paragraphs brought tears.

I can't wait to see you. Term here ends on June 6 and I am counting the days. Mama says I can get a plane ticket out to California on that day, as they will not be able to get back from Africa to see me before the summer starts. I will go to the airlines on my next half day and get the ticket and send you the information. Grandpa, the first thing I want to do is ride to the lake. Will you take me? Please?

I love you both very much and miss you a lot. Please write me as often as you can, though I know you're very busy.

No wonder she was so good at being alone. It was all she'd known for most of her childhood. The loneliness she'd felt in that boarding school came back in a dull ache of old pain. Samantha sat on the bed, clutching the paper in her hand, staring blindly down at it. She'd put on a positive front for her grandparents, but she'd cried herself to sleep during her first year of high school. Some of the girls in the school had been kind, but most had left at holidays and weekends to be with their families. The hallways of the school had echoed with their absence.

The memories of her summers on the ranch had carried her through the school years. She'd boarded a plane every June with a feeling of anticipation and delight that stayed with her across the Atlantic, across the country, until she got off the plane and ran into her grandparents' arms.

It struck her that in her race for success, her single focus on her career, she'd forgotten how much the ranch had meant to her. This box of mementos was a reminder of how rich with experiences and happiness her time here had been. It was the one piece of her childhood that she cherished.

For a moment, Samantha wished she'd never come back to the ranch—she wished she'd sold it without ever visiting. By staying here, surrounded by the beauty of it, immersed in her memories, she was attempting the slow amputation of a part of herself. It would have been a lot easier to sever this connection if she'd never been back here, if she'd never come home at all.

SAMANTHA DIDN'T WANT to wake up from her dream. She was back at the lake with Jack, lying in the sun on a boulder by the shore. He was in the water and he swam over to her, looked up at her and held her gaze, his blue eyes radiating the most pure, intense love. A blissful feeling of contentment and gratitude flowed through her. Then she was sitting bolt upright in bed, knowing with certainty that something was wrong.

Samantha's heart thumped audibly in her chest as she strained to hear what had woken her. Suddenly she realized that the room was dimly lit with an orange glow and in that instant the sounds and smells came together in her mind as one cohesive thought. Fire!

She scrambled over to the window and looked out over Grandpa's back pasture. The light and heat were closer than she'd thought. The woodshed, directly behind the back wall of the house, directly below her room, was burning. The metal roof was glowing an eerie yellow and orange flames were licking hungrily at the clapboard siding of the old farmhouse.

"No!" Fear and anger surged through her and Samantha reached for her cell phone, dialing 911 as she pulled on jeans, boots, a sweater. She ran down the stairs trying to remember if she'd seen an old garden hose anywhere. She grabbed her flashlight off the kitchen counter, and as she gave the dispatcher her information, she ran around the side of the house and down the dirt path to the old barn. There had been a lot of junk in there the day she'd found the ladder.

Shining the light around the shadowy depths, she tried to remain calm and focused on the task at hand. There was nothing in the main aisle, but she leaned over the old stall doors, the beam of the light illuminating piles of old farm equipment. Finally, in the third stall, she saw a hose coiled underneath a pile of lumber. She jerked the door open, shoving and heaving at the wood until she freed the tangled lengths.

Running back down the path toward the back of the house, stumbling under the awkward weight, Samantha prayed a litany of requests—*please no wind, please don't let the house go up, please let the faucet work*... And then she was around the corner to the back of the house and up the slope to the spigot in what used to be Ruth's kitchen garden. Her hands were shaking as she fumbled with the hose. It seemed to take hours to screw it onto the faucet and crank the handle.

Relief flooded her when she saw the water spurt out and then she was running toward the shed, icy water soaking her from the nozzle in her hands. She started on the wall above it first, hoping she could stop the flames from creeping over any more of her grandparents' beloved home. The water seemed to be helping, but the overgrown weeds and shrubs around the shed were like kindling and soon they were hissing, catching and crackling. Samantha sprayed water in a circle around the sides of the shed to keep the fire from spreading. But as she sprayed one section another caught. She kept praying for the fire department to arrive, and for no wind.

"Samantha! Are you okay?" It was Jack shouting, flashlight in one hand, axe in the other, plummeting down the trail. Another man followed more slowly with what looked like a shovel and a second hose.

Jack stopped at the faucet, turned the water as far as it would go and over the hiss and pop of the flames he shouted, "Samantha, spray the water on the wall closest to me! Walt, shovel up the soil around the ground fire. Throw dirt on it to stop it. I'm going in!"

Samantha did as she was told, and the other man, Walt, ran up with the shovel and soon dirt clods were landing on the flaming grass. Jack ran toward the shed, holding the axe above his head like some ancient warrior. He drove it in between the back of the shed and the wall of the house and then leapt back again as the wood crackled and the flames roared.

"Keep the water coming!" he shouted. So she did, and the flames on his side of the shed seemed to hiss and give in. He drove the axe again and again until the side of the shed came away from the house, with Jack just barely darting out of the way.

"Be careful!" Samantha shrieked, aiming the water between Jack and the flames.

Jack ran around to the opposite side of the shed and Samantha sprayed water while he hacked and chopped and eventually that side of the shed tipped away from the house, too. Then the whole structure collapsed forward. Samantha turned the water onto the back of the heap, watching the water pour over the woodshed ruins. Jack and Walt used shovels to pull apart the smoldering boards and coals, making sure there was nothing left but charred wood and ash.

Sirens ripped apart the quiet of the country night. Samantha heard shouting by the front of the house. Doors slammed and footsteps crunched on gravel. The beam of a flashlight lit up the corner of the house with a bobbing glare and three firefighters jogged into view. They slowed when they saw Samantha holding the hose over the embers and Jack and Walt wielding their shovels.

Two more people ran up. As they got closer

Samantha recognized the sheriff, Mike, along with a paramedic carrying a large medical bag.

"Are you okay, Samantha?" Mike asked. "Why don't you step back and let these folks finish this off?"

"Okay," she said as one of the firefighters took the hose from her. Now with nothing to do she was suddenly aware of how cold and wet she was. She shivered. "Thanks for coming, Mike."

The paramedic pulled an emergency blanket from his bag and settled it around Samantha's shoulders. "Come sit down," he said gently.

"I'm okay." She read the name on his uniform. "Louis. Thanks."

"No problem. We…"

Just then the radio at Mike's belt blared out something barely audible. Samantha recognized the word "backup."

Mike looked down at his radio and then reached for his gun. "My deputy's out front. Something's happened!"

"I'll go with you." Jack was by her side, a grim expression under the soot that coated his skin.

"No, stay here," Mike commanded, before running toward the corner of the house. "I mean it!" he yelled back over his shoulder. Samantha watched him disappear around the corner, wondering what gave certain people the courage to run headlong into danger like that.

Then Jack was walking over to her. "It's gonna be all right, Samantha," he said, slipping his arm around her to stop the shivering. "You did great. You stopped the fire."

She sat huddled next to him, listening to his soothing words and worrying about Mike. She could tell Jack was worried, too, because he kept glancing at the corner of the house. Then they heard more shouts, and the slam of a car door. Footsteps hit the gravel along the side of the house and Jack stood, moving in front of Samantha as if to protect her. But it was Mike again. Out of breath, looking triumphant.

"We got him," he said as he slowed to a halt. "We got Rob Morgan."

They stared at him in uncomprehending silence and finally Samantha asked, "What does Rob Morgan have to do with any of this?"

"Apparently everything," Mike answered. "He set the fire."

"Why would Rob set my house on fire? What is he even doing here?" This was starting to feel like a strange dream.

"My deputy found him on the other side of the house. He was climbing the fence into the front pasture."

Jack voice was low with fury. "That little weasel."

Mike held up his hand to placate Jack. "I know,

I know. But he's been caught. Samantha, evidently he saw your ranch as a fast way to pay off a bunch of debt. Looks like he was hoping you'd sell your land to him right away, no questions, no doubts. When you didn't, he got desperate, and tried to scare you off. I guess he figured you'd be frightened and come running to him, and he'd get a good deal."

"If he thought she'd run away, he obviously doesn't know Samantha." Jack stepped off the porch, hands coiling into fists. "He's in the patrol car?"

Mike took a long look at his friend. "My deputy has him there. And he's not going to let you near him."

Jack glared at Mike, but sat back down by Samantha.

Samantha felt like there were snakes coiling in her stomach. She couldn't make sense of the information Mike was giving her. "Did he write the notes? Throw the rock?"

"It appears so." Mike said quietly. "I'm sorry, Samantha."

"He seemed so nice. And he was Grandma's lawyer. Jack thought Rob might be the vandal, but I didn't believe him. It's so hard to understand any of this."

"Well, in my experience, even nice people can do terrible things if they're desperate enough," Mike explained. "It sounds like the guys who Rob owes money to were putting a lot of pressure on him. If it's any consolation, I only caught him because he regretted what he'd done. He figured he'd light the fire and you'd wake up immediately, and it would be one more, *small* scare. But you didn't wake up, and on his way down to his car he could see the flames, but not you. He was running back to put out the fire just as you arrived with the hose. When I spotted him he was trying to sneak through the front pasture, back to his car."

"Well, I suppose that's a small consolation," Samantha said bitterly.

Mike went on. "You were smart to put the goats in the pasture there. They were making such a ruckus—that's what got my attention that anyone was out there."

"They were Jack's idea." A wave of exhaustion flooded her and she just wanted this night to be over. But there was one more thing she had to do. She turned to Mike. "Can I talk to him?"

"To Rob?" Mike looked doubtful. "Are you sure?"

"Samantha, he tried to hurt you. Don't…" Jack was beside her.

She looked at Jack's soot-covered face, the concern etched in lines, and remembered her harsh words to him last weekend. She'd defended Rob.

Accused Jack. "I'm so sorry," she said. "I believed him, not you."

"I haven't given you cause to believe much of what I say." His voice was so much more gentle than she deserved at that moment.

She had to see Rob. Had to look him in the eye and try to fathom how he could have done this to her. Samantha took the sheriff's arm and they walked around the side of the house. "Mike," she said, "how did I not see what Rob was up to?"

"Samantha, I know Rob a lot better than you and never thought he'd go to these extremes to get the ranch. If I didn't see it, how would you have?"

"Jack saw it."

"Jack *suspected*. Now come on. It's over. So let's go give Rob Morgan a piece of your mind."

But when she saw Rob hunched in the back of the police car, filthy and crumpled and apologetic, she didn't really have that much to say. It was sad to see him so broken. As he explained about his debt, and apologized over and over, all she could think was that life was complicated. And people made bad decisions every day— even good people.

She finally interrupted what must have been his tenth apology. "Rob, I hear that you're sorry. I'm sorry, too. I'm sorry that you thought money was more important than my safety. And I'm sorry you got yourself into so much trouble that your life has come to this." She gestured to the police car.

He looked at her in silence for a moment. "You're a class act, Samantha. You really are. Your grandmother was, too."

"Good luck, Rob," was all she could think of to say, and Mike took her arm and led her back to where the firemen were raking through the debris alongside the house, making sure every last spark was out.

CHAPTER NINETEEN

SAMANTHA SAT ON the back porch steps. She was tired, and strangely numb, and when Mike poured her a cup of coffee from a thermos, she accepted it gratefully.

She watched Jack talking to the firemen but it seemed as if he was getting farther and farther away. She started to feel dizzy so she put her head between her knees. One of the firemen took her pulse then he pulled out a sports drink with electrolytes in it and had her drink some.

Jack approached her perch on the back steps and held out his hand. Samantha took it without a word of protest, and the rough strength of him gave her enough energy to stand. He guided her up the trail to his house.

Maybe it was weak, but there was no way she was going to sleep in the farmhouse alone tonight, and she was grateful he didn't even ask. Once they were in the house Jack filled the guest room tub with steaming water and left her alone to soak.

It was hard to relax, but the lavender scent of the soap and the hot water calmed her pulse and some of her adrenaline seeped out into the bath-water. When she was finished she found a pair of men's pajamas and some fuzzy wool socks folded neatly outside her door. She put them on and headed downstairs to say good-night.

Noise came from the kitchen and she followed it to find Jack there, leaning on the counter. He'd showered but his eyes were still reddened with smoke. He handed her a mug of steaming herbal tea and a shot of scotch.

"I wasn't sure which one you needed, so I made both."

"I probably need both." The tea looked dangerously hot so she took a sip of the scotch. "Thank you, Jack." She smiled, trying to convey her gratitude. "It seems like I'm saying that a lot lately. I bet you were hoping I'd stay in the city this weekend so you wouldn't have to do quite so much rescuing."

Jack laughed softly. "Well, it gets pretty quiet here. You're the most excitement we've seen in a while."

"Glad I'm good for something." She smiled ruefully.

He smiled back but then became more serious. "Last weekend I promised you I'd be completely honest with you, Samantha," he said. "And all week I've been thinking about what that means. So I'll be honest now. But you might not want to hear it."

Samantha didn't know what to think. "Go ahead," she told him.

"Okay." He actually looked nervous. "Here goes. I want you to know that at first I didn't tell you I'd like to buy the ranch because it seemed impolite so soon after your grandmother's passing. Does that make sense?"

"Yes." It did, actually, knowing Jack.

"Then I thought I might ask, but I didn't because each time we were together it was fun. I liked being with you and I didn't feel much like talking business, even though I knew I should."

"Okay." She hadn't wanted to talk business, either. She took another sip of scotch, waiting.

"I was never trying to intentionally deceive you. I hope you can believe that. But the basic fact is, if you don't want the ranch anymore, I would like to be the one who buys it—or at least have the chance to make an offer. I need all those pastures. Through renting or owning, I need them somehow."

She nodded.

"And about my conversation with Rob, it was something I promised Betty I'd try. We were hoping to get him to see reason about developing around here. Because fighting off his crazy schemes is getting a little tiresome. And expensive."

Samantha sighed. "I'm so sorry I said those things about you being the vandal. I was really angry, but that doesn't excuse anything."

Jack took a sip of his drink. "It's okay. You had reason to be angry." He came toward her, and Samantha watched him over the rim of her glass, marveling at how much she wanted him to kiss her.

"Now that everything's out on the table, can I be honest about one more thing?"

Samantha put her glass down and Jack took her hands carefully, wrapping them in his own.

"I didn't think about much else this week besides kissing you."

Her voice came out breathless. "Well, that's honest."

"So can I kiss you now?"

"Yes." Her answer was just a whisper. Jack's eyes darkened with need and her pulse sped up. His broad hands came up to her shoulders and gently pulled her close, his long arms wrapped around her and he buried his face in her hair. Samantha knew she shouldn't let this happen, but the scent of scotch and smoke clung to him and she held him tightly, reveling in his hard strength.

When he leaned back and tipped her chin up, she felt his breath on her mouth, saw the midnight blue of his eyes, and all reason fled.

He kissed her, gently at first and then with a rough need. Samantha put her hands to his face, tracing his strong jaw with her fingers, and kissed him back, amazed at her own fervor.

"Samantha," he whispered, pulling back to look

into her eyes with a warmth and fire that stilled her. "I didn't ask to buy the ranch because I wanted you to keep it—I wanted you to stay."

She stared at him in shock and he smiled the slow, satisfied smile of a gambler who'd put all his chips on the table, finally content to trust his luck.

"I… I didn't know," she whispered, trying to absorb his revelation.

He leaned over and whispered back, his mouth so close that his breath caressed her ear, "I've wanted you since that first day. I've wanted to kiss you every day since then."

She'd never felt the power of words like this. Each syllable teased her and heated her until she felt like she'd agree to anything he asked. But he didn't ask. He just took. Brought his mouth to hers and bit her lip gently, then caressed the tiny bruise with his tongue. Kissed her deeply, hands tangled in her hair, curved around her jaw, his mouth savaging hers. The feel of him surrounding her was her undoing.

Jack wrapped his hands around her waist and lifted her onto the kitchen counter. He stood between her thighs and ran his hands up her back to her shoulder blades, kissing her again. His taste was potent, scotch and heat, and she kissed him back fervently, reveling in the feel of his mouth.

Samantha closed her eyes and then there was

nothing but feeling. And no matter how he kissed her, she was somehow left wanting even more.

Her hands gripped his shoulders, then his back, as she tried to pull him closer. Jack wrapped his arms around her and pulled her off the counter so she was clinging to his shoulders, her legs wrapped around his waist. He carried her up the stairs, kissing her the entire way.

He'd wanted her to stay. The words freed something inside of her. She pulled at his shirt and the buttons on the worn flannel scattered around them and her hands were on his chest, feeling the soft hair there, sliding down over the taut strength of his stomach. She bit into the muscle of his shoulder and he gasped in pleasure, staggered a step and bumped her into the door frame.

"Ouch!" There was a sharp pain in the back of her head.

"Samantha, I'm so sorry…" Jack kissed her cheek and set her down on the ground carefully, rubbing his palm gently over the back of her head.

Her head ached and her desire fizzled. What was she thinking? The bump had jolted her back to reality—this thing between them couldn't happen. They'd been here just last weekend. And when she woke up the next the morning, savoring the memory of those kisses, she'd found Jack confronting Rob Morgan. It had felt horrible, and Samantha had spent all week feeling so profoundly relieved that they'd only kissed.

And now, Jack said a few of the right words, after so many wrong ones, and she was going to sleep with him? Was she ever going to learn to be more careful? She thought about Rob and the fire. The way she'd trusted him from the beginning. The way she'd trusted Mark.

Even though tonight's events had proven that Jack was right about Rob, who knew what tomorrow would bring? She didn't want to regret, didn't want to feel the hurt she'd felt last weekend, or worse. She looked at Jack's torn shirt, amazed at the damage she'd caused. She'd completely lost control and that just wasn't safe.

"I can't." It came out almost as a sob. "This doesn't make sense. We can't do this."

They stood, her forehead to his chest, catching their breath. Samantha kept her eyes closed. She knew that if she looked at him, and saw the fierce desire in his eyes, she wouldn't be able to walk away.

"We can do this," Jack said quietly. "If we want. But we should stop, if there's doubt. I can wait for you, Samantha."

"Don't wait," she told him, fighting the tears that were welling up. "There's no point. Good night, Jack." She turned and stumbled down the hall toward the guest room on reluctant legs.

SAMANTHA DIDN'T WANT to open her eyes yet. As she drifted toward the surface of sleep, she nestled deeper into the down pillows and pulled the comforter close. The light behind her eyelids and the tantalizing smell of coffee told her it was morning, but her mind was having trouble catching up. Something felt different. Slowly, like fish rising to the surface of a pond, events of the previous night began to ripple through her tired brain and she opened one eye, then another, to find herself in Jack's guest room, its arched windows showing her the peaks of mountains and the green of pines.

She took in the vaulted ceilings with their wood beams, the fireplace, the plaster walls glowing softly in the morning light. She sat up in bed and her hands went to her flushed cheeks as she remembered the many kisses they'd shared.

A visceral memory of how good it felt to run her hands over his muscular body shredded what composure she presently had. She wanted Jack in a way she'd never wanted anyone before. And he wanted her, too. And she'd told him no. She'd told him there was no point, no future. And she'd done the right thing. So why did she feel so much regret right now?

Samantha rolled over and pulled the covers over her head. After Mark, she'd promised herself to be more careful, to protect her heart. Yet she could feel herself stepping right back onto the Jack Baron emotional roller coaster. Despite her brave words last night, she knew that it was going to be very hard to walk away. "You idiot," she groaned into the pillow. "You absolute idiot."

JACK WAS MAKING cappuccino in a cowboy hat. Samantha leaned on the kitchen island and took in the sight of him in his flannel and denim, wrestling with the home espresso machine.

He offered her a cup and she saw that he'd swirled the coffee through the milk to make a pretty leaflike pattern. "You are full of surprises, Jack Baron!"

He shrugged. "When I moved here I missed espresso. The only option was to figure out how to make it myself."

"If I had known, I would've been banging on your door begging every weekend!" Samantha took a sip. It was heaven.

"Hey, if it keeps you coming around, Frisco, I'll keep making 'em."

His words warmed her more than the coffee, but she knew the right thing to do was to stop him from thinking that way. She shouldn't keep coming around. It just didn't make sense.

"Jack, thank you for last night."

He turned with his own cup in his hand and leaned on the counter, all long grace. "No problem."

"And I'm sorry… I mean…" She realized she

was stumbling around trying to find the words. "I don't regret anything. It felt so incredible, what we did together. I... It shouldn't go further."

"Okay," Jack said mildly. He took a sip of coffee, set the cup down on the counter. "Did you hear what I told you last night?" he asked.

"I heard you say a lot of things." And some of them had just about melted her.

Jack stood and came toward her, and the purpose that sharpened his eyes to the deepest blue was back. He took her mug and put it on the kitchen table, and lightly rested his broad hands on her shoulders. "I said that I wanted you, Samantha. And I still do, more than ever."

He paused and slid his hands down to take hers. "Last night was incredible. And I didn't want to stop what we were doing. But I don't want to be with you when you're distracted by doubts. When I make love to you, you'll be there with me one hundred percent. I won't have it any other way."

"When?" Samantha teased to cover the fact that her knees were about to give way. She found a stool and sat down before she fell over. She picked up her coffee mug again. "You sound pretty certain about that, Cowboy."

Jack's eyes lit with a smile as he leaned against the counter. He was six feet of pure confidence. "I guess I am." He seemed amused at the idea. A thoughtful look crossed his face. "I guess I am," he repeated.

He kissed her on the top of her head and she leaned her forehead against his chest, breathing him in, wanting more of what she shouldn't have.

He kissed her hair once more and then tipped her face up so she looked into the warmth of his eyes. "I have to go feed the horses and get a few things done. But can I do that honesty thing again first?

She laughed. "Um…sure. Do the honesty thing." It had certainly worked out well for her last night.

"I want to take a trip with you."

"A trip?" She pulled back and retrieved her coffee. "Where to?"

"Into the mountains. On horseback. Do you camp, Frisco?"

"No. Well, I did, with my grandparents. But since then I've developed an addiction to boutique hotels, sheets with high thread counts, that sort of thing."

"Will you try? I want to be in the wilderness with you."

She wanted to be in the wilderness with him, too, but that didn't mean it was a good idea. She couldn't stay on the ranch and be with him even if she wanted to—it wasn't realistic. So why make the whole thing worse by spending even more time with him?

"You're scared, aren't you?" he asked, and his eyes were piercing. He leaned in and kissed her, searing her skin, making her want, making it hard to think straight. She clung to him.

"I know it doesn't make sense, Samantha. I know it isn't necessarily gonna make things easier between us, but I want to have that time. Away from the ranch and away from everything that's happened here lately."

Samantha turned away from Jack and went to the window, looking out at the morning light on the peaks. Maybe the kiss had rattled her brain. Because all she could think was that someone like Jack would never come into her life again. Of that she could be certain. "Yes," she answered, marveling at her own daring as she said it. "I'll go."

CHAPTER TWENTY

JACK HAD A very nice view of Samantha's straight
back as they road up the narrow mountain trail.
She was easy in the saddle, talking to Apple and
looking around at the scenery. He left her to her
thoughts, letting her take in the high meadows that
gave way to the brief foothills of coarse rock dotted with sage, mesquite and an occasional hardy
cactus. She'd been through so much stress. He just
wanted her to find peace under the huge sky and in
the endless supply of clear, pine-scented air.

The campsite was on a bluff over a big creek.
The water had cut a deep bed for itself over the
hundreds of years it had run there. Aspen lined
the edges just a few yards farther up, but he deliberately chose a spot under open sky so they'd
be able to watch the stars at night. In the autumn
there were meteor showers, and he was hoping that
they'd have a chance to catch one of nature's most
spectacular shows.

They talked quietly as they set up camp and
turned the horses out to graze in the meadow.

The late-afternoon shadows told him the sun was setting so he took her hand and led her uphill to where a large boulder jutted out and up. They clambered onto it and watched the fiery colors lighting up the high peaks.

Jack watched Samantha take it all in. Her skin was a rosy velvet after a day in the sun. Her lips were full, and curved in a faint smile. For the first time he noticed a dimple on the side of her mouth and knew he'd look for it deepening the next time he made her laugh. He couldn't resist brushing a knuckle over it and she turned to look at him questioningly. "What's going on in that formidable brain of yours, Samantha?"

She gave him a bemused look. "I don't think it's possible to call it formidable at this point. But I guess…" She looked back at the mountains as the last rays of the sun flung themselves over the highest crags, lighting them golden. "It's just that this is so beautiful. You'd think that after the fire and everything with Rob, I'd be upset. But instead, I don't know when I've felt so peaceful."

"I'm glad you feel it," he told her. "I do, too. That's what made me decide to live here, you know. I drove everywhere—Colorado, Wyoming, Montana. I knew I wanted mountains but nothing seemed right. Then I got here and I spent a day hiking around and I knew."

"That must be nice, knowing like that. I feel like I don't know much of anything anymore." Her expression was solemn.

He put his arm around her and pulled her close. "You will. You'll figure it out."

They watched as the sun disappeared behind the peaks and felt the sudden chill of its absence wash over them. She shivered and pulled her jacket closer.

"It's getting late," Jack said. "Let's put on some warmer clothes and I'll make some dinner. Then there's something I want to show you about this place." He offered a hand to help her up and they walked toward their camp.

Soon they were building a small fire and the smell of cooking steak filled the air. Jack looked at Samantha across the flames, curled up with her arms around her knees and he knew, more certainly than he'd known anything before, that there was nowhere in the world he'd rather be right now.

Maybe she'd be gone by tomorrow afternoon, maybe she couldn't say when she'd be coming back, but for now it was enough to be in her presence, to drink in her beauty, to see her smile and unwind a little around him. As her defenses fell away in the clear mountain air, the warmth she kept so guarded most of the time shone through, and it was the most beautiful thing he'd ever seen.

SAMANTHA WATCHED AS the campfire flames wove in and out of oranges, yellows and some deep and indefinable blue. The golden light illuminated Jack's cheekbones; his fierce, angular face was a web of shadows and light. He looked like some kind of primitive god, but one dressed in jeans and Gore-Tex. It almost took her off balance, the way every cell in her body yearned for this man.

It was a weekend of flames, Samantha thought. Last night they'd been brought together by a fire and now she could feel the warmth from the campfire on her face, and a steady heat within her, banked now, but ready to flame again at his touch.

Samantha didn't know how such a fire could ever be extinguished. Maybe, she thought, if she finally had a fling with him, she could put it out, or at least tamp it down. Life would be so much more comfortable if she could.

"A steak for your thoughts." Samantha jumped a bit as a slab of meat on a tin plate was placed in front of her. "It's not exactly fine dining," Jack said as he returned to his side of the fire and speared the second steak off the grill.

Samantha inhaled the rich, smoky smell and cut into the thick steak. He'd cooked it to perfection, and it melted in her mouth as she chewed, savoring the deep flavors. She opened her eyes to find Jack watching her with a slightly dazed expression. "It's delicious." She cut into another bite. "And you are wrong, this is definitely fine dining."

He chuckled at her lavish compliment and cut into his own meat. "I'd still like to know what you were thinking back there."

"It wasn't important." Fortunately it was too dark for him to see her blush. Something caught her eye in the deepening dusk and she glanced up in time to see a star sailing across the heavens. "Shooting star!" she exclaimed, pointing toward it as it disappeared. She was grateful for the change of subject.

"You must be on the lucky rock." Jack walked around the fire and sat beside her. They put their plates aside and Jack pulled the saddles over so they could lie back against them and watch the sky. "It's a meteor shower. Look, there's another one!" He pointed to a tiny glimmer that was zipping along the horizon.

Jack's hand found hers. His grip was warm and strong and Samantha had the strange and unfamiliar feeling that she was right where she should be.

The sky was awash in a glory of glimmering stars that cascaded from horizon to horizon, crystalline sparks sharp in the clean, thin mountain air. Another traveler shot across the sky, this time leaving a trail of light behind it. She gasped and Jack laughed.

"Isn't it incredible?" he asked.

She loved this sky, with its flying stars and its

clarity. She loved the solidity of the granite beneath her, and the sound of the nearby creek bubbling through the quiet of the high mountain night. This was a big reason the thought of selling the ranch wove knots in her stomach. She'd made the mistake of falling in love with these mountains, these meadows. And now she was falling in love with Jack. Samantha gasped and sat up suddenly.

"You okay?" Jack tilted the brim of his hat up to study her face, concern etched on his own. "Samantha?"

She shook her head, trying to fight the growing certainty of her feelings as she stared at his long, lean frame stretched so gracefully on the rocky ground. A flash of firelight lit his face and she could see the dark intensity in his eyes as he sat up and repeated the question. "Are you okay? Are you cold?"

She hadn't known she had these feelings. She didn't want these feelings. There was no way she could be falling in love with Jack Baron. He was a crush, an attempted fling, a friend, a pipe dream, but not someone she could ever truly be with. She wanted him desperately, there was no doubt about that, but she'd vowed she wouldn't set herself up for such certain heartache.

She took a few deep breaths until she was able to answer in what she hoped was a nonchalant tone of voice, "Maybe I am a little cold."

He stood immediately. "Well, I can fix that for you." He held out his hand. "Come on."

She hesitated. "Where?"

"Have you always been so damn cautious, Frisco? Get up here and I'll show you!"

Laughing at his accurate assessment of her personality, Samantha took his hand and let him pull her up. He grabbed a towel from his saddlebag, and flung it over his shoulder.

She let him lead her over to the creek. A small trail down the bank was just visible in the growing starlight. Jack started down the path, stopping in front of her to support her as she climbed down the uneven path.

When they reached the water she stopped at the sight of the stars reflected in the rippling surface. The air felt a little cooler, a little damper down here and she could smell the moist earth under her feet. She eyed Jack's towel as he turned to face her. "We are not going for a swim. It's freezing!"

He took a step closer and she could feel the heat radiating from his tall frame. He kissed her lightly on the mouth. "Have faith, Samantha. I'm not going to freeze you. I want to show you something special about the mountains. Something not a lot of people know about. Will you follow me?"

She did, and he led her along the pebbly shore of the creek and around a bend. The banks were higher and steeper here, more like small cliffs.

They walked a few more yards and Samantha heard a trickle of water that became louder. Jack stopped and motioned toward the bank. Rivulets of water were running down an overhang, making a waterfall. The area under the waterfall had been walled off with rocks, creating a deep pool alongside the edge of the creek.

"Touch it," Jack said, and she leaned down to the surface of the pool. The smell hit her first. Sulfur, a faint rotting egg smell that was just weak enough to be somewhat inoffensive. Her hand grazed the surface and she pulled it back in surprise. The water was hot. The rocks created a hot bathtub that sat still and steaming by the rushing creek.

A rush of wonder filled her. "A hot spring! I've heard about these." She put her hand under the dripping waterfall and pulled it back instantly. It was scalding.

"Careful! The waterfall comes straight out of the ground. It's incredibly hot."

"You're not kidding." Samantha stepped back. "This is amazing. Thank you for showing this to me."

"Showing? Honey, if anyone ever needed a long soak in a hot spring it's you. You're going in."

"Me? You're kidding." She looked doubtfully at the dark water in the pool. "I can't go in there!"

"Why not? The creek water mixes in with it. You felt it, the temperature's perfect!"

She glared at him, though she doubted he could see it in the dark. "I'm sure it's perfect, but it's also dark and I can't see what's in there. God knows what's crawling around on the bottom of that pool!"

Jack pulled a flashlight out of one of the pockets of the shearling jacket he'd put on. He shone it into the pool and Samantha could see into the water. It was about three feet deep and crystal clear. The bottom was pebbles and sand.

"See? No strange, hot-spring-dwelling critters in there. And just to make sure they stay away…" Jack reached into another pocket and took out a handful of small safety candles. He lit one and then another and began setting them on the various rocks and ledges that surrounded the pool. They illuminated the area with a soft, flickering glow.

She watched him, impressed with his preparations. "But my swimsuit is back at the camp…" She knew her protests were getting weaker.

"It's just you and me out here, Samantha. If it helps, I'll sit down here on this rock while you're in the tub. That way you'll have all the privacy you need. Any more excuses?"

None she could think of. A thrill ran up her spine. She never did things like this! She truly wanted to get into the water on this beautiful night under a sky full of shooting stars. She knew that the soak would ease her aches and pains after a day in the saddle, but more than that there was something seductive about this still water that came from so deep within the earth. It was as basic and primitive as what she felt for Jack, a feeling that seemed to flow down to the marrow of her bones.

Jack moved over to the rock he'd mentioned and sat down, leaning his back against another boulder and looking up at the stars, seeming completely relaxed in their wild surroundings. He didn't speak, and after checking and double-checking that he wasn't looking, Samantha unzipped her parka and laid it on a rock. Sitting down, she pulled off her boots and socks and felt the rough gravel cold beneath her feet. The chill autumn air snapped against her face and she could see her breath in the candlelight. Bracing herself, she quickly yanked her sweater over her head and pulled her jeans down. The cold rippled across her skin, leaving her shaky and invigorated at the same time.

Standing in her bra and panties, she stopped and looked around at Jack, but true to his word, he was gazing off into the distance, seemingly unaware of her stripping a few feet away.

Her skin rose in goose bumps and she felt suddenly on high alert, aware of the ground beneath her feet, the arch of the sky above, the sound of the creek tumbling over rock, the living and breathing of the night and it's creatures all around her. She unhooked her bra, stepped out of her panties and got into the water.

Its heat was a welcome embrace as she eased herself down to lie in the pool. Heavy with minerals, the water enveloped her limbs and washed over and around her in the softest caress. Nerve endings that had felt so raw from work, from the fire, from her feelings for Jack, were soothed. She leaned back on a rock, let her hair float on the hot surface and closed her eyes, realizing that somehow, once again, Jack Baron had known exactly what she needed.

JACK ALWAYS KEPT his promises. That's what he told himself as he listened to Samantha undress behind him. But he hadn't realized until now that pieces of clothing had their own unique sound. Her jacket dropped with a hiss of nylon, and her boots came off with a swish and a thump. Her sweater landed on a rock nearby with a small shuffle and the zipper on her jeans seemed amplified by the silence of the wilderness at night. With each new sound he clenched his fist tighter, balling it into the outside of his thigh until it hurt, trying to ignore the desire that was building in him.

He wanted this woman. He wanted her fire and spirit and fierce independence. And at the same time, he wanted to bring her to trust his touch, to rely on his protection sometimes. She'd never had a lot of security in her life—that was clear. She'd been pushing through life essentially on her own since she was a kid. He wanted to be her safe haven, that secure place where she could go to let down the brilliant defenses she put up to keep the world at bay.

And now she was naked behind him and in some moment of chivalry, or idiocy, he'd promised to stay away, and it was very likely going to drive him insane. He wanted his hands on her so badly it hurt. He stared out into the night, forcing himself to concentrate on a search for shooting stars, on the outline of the mountain range beyond, on anything but the woman behind him who had eased into the hot spring with a spontaneous gasp of pleasure that had the blood beating hot and fierce in his veins.

BEHIND CLOSED EYES, Samantha pictured Jack. How could she not be drawn to his easy grace? The way he'd moved so casually around the campsite creating delicious food on an open fire, the calm, capable way he cared for the horses. The way he took care of her when she didn't even realize herself what she needed.

She could imagine his life most days. One man on a horse, alone and content in the mountains. If a life could have an opposite, his was the opposite of hers. But right now she didn't care. She loved him. And now that she was getting used to the idea, it somehow didn't seem so scary.

She looked up at the night sky and whispered, "Jack, look!"

Another falling star blazed a trail overhead, momentarily lighting the sky around it.

Samantha scanned the dome of stars above her, hoping to see another one. The water picked her up and floated her on gentle arms. She felt the night air sharp and chill on her nose, her cheeks and her breasts as she surfaced. The contrast was like a lover's touch, making all nerves stand on end. This night was magic and it was all because of Jack.

She wanted him. She'd wanted him last night and all day and the soft touch of the hot water made her want him more. Maybe it was a bad idea. Maybe she should use the same willpower she'd used last night to make herself keep her distance. But something was different. She was different. She turned to look at him just as the moon reached up over the distant hills and lit up the entire landscape in blue-gray light.

"Jack," she said, her voice sounding unfamiliar against the rush of the water.

"Yeah?" She could hear him shift on the rock, but he didn't come close.

She tried again. "Jack, please, will you come in with me?"

She heard the crunch of gravel as he stood, but he still said nothing. Just when she was wondering if maybe he hadn't heard her, he came forward with

long strides and knelt down beside her. His voice
was hoarse. "Are you sure you want my company?"

The certainty hit her with a force that left her
breathless. She'd never felt so sure of wanting anything, ever. In fact, if she couldn't touch him, and
if he didn't touch her very soon, she felt as if she'd
just burn up in the pool.

She looked into his shadowed eyes, at the question in their dark depths, and put her hands up to
his cheeks in answer. Pushing herself up she kissed
him, feeling his mouth go hot above hers when he
kissed her back, hard.

He pulled away abruptly and Samantha sank
back into the water, watching silently as he pulled
off his hat and jacket and threw them down on a
boulder by the creek. His chest was lit by moonlight
as his shirt landed by his feet. Boots and jeans came
off in a blur. She bit her lip hard as he stood over
her naked, so confident and at home in the night air.

Jack stepped down into the pool beside her and
she sat up, uncertain of what to do next. But he
solved that problem by reaching for her, scooping her up onto his lap, one hand supporting her
back as the other cradled her legs. She could feel
him rigid beneath her and she ran her hands up
the silken skin and hard muscles of his chest, en-
chanted by his broad, strong shoulders, the planes
and angles of his work-sculpted torso. He let her

explore. When she got to his neck she brought his mouth down to hers.

Any lingering reasons why she shouldn't do this were wiped out by the taste of his kiss. His hand left her back and held her neck and he kissed her again—an expression of pure need. Her heart felt swollen with it and tears started behind her eyes as she let her new feelings for him pour through her.

A moan escaped her throat as his mouth blazed a trail over her skin, electrifying her neck, her collarbone, her shoulders and the path between. Jack's hands slid down into the hot water, finding her breasts, cradling them in his broad palms. She gasped as his calloused fingers circled her nipples and she quickly turned to face him, bringing her hands around his neck, trying to bring his mouth even deeper into hers.

She brought her hands down to his hips, his thighs and then to his erection. She wanted to make him gasp, wanted to arouse and amaze him. His arms were silk and steel wrapped around her back, holding her up when she would have collapsed against him in desire. He slid one hand down between her legs and then it was hard to know whether it was her skin or his or the hot velvet water that she was touching.

Finally with a cry of frustration, Jack pulled away from her, and held her at arms length. "Samantha, do you want…" he began.

"Yes." For once in her life she was not going to plan or control or worry. She was going to grab on to whatever time they had together and cherish every second.

Relief crossed his strained features and he scooped her up in his arms, standing in one fluid motion so she gasped at the crisp night air prickling over her skin as she left the water. Jack pulled her close to his dripping chest and carried her a few steps back up the creek toward their campsite. Then he stopped and dropped his head to her forehead with a low, humorless laugh.

"I want you so badly, it's killing me. But it's a hike up to the tent, and even for you, irresistible as you are, I don't think I can do it without my boots on!"

A giggle escaped her and then another, as she clung to his chest while he attempted to step into his boots without lowering her to the ground. Though she couldn't see much of him from her position in his arms, the image of him buck naked except for his worn cowboy boots was too much, and the giggles turned to peals of laughter as he hopped into the second boot, swearing softly to himself.

He stopped hopping, boots evidently on, and looked at her seriously, his gravity betrayed by the twitch of humor at the side of his mouth. "I'll ask you not to mock me at this moment, as my dignity is a little fragile."

Tears poured down her face as she shook with suppressed humor against his chest. "I'm sorry," she finally gasped as he started up the trail. "It's just so cold and then you..." Another wave of laughter overcame her and she shook silently before blurting out "You're naked in your boots!"

He grinned down at her as he heaved them up the final ledge to the meadow where their tent was. "Hey, at Chippendales the ladies would pay good money for this look. And you, I'll remind you, are even more naked than me." He smacked a rather unromantic kiss on the top of her wet head and strode toward the tent, stopping to spin her around under the stars, making her skin ripple as the cold breeze rushed past.

"Jack, I'm freezing!" She clung to him as he unzipped the door. He leaned in and dumped her unceremoniously on the pile of sleeping bags and blankets inside. Samantha quickly scrambled under the down bags, rubbing her shoulders and arms with her hands, trying to get the chill out. She heard Jack pull off his boots and he lowered himself down next to her.

He slid beneath the thick down sleeping bag and reached for her, and she turned toward his heat, her need for him greater than the pounding of her nervous heart. The rough callouses of his hands were a sharp contrast to his soft touch as he pulled her close to his broad chest and then rolled so he was

above her. He held her as if she was something
fragile rather than a heated, wanting woman.

"What is it?" she questioned, turning her head
to look up at him and running her fingertips over
the rough stubble of his angular jaw.

"You're incredible, Samantha." He traced her
cheekbones with his thumbs, cradling her head in
his hands. "You take my breath away every time
I see you. It's been like that from the beginning."
Her eyes flew to his, surprised by the emotion she
could hear in his voice, but his expression was un-
fathomable in the rich darkness.

A lump rose suddenly in her throat and, word-
less, she reached her hands around his shoulders
and pulled him toward her. Her hands were shaking and her stomach felt tight with nerves, but the
warmth of his skin under her fingers calmed her.
He leaned down, bracing his weight on his fore-
arms that rested on either side of her head, his fingers tangled in her hair. When she felt his muscular
torso cover her, and the thrill of her skin and his
touching down the length of their bodies, the very
last ghosts of doubt fled.

And then his gentleness vanished and his mouth
was on hers, forcing her own to open for him. His
kisses inflamed her until her skin felt alive, her
body aching with a need that was as primitive and
essential as the wilderness around them.

Her hands roamed over his long back, around the

taught strength of his thighs, and her touch had him gasping her name. His hands savaged her, holding her down as he brought his mouth to her breasts, her hips and along her legs. At the feel of his hot mouth on her she went wild, moaning his name as she reached for him, her nails grazing his shoulders. She pulled him up and he paused in sudden stillness, crouched over her. "You're sure?"

He had to ask? She would dissolve if she couldn't have him…just evaporate out into the cold night air and disappear.

"Condom." She gasped. "We have to…"

"No worries." Jack reached into the duffel bag and pulled out a foil packet. "This time I'm the organized one."

"Thank goodness," Samantha breathed. And then he was inside her, all heat and strength.

Samantha pulled him even closer, loving each powerful push of his hips and the way he filled her and moved her. Her back arched up to meet his hands and she heard him say her name. It felt like she could never have enough of him, would never be sated. Then bone and muscle surged in rippling heat and he was there with her, shuddering and shaking and then still.

They lay silent for a few moments and then Jack turned and pulled her to him so she lay with her head on his chest, his arm cradling her to the warmth of his body. Samantha knew she should say something, but no words came, just a languid bliss. She snuggled closer and felt exhaustion weighting her bones, sinking her into sleep.

JACK FELT SAMANTHA drift off and smiled in lazy acknowledgment. When she'd invited him into the pool with her he'd been determined to go slowly and carefully. He'd thought she'd need that, to ease her out of that reserve she wore like a suit of armor. Nothing had prepared him for the way she'd touched him, and the way she'd come undone under his hands. And now that he'd seen the wildness she hid deep inside, he knew he'd never be the same. The pattern and passion of her had been branded on his skin and his mind and left behind a scar that would haunt him when she left. *If she left*. He knew he'd do whatever he could to talk her into staying.

CHAPTER TWENTY-ONE

SAMANTHA SAT UP in the dim light of dawn. Jack was lying on his back, one muscled arm thrown over his eyes, a sleeping bag thrown carelessly over him. He seemed oblivious to the cold and Samantha was jealous as she yanked her bag more closely around her chilled shoulders.

The icy air awakened her mind and the force of what they'd done washed through her. She put her hands up and felt her flushed cheeks, and an involuntary smile started that widened as her body remembered Jack's touch with vivid delight. She tried to grasp what had happened. Memories coated her skin and she could almost feel the imprint of his fingers, his limbs on her body as if he'd marked her as his own.

She lay back down with a heavy thud. Questions tugged at her mind, tempting her to hash over the meaning of it all. But for once, she didn't want to analyze. Besides, the meaning was simple. She, Samantha Rylant, ambitious, organized, practical and unadventurous, just had incredible wilderness sex with a gorgeous cowboy. She grinned. Who knew she was capable of doing such a thing? She wiggled down in her sleeping bag and as soon as she warmed up, she fell back into a deep, relaxed sleep.

When she woke again the sky was lighter and a few dim rays from the morning sun were turning the walls of the tent golden, dust motes dancing in the air. Jack was up and outside already, a tangle of sleeping bags left behind. She rolled over onto them and inhaled his lingering scent.

She could hear his footsteps and smell coffee brewing on the campfire. He was so natural out here, so clearly a part of the scenery. She tried to imagine him at his old job in New York in a suit and tie. She smiled to herself. She couldn't picture him in anything but jeans and a cowboy hat.

She groaned inwardly, thinking about facing him. Would he regret last night? Did she? How could she regret it when just the memory of making love had her breath catching and her bones turning liquid? But what should she do next?

The sum of her experience with flings was almost zero. The Samantha of a few short weeks ago would never be here at all, would never consider waking up on this mountain in the middle of nowhere with two horses, Jack Baron and some very rumpled sleeping bags.

But was this a fling? She knew the real answer, and it scared her.

She flopped on her back and stared at the tent

ceiling, watching the light grow brighter as the sun rose.

Unable to resist the smell of the coffee any longer, Samantha pulled on jeans and a sweater, and stepped into her boots, which Jack must have brought up from the creek at some point. He'd left them outside the tent, with her clothing folded neatly beside them. Just that small intimacy thrilled her.

Jack was putting sticks into the fire. He looked up. "Morning." His welcoming smile lit up her heart, erasing the doubts that had been there moments before. He held out a mug of coffee and she walked over to him, gratefully taking the cup and drinking a deep swallow of the bitter brew.

"Hey," she answered, trying to appear as if waking up with a man after incredible sex was not a big deal. She waved a hand, taking in the sunshine, the view of the valley below, the creek, and the aspen. "Nice place you got here."

He regarded her intently. "How are you this morning?"

Trust Jack not to waste time on small talk. "I'm okay." She watched the fire and felt her cheeks flush as memories of last night came flooding back. She looked up, forcing herself to meet his gaze. That deep blue she could study forever. "I'm good," she admitted. "Very good, actually. And you?"

He walked over to her and pulled her into a tight

embrace, then bent down to kiss her gently on the mouth. He looked into her eyes and she saw passion and tenderness mingled there. "I'm good. Very, very good. Thank you." He kissed her again, then turned away and began rummaging for something in the saddlebags.

Samantha watched him without speaking, trying to imagine what he must think of her. Did he do this kind of thing often? Did he think that she did? She wished she could turn off her churning mind for just five minutes but it was impossible. The questions piled up, with no answers in sight.

They were quiet over breakfast and Samantha was relieved. She had too much emotion to sort through to speak. Instead she tried to memorize all the details of their campsite. On first glance it was a simple mountain meadow, dotted in brush and the big mule-ear daisies that loved these high hills. Samantha knew she would remember it as one of the most important places she'd ever visited.

After they packed up their bags and saddled the horses, Samantha buried her face in Apple's lush mane for a moment, inhaling her comforting horsey scent.

Part of her, a large part, wanted to just keep riding into the mountains. Disappear with Jack at her side, knowing that together they'd have all they needed. Unfortunately she knew love didn't really work that way. Back to reality, Samantha thought, and the bittersweetness of it all flooded hot tears behind her eyes. She blinked them away and pulled herself up onto Apple's back.

The path home wound up a hill studded with granite and pines that had been twisted by years of heavy snow. As they topped the rise and began to pick their way down the steep descent, the view had Samantha slowing Apple to a halt so she could take it all in.

In the early-morning light, peaks and valleys unrolled beneath them in a vast landscape of bold illumination and deep shadows. Aspen painted dashes of yellow in front of the rich green of conifers. She hadn't left for the city yet, but the crisp scent of pine, of sunbaked granite, of mountain breeze was already making her nostalgic. The air here seemed to fill her veins, soothe her thoughts and calm her nerves.

Samantha wished there was a way to take this feeling back home with her. She could use some of this serenity during her busy days in crowded, bustling San Francisco.

THE SIGHT OF the barn made the horses happy, but Samantha didn't share their enthusiasm. How was she going to let go of the past twenty-four hours of pure magic and head back to everyday life?

The trouble with these new feelings for Jack, she decided, was that they messed with her focus. She had this inner drive that had pushed her forward all these years and given her so much success at work. Now, for the first time, she didn't want to work. She wanted to lie in a field with Jack and watch the day spin by. She wanted to hike in the mountains holding his hand. This, she thought, illustrated perfectly one of the many downsides to falling for someone.

They walked the horses up to the rails by the barn and dismounted. It had been a lot of riding and Samantha was pretty sure she heard her bones creak when her feet hit the ground.

Jack slipped a rope around Apple's neck and slid her bridle off. Apple obligingly stuck her nose into the soft halter and stood still as he buckled the strap. He tied her rope to the rail and then moved over to start on Larry. "So did you like your camping trip?"

His eyes were shadowed by his cowboy hat so she couldn't read his expression, but she could tell that he too was melancholy that their trip was over. "It was perfect," she said and walked over to him, putting her hands on his shoulders. "And you? Did you like it?"

In answer he leaned down and kissed her, his lips lingering softly afterward. "It was a phenomenal night and I'm grateful for it." He pulled her toward him, cradling her against him, taking her hat off so he could caress her hair and kiss her face.

"I need you," he whispered in her ear and her body echoed his words with rippling want.

"Can we?" she asked. "Before I have to go?" In answer he scooped her up and she clung to his neck as he carried her into the relative privacy of the barn, covering her laughing protests with kisses.

One more time. Maybe it was irresponsible. She should be leaving for San Francisco, but she wanted one more incredible memory to add to her hoard, to cherish and pore over in the future.

Jack carried her as if she weighed nothing, and she felt the muscles of his shoulders rippling under her arms. She loved the strength and surety of him. He strode through the barn and into a stall full of clean straw and in one smooth motion, turned and leaned her against the wall. Her legs went round his waist and his kisses were hot on her mouth and melted her defenses, letting hunger, longing and loss rage through her. His wide palms and long fingers wrapped around her, pulling her in as if he couldn't bring her close enough. His touch became more aggressive, until he was setting a rhythm and she was blindly following, trapped against him while his hands drove her hips on.

There was a point where she realized she'd never be able to stop, that her whole being was centered around the pace he was setting, the steel strength of his mouth under hers, the intense control his strong hands and arms were exerting to drive her inexorably over the edge.

And then it all broke apart in ripples of heat and energy and he stilled her and sheltered her as she plummeted into oblivion, her release coming in sobbing breaths. She buried her face where his neck met his shoulder as the waves faded and he wrapped his arms around her, holding her close and steadying her breath.

She wanted him to have the same wonder, the same exhilaration, so when she could move again she slid down to support her own weight while her hands travelled his skin, under his shirt and along the waist of his jeans to caress the soft skin of his hip. He spoke her name in a whisper again and again as she unbuttoned his jeans and wrapped the hard length of him in her small hands. This was an intimacy she hadn't known, and when he dropped his forehead to her hair and gasped his pleasure, she felt a sort of reverence that her touch, her hands, could put him in this state. He guided her, helping her learn the way, until with a harsh cry he throbbed and shook under her touch.

Jack lay behind her on an old blanket in the straw, his heated skin warming her back, his face buried in her hair. Everything about this scene was perfect except one thing—she couldn't picture what came next.

She'd allowed herself this time in the mountains

with Jack because she thought she was capable of seizing a moment that might not come again. But in *this* moment, the one right before goodbye, it was becoming clear to her that she was not at all capable. The past twenty-four hours had been amazing, life altering, but now, faced with leaving, she couldn't stand to end it. Even if an ending was all that was possible.

Samantha could see the light changing through the barn window as afternoon moved closer to evening. "Jack," she whispered. "I have to go home."

"You are home," he whispered back, nuzzling her neck.

She smiled at the sweetness of that, but tears stung. "I'm not, Jack. I have work in the morning. Work I can't miss." She slid out from under his arm and sat up. "I'm sorry, but it's getting late and I have a long drive."

Jack yawned and gave her a sleepy smile that melted any part of her that hadn't liquefied already. "Okay, let's get you on the road." He sat up and they straightened clothes and walked hand in hand out to where the horses were tethered. "Do you want me to walk you home?" he asked.

"That's very sweet. But no, stay here and take care of these beauties." She gave Larry a pat and then went over to Apple and gave her a quick hug. "I'll miss you," she whispered in the chestnut's ear.

And then there was nothing left to do except say

goodbye. "I don't know how to do this," she said, turning to Jack.

"Will you come next weekend?" He tucked a curl behind her ear. Kissed her lower lip and lingered there.

"I'll try." He kissed her again. "Probably." He kissed her again and she smiled. "Okay. I'll be here."

"That's what I was hoping to hear." His face creased into the smile she loved. "Hey, Frisco," he said softly, smoothing her hair back from her face. "We're going to figure it out. Trust me." He kissed her forehead and stepped back.

Samantha wished she could believe him. But even Jack, in his superhero cowboy garb, couldn't rescue them from their incredibly different lives.

She squeezed his hand once and let go, feeling the loss instantly. "Have a good week, Jack."

Her legs felt shaky, whether from all the riding or all the feelings, she wasn't sure. She turned and made her way carefully down the path. Time to gather her things and head to San Francisco. Would the city look different, she wondered, now that she had changed?

CHAPTER TWENTY-TWO

MARK STOOD UP. She could see the anger seething under his calm façade. "You still work for me, you know."

"How could I possibly forget?" Samantha gathered her folders and stood, too—no way would she let him loom over her.

Mark's fair skin turned a deeper shade of red. "You usurped my authority in here today." He gestured around the now-empty conference room.

"Not intentionally, Mark. I just disagreed with you. I think you're being a little tough on everyone. The people on our team are working incredibly hard for you, Mark. They have fantastic ideas…"

"I want results. Not ideas. And I want them now! Telling everyone to leave early on a Friday to go drinking is not going to get this project done!"

The tight control she'd been keeping on her temper was losing its hold. "First of all, five o'clock is not early. Second of all, we work in a creative field, Mark. At least it used to be. People need to feel enthusiastic and inspired, so they can come up with the type of cutting-edge ads that have made our reputation. I am not trying to *usurp* your authority, but I am trying to keep them jazzed. Pressuring them with the kinds of unrealistic deadlines that you've been setting is not going to do that!"

"Well my deadlines wouldn't be so unrealistic if you'd stay here in the office and get your work done like you used to instead of taking off to play cowgirl all the time."

His words hit her in the stomach and turned her tension into something boiling and raging. Her voice dripped sarcasm and she didn't care.

"Forgive me for finally using a few days of the three months' vacation time I've earned to deal with my inheritance. My apologies for needing a little time to cope with my grandmother's death!"

"Samantha." His words stopped her as she turned to leave. "I just don't know how to deal with you anymore. You never used to argue with me like this."

He was staring at her, uncomprehending. And then it hit her. He really didn't get it. He really, truly did not understand that his actions might have caused a few of the changes in her that he was noticing.

Who knew why? Maybe in his mind, in his world, he didn't think what he'd done was that bad. Whatever the reason, it meant she'd never really known him at all. Which meant that all the heartache, and all the angst she'd felt at his betrayal, was really for someone who didn't exist. Someone she'd imagined Mark to be.

It was as if a fifty-pound weight had been lifted from her shoulders. As if someone had flipped a light switch to illuminate a shadowed room. She didn't need to care about him anymore and it was a lovely feeling.

Mark was still staring. Only seconds had passed, but everything was different. "You know what, Mark? Never mind, it doesn't matter anymore." She turned on her heel before he could say anything to spoil her newfound peace.

As she walked down the hallway toward the elevators, a deep voice interrupted her. "Samantha, can you come in here for a moment?" It was Harold Armstrong, Mark's supervisor and managing director of the San Francisco office of Taylor Advertising. Samantha's stomach fluttered with nerves. Harold had barely spoken to her since the Los Angeles meeting they'd attended together. Maybe he'd heard about the way she'd disagreed with Mark during their meeting today. Her serenity gone, she wondered if she was about to be fired.

Samantha stepped into Harold's luxurious corner office and sat down in the comfortable chair that he pulled out for her. Harold closed the door and sat down in another seat, clasping his hands as if collecting his thoughts. He took off his black-framed glasses and polished them, ran a hand over his balding head, and finally looked at her. "I'd like to make you an offer, Samantha."

"Okay," she said cautiously. This wasn't the reprimand she'd been expecting.

"The truth is, things haven't been going very smoothly since you started taking time off."

"Harold, I'm…" she started to explain, but he held up his hand.

"Wait, I'm not blaming you, just hear me out. Speaking confidentially, of course, it's become clear that people just don't listen to Mark quite the same way they do with you. People don't work as hard when you're gone. They don't have as much to say in meetings, and when they do talk, their ideas aren't as creative. You inspire them, Samantha."

She was flattered and surprised that he'd noticed her work. "Thank you."

"So we're thinking of shaking things up a bit around here. We want to promote you to senior vice president. You and Mark will be equals and you'll report to me. We'll keep you on your current projects, and we're planning to move Mark on to some other aspects of the business, where perhaps he'll be better suited. What do you think?"

Samantha tried to control the elation she felt. She'd wanted this promotion for so long, and worked so hard for it. She'd given up nights and weekends and vacations to get ahead, and it was finally paying off. Senior VP in only six years at

Taylor. It almost never happened so fast. And then there was the added, miraculous bonus that Mark wouldn't be her boss anymore.

"Harold, thank you, I'd love to. Of course I accept!"

"Fabulous. I'm so glad." Harold shook her hand, briskly. "Make an appointment with human resources some time next week. And have a good weekend!"

"It will certainly be better now. Thank you again, Harold."

Samantha floated down the hall. She was so filled with gratitude and triumph that she was sure her feet did not touch the ground. Deep in her thoughts, she didn't notice Dana until she almost bumped into her. Dana held out her hand in alarm and a large diamond caught the light and glistened. An engagement ring. Samantha waited to feel some angst, or jealousy or regret, but she felt nothing. It was such a huge relief to feel *nothing*.

Dana looked at Samantha questioningly and moved to walk past her. For the first time, Samantha felt sorry for her. What would it be like to have Mark as your future husband, knowing he was capable of lying and cheating? Knowing that you were going to spend your life with him, and raise a child with him, while always wondering if you could trust him?

"Dana, wait."

"Yes?" Dana looked worried.

"I just wanted to say congratulations. And good luck."

Dana looked at her in surprise. "Uh, yeah… thanks," she said, and wandered off down the hall in search of Mark. Samantha watched her go, feeling so glad that *she* was no longer the person who waited around for Mark after work. So glad she no longer worked for him, either. So glad that somehow life was setting her free of him once and for all.

CHAPTER TWENTY-THREE

THE SUN BEAMED in through the hallway window, enticing Samantha to lean against the frame and look out. From this side of the ranch house she could see back toward the valley, and the roofs of Benson peeked out from behind the tops of pines. Beyond the town, the highway ran like a snake through Owens Valley. The roads, the pastures, everything she could see was quiet and still, so early on a Saturday morning.

She picked up her coffee and headed out to the back porch. Huddled under a blanket against the morning chill she sat on the step looking over the property. To her right was the hulk of ashes that was once the woodshed. Beyond that, the kitchen garden, choked with weeds. Grandma Ruth had loved that kitchen garden. She'd start putting in the crops soon after the snow melted. She was constantly experimenting with what she planted.

Samantha let her eyes wander upward, past the empty pastures until granite began to take over the mountain meadows. Her ranch. Her land and her mountains, stretching all the way to Rock Lake.

Lake Beautiful Ruth. Samantha closed her eyes as memories of her trip there with Jack overwhelmed her. She exhaled, trying to breathe out the pressure of the decision she was about to make.

How was she supposed to handle this? She didn't want to let the ranch go. She didn't want to let Jack go. But her dream had come true. She was now the youngest senior vice president at Taylor Advertising. The youngest ever. And yesterday she'd learned that the pitch she'd somehow powered through the day she found out about Mark and Dana had been successful—Peter Claude Skincare was now their client. Her client. The biggest client the San Francisco office had ever landed.

Since then, her phone had been ringing constantly and her email inbox filled up hourly, foretelling what her life was going to be like from now on. There wasn't going to be much time for weekend trips to the ranch now. She had no choice but to say goodbye to all this. To say goodbye to Jack.

Tears came again as she thought about the irony of it all. The moment she finally took a risk and allowed something to happen with Jack, the moment she'd really started to enjoy the ranch and the mountains, was also the moment that life had given her everything she'd been working for in San Francisco. *Be careful what you wish for,* she thought bitterly.

A dog's distant bark, sharp and abrupt in the

morning air, had her turning her head in the direction of the sound. She could hear the crunch of footsteps on gravel and she imagined Jack striding around the truck, pulling open the passenger door to the cab.

"Hector! Zeke!" His deep voice carried perfectly. "Scoot over there, Hector. You're getting fat as a hen, you old rascal. Down, Zeke! Sit!" The slam of the truck door and the growl of its engine echoed down the valley and she knew she couldn't wait any longer.

She needed to screw up her courage, walk up that hill and say goodbye.

A SINGLE BARK from Zeke had Jack turning around. Samantha was coming up the drive toward the paddock. He'd hoped she'd show up early today. He wanted to take her for a ride to the lake. He'd even bought supplies for a picnic lunch. They could cool a couple of beers in the water while they swam, though come to think of it, he couldn't quite imagine Samantha drinking a beer. Maybe he had some white wine in his refrigerator. He'd have to check.

He started toward her, trying to keep his smile from reaching ear to ear. Her black hair was blown sleek and straight and she'd wrapped a pale pink scarf around her neck to block the morning chill. She was so beautiful, such a welcome sight that he didn't quite know where to look.

"Hey, Frisco," was all he could think to say. He opened his arms and she stepped in and it felt so incredibly good to hold her again. He dropped his head and breathed in the fresh scent of her hair, felt the delicate strength of her in his arms, just like he'd remembered.

She was shaking. He stepped back and held her at arms length and saw tears tracing their tracks down her face.

"Samantha, what's wrong? Is it the house? Are you okay?" His mind swirled. Was Rob Morgan trying something new? That was impossible.

"Jack, do you still want to buy the ranch?"

His heart dropped. He actually felt it drop and slam into the bottom of his stomach. "What are you saying?"

Her green eyes were dark with brimming tears. "I got a promotion last week. It's the job I've always wanted. It's what I've been working so hard for." Jack stared at her, trying to understand how all this fit together in her head.

"That's great! Congratulations. But it doesn't mean you have to sell me the ranch."

"I won't have time to come out here anymore." Her voice had a quaver in it he'd never heard before.

"Not come here? Aren't you being a little extreme?"

"No. I'm not. I'm the youngest person ever to become senior vice president in my office. I'm going to have a lot to prove. And we just landed a huge new account. I'll be working. All the time."

"What about what happened between us last weekend? That didn't mean anything to you?" He knew he sounded like a girl and it pissed him off even more.

"It meant everything, Jack. It still does. It always will." Tears rolled down her cheeks and she swiped at them impatiently with her sleeve. "I'm so sorry. I loved last weekend. I'll never forget it. This has all been so amazing. I didn't even know I could feel this way."

He couldn't stay calm. Couldn't think clearly enough to say things politely. "So do something about it. Don't just walk away. It doesn't make sense."

"It does make sense." Her full mouth was set in a stubborn line. "We've each worked so hard to find our path through life, and simply because we found each other doesn't mean we should give that up."

"I disagree." He couldn't believe this was happening. "Jobs come and go, Samantha."

"Are you willing to give up yours for me, Jack?"

She had him there. He couldn't give up the ranch and everything he'd worked for. "It's different," he tried. "My job has to be located out here. Or in the country somewhere. But you could do yours anywhere."

"I couldn't. Not this job. Not the one I've worked

so hard for. Jack, I've thought about it all week. We have to accept that, whatever we might feel, this is just not practical."

"Practical?" he spat back. "No it's not. Is love supposed to be?"

Samantha looked completely caught off guard. "Well, to have a relationship with someone…it can't be about attraction alone. It has to make sense, it has to fit into your life, it has to…"

"Be something you can control?" Jack covered the ground between them in two strides and took her shoulders, shaking her just a little with the force of his grip. "I don't think so, Samantha. I think this is way beyond either of our control." He looked into her eyes, trying to see into her soul. Trying to reach her. "You want to have your hands on the wheel at all times. With me you don't and it scares you. You're scared of what's happening to you because you can't control it, and you can't organize it into some neat little package."

Her eyes flashed as her temper flared up. Probably because she knew he'd spoken the truth. "I'm not scared, Jack. Just realistic."

"What's realistic is to stay here and find a way to make it work."

She stared at him as if he'd suggested she visit another planet. "You don't understand, do you? This job, this promotion, has been my dream for so long. I can't just walk away from it now that it's finally come true."

"What about this?" Jack gestured to the mountains around them. "What about this dream?"

"This was my grandparents' dream. It's your dream. It was never my dream." Her jaw was set in a stubborn line.

"Dreams can change, Samantha. Has that ever occurred to you? They're about what you wish for in the moment. Not what you wanted six years ago when you were a kid fresh out of college. They're not set in stone."

"I got what I wished for," she said firmly. "And I need to see it through."

Well, he couldn't argue when she was that blunt. He played his last card. He was that desperate. "I care about you, Samantha. And I think you care about me."

"It's not enough, Jack. We know that. Think about your marriage. Were your feelings for Amy enough for her to be happy here?"

That stung. He turned away and grabbed the halter he'd hung on a fence post earlier and tossed it into the truck bed. Just to have something to do.

When he turned back around, she wouldn't meet his eyes. "Maybe you can recommend a real estate agent, or another attorney we can use for the sale," she said softly. "I'll get the ranch appraised as soon as I can. We might as well get going on this."

He couldn't move because if he did he might do something crazy. Yell, or shake her or pick her up and run off into his house with her. So he just stood there, his hand on his truck, not wanting her to leave.

Samantha gave him a worried look and then glanced at her watch. "Well," she said, "I'd better get going. I have packing to do."

His voice didn't seem to be working and like hell was he going to make small talk with her anyway.

She seemed to understand that he had nothing more to say. She swiped at her eyes with her sleeve, looking irritated with the tears. "Goodbye, Jack. Thank you, for everything. I'm glad we met."

He just stood there watching her go. When she disappeared down the trail, it felt like she'd ripped out his heart and taken it with her.

THE LOOK SHE'D seen on Jack's face when she'd said goodbye haunted her. Samantha had always assumed it was just her own heart she was risking by getting involved with Jack. Now she saw that she'd hurt him as well. She knew his confident, almost cocky nature. And she knew that it had taken a lot for him to ask her to stay, yet he had asked again and again. And she'd still said no. But the harsh reality was that she couldn't stay. Her time on the ranch had been an incredible detour, but it wasn't her real life. She had no choice but to get back to that now.

Her car was packed with mementos she knew she'd cherish forever. The letters she'd found, old photos, one of the old afghans Ruth had crocheted in the 1970s, back when everyone was making them. There'd be more moving to do later, but the most important items were in the car, ready for the journey to San Francisco.

And that was it. Her heart hurt so much right now, she knew she wouldn't have the courage to come back here. Luckily, most other things could be done from a safe distance. Appraisers and real estate agents could take care of the sale, and movers could be hired by phone to pack the house and take everything to a storage unit in San Francisco. It was amazing how, once she'd made her decision, it was so easy to wrap up the loose ends. She wished her feelings could be taken care of so easily.

The evening light gave a soft glow to the pastures around the driveway. It painted the high peaks in gold-tipped shadows. Samantha could hear the goats that Jack had brought her munching and bleating nearby. She walked over to the fence and watched them eat. They brought so much tranquility with the rustle of their hooves in the dry grass.

The tiny white goat scampered over to rub its forehead on her hand. "Hey, little one," she crooned, rubbing its soft ears. "Hey, you little sweet thing."

"Maaa!" it bleated with incredible volume and Samantha jumped back with a yelp of surprise, smiling in spite of her dark mood.

"Scared by the world's smallest goat!" she told it. "Just more evidence that I'm not cut out to be a rancher." Grateful for the levity amidst so much heartache, she turned to go.

Leaning on the car, keys in hand, Samantha tried to take it all in. For a few incredible weeks she'd owned a large part of all that she could see. The beloved farmhouse, the pastures, the hills above, and the lake and mountains beyond that. She'd shared time with horses, goats and the most gorgeous man she'd ever known.

"Thank you, Grandma," she whispered. "You gave me one of the greatest adventures of my life."

Images of her grandparents working on the ranch flooded her mind. The era of their toil and love had come to an end, and she felt guilty that she wasn't the granddaughter they'd deserved, the one who could follow in their footsteps. But she was grateful the land would pass into Jack's capable hands. He would continue to shepherd it safely into the future. She hoped her grandmother would approve.

She looked down the driveway and saw the stump of the old pine tree, its torn wood still raw and jagged. Jack had tried so hard not to laugh when he saw her poor car that evening. More images followed. Jack's laughing, mocking eyes when they'd first met, the tenderness in his voice when he'd patched her up after she fell off the ladder, the way he looked after he kissed her that first time. She remembered the heat of his passion, and the way desire changed his voice.

She wanted to memorize it all. She wanted a vivid picture of this ranch, this land and the incredible man she'd gotten to know and grown to love. Then, no matter how busy she got, no matter how much time she logged at the office in her new job, she'd be able to pull the memories out, to revisit the precious time when she'd owned a ranch and loved a cowboy.

But right now the memories hurt like fresh wounds and she instinctively turned away from the pain, opening the car door and getting into the driver's seat. She took one more glance up toward Jack's property, and blew a kiss in his general direction. Tears poured in rivers down her cheeks as her car rolled down the drive.

CHAPTER TWENTY-FOUR

JACK LEANED HIS head on the column of his front porch, then he banged it once, hard. He didn't know who he was angrier with—Samantha for her decision to leave, or himself for missing her so much. Or maybe he was so pissed off because she was right? Their being together went against all logic and all reason. He should know better than to head down the same dead-end road he'd been on with Amy. A road that had ended once already in divorce and disaster, as Samantha had so kindly reminded him yesterday.

He took a long swallow of the beer in his hand. Somehow, all yesterday evening, he'd expected her to reconsider. He'd hoped she'd decide that there was no career, no ambition that was more important than them being together. But at dusk he'd watched her car disappear down the driveway, leaving him with his memories, burned into his brain, etched onto his heart. He had a feeling they weren't fading away anytime soon.

Jack had moved on to his second beer when Betty's truck roared up his driveway.

"Morning," he said as she emerged from the cab and hurried over to him with a basket that he very much hoped contained some freshly baked muffins. She gave him a hug, handed him the basket and cuffed him hard upside the head.

"Ouch, Betty! What are you doing?" He rubbed the side of his head in surprise.

"That," she said, pointing to the basket, "is because I heard that Samantha left. And that," she continued, pointing toward the ear she'd just smacked, "is because you're a fool, Jack Baron, and it's time I told you so."

"A fool!" Jack looked at his old friend in disbelief. "Betty, I may be stupid sometimes, but I can't think what it is I've done that was bad enough for you to drive up here just to wail on me!"

Betty looked like an angry hen as she paced in front of him. "You let Samantha go! Anyone can see that you are meant for each other and yet she's gone back to San Francisco and you're getting drunk on your porch at ten-thirty in the morning!" Betty stopped and faced him with a small huff and waited, tapping her toe impatiently.

"Whoa, slow down. Who made you my keeper?"

"I did. Ever since I saw the way you look at her. The way you talk about her. You love her."

"She doesn't care, Betty. I told her how I felt and it made no difference. She's selling the ranch. To me." He took another swallow of beer. "Huh, be careful what you wish for, right?"

"Enough! Stop feeling sorry for yourself." Betty softened her voice. "Jack, you can't give up. You have to try!"

This was the last straw. He was tired, he'd just been dumped, and now his ear was sore. "Try? Betty, all I've done is try. I took her riding, I took her camping, I pulled boards off her windows and put them back on again. I've put out fires, chopped up trees. I've done nothing but rescue and help…I even drove a bunch of goats in my trailer for her. Do you have any idea what a mess I had to clean afterward? And I asked her to stay…over and over like some pathetic wimp. So don't tell me I'm not trying!"

He realized he was waving his hands in wild gestures to punctuate his speech. "Sorry, Betty." He mumbled and ran a hand through his hair. "I'm just so frustrated."

Betty gave a hearty chuckle. "Oh, honey, you are a mess." She pointed to the chair next to her. "Now sit down and listen—carefully."

Jack took a swallow of beer and sat down. Betty took his hand.

"Look, Jack, asking Samantha to move here, to give up her entire life for you, is asking a lot."

"It shouldn't be, if you're in love with someone."

"Oh, Jack, you of all people know that's not

true!" She took his beer away. "Now, you need to stop drinking and start thinking. Samantha's trust was trampled on her whole life as a little girl. Ruth told me all about it. She was left here every summer while her parents went gallivanting all over the world. She was shipped off to boarding schools or dragged from country to country year after year. Those kinds of experiences change a person!"

"But I can't change what happened to her."

Betty sighed in exasperation. "Men! Why are you all so literal? Jack, she's not going to move here with you because she learned a long time ago that she has to stand on her own in order to be okay. Her independence is what makes her feel safe. So if you want her, you need to show her that she can have all that—safety, trust, *independence*—right here with you."

Jack stared at Betty, stunned, trying to take in everything she was saying. It made a lot of sense, actually. "But I'm not sure how to do that."

"If you really love her, you'll figure it out. Think big gestures, Jack. Not just flowers or kind words, though they help. Do something bold and brave. Now, give me a kiss, I've gotta get going—I have more things to accomplish today besides fixing your life!" She raised her cheek to accept the quick kiss that Jack gave her and then sauntered back to the truck, obviously very pleased with herself.

Jack called to her. "Betty!" She turned and looked over her shoulder at him.

"Yes, Jack?"

"You're a meddlesome woman, Betty! But thanks. Thanks a lot."

She beamed at him and climbed into the cab of the truck. "Don't forget what I said, Jack! A grand gesture!" And she was gone down the driveway in a cloud of dust.

Jack opened the basket and his spirits rose when he saw what was inside. He'd never realized that blackberry muffins went so well with beer. He spent the next few hours, sitting on his porch, combining the two. And sometime during the last beer, and the last muffin, a glimmer of inspiration flickered in his hazy brain. Betty had told him to come up with a grand gesture. He just might have one that could show Samantha what was possible. That city and country, work and play, independence and love, could coexist right here on her ranch.

CHAPTER TWENTY-FIVE

THE CELEBRATION WAS at one of her favorite San Francisco landmarks. Well, landmarks for those who really liked cocktails, that is. Located at the bottom of a historic post office, it had a speakeasy ambiance and some of the best martinis in the city.

Maybe because of her new senior vice presidential status, Harold had asked Samantha where to hold the victory party for the new Peter Claude account, and she'd chosen the Metro Club.

Sitting at the beautiful oval bar with its swirling art deco pattern, Samantha sipped her Manhattan and tried to smile as she accepted congratulations from her colleagues. It was a celebrity night for her. Everyone knew she'd helped Mark lead their team to such a successful pitch, and news of her promotion had leaked as well.

"Senior VP in only six years, huh?" Tim from the art department sailed up and gave her a crushing hug. "I'm so proud of you, sweetie!" In an exaggerated stage whisper he added, "Everyone knew you were doing Mark's work for him anyway. It's about time they gave you this darn promotion!"

"Shhh…" Samantha giggled. Tim was one of her favorite people to work with, and she was flattered by his statement, but it was definitely bad office politics.

"Samantha!" Lucy, who'd started recently in their media department, clinked glasses with her. "I'm so happy for you. And don't forget, you're meeting with me at 7:00 a.m. sharp tomorrow, so don't drink too many of those!"

Lucy needn't have worried. There were so many people coming by her perch to say hello that Samantha didn't have much time for her drink.

Sitting there, showered in so many good wishes, Samantha knew she should be happy. All week she'd been telling herself to be happy. But ever since she'd said her goodbyes to the ranch, and to Jack, she'd felt mainly sadness and loss. And things she normally enjoyed seemed hollow. Empty.

During one of the busiest weeks of her career, she kept finding herself staring out the conference room windows, or doodling on her notepad. And the pictures she scribbled were always of mountains.

The funny thing was, she'd wanted this promotion for so long, and had worked so hard for it, but now that she had it, it worried her. It used to be that Samantha loved the routine of her life. She loved her career goals, the security of success, the predictability of her days. But now, when she looked ahead at the months and years to come, she saw the heavy workload, the endless meetings, the busy schedule stretching on and on. And it all seemed disturbingly dull, as if her life was going to consist of jumping from calendar entry to calendar entry, rather than actually living.

Of course, there would be some time off from work to play in the city. But San Francisco had lost some of its appeal recently. Maybe the fog that had shrouded the city all week had something to do with it, but Samantha felt a bit like Dorothy in the old *Wizard of Oz* movie. Right now San Francisco was her Kansas, where everything existed in black and white. And her time on the ranch had been her Oz, vivid with Technicolor. Samantha had been like Dorothy, trying to get back home, to the security of the place she knew best. The problem was, now that she was here, she was finding it hard to accept the familiar gray landscape. Instead, she longed for the adventure and color of the ranch.

Samantha shook her head to bring herself back from her long metaphor, and took a sip of her neglected Manhattan. She needed to mingle, to be seen around this party, but her heart wasn't in it. She wondered how Jack was, and what he was doing right now. She thought about the old farmhouse, sitting dark and dilapidated in the mountain night. What would become of it?

"Samantha?" It was Harold's voice. Apparently

he'd given some kind of speech, and now he was holding up a portable microphone in her direction. From the puzzled look on his face, it seemed he'd called her name a few times already.

"Oh!" she exclaimed. "Coming." There were a few chuckles from the crowd at that and Samantha crossed the room and went up the steps of the dais that Harold was speaking from.

She cleared her throat, trying to think of something to say. "I want to start by thanking the people on my team. I mean, *our...*" she gestured vaguely in the direction where she'd last seen Mark "...team. They put in long hours, worked with wonderful creativity and spirit, and they are the ones who deserve the accolades for getting this account. Please give them a round of applause!"

While the clapping filled the room, Harold leaned over and put his hand over the microphone. "Why don't you say a few words about your promotion?" He suggested with a warm smile.

Why didn't she? Because she had no idea what to say. Every time she thought of it she pictured a long, straight, gray road, lined with cubicles and conference rooms, computer screens and calendars. It twisted her stomach and her mind was devoid of words. The room had quieted and she looked around nervously.

"Harold has kindly asked me to say a few words about my new promotion."

"Youngest SVP ever!" Tim called out. Laughter scattered through the room and a few people clapped.

Samantha cleared her throat, trying to dislodge the odd lump that was growing there. "Yes…about that." And then she knew, more surely than she'd known anything, ever, that she couldn't go down this colorless path.

Yes, she was terrified of change, but she was even more terrified of the sameness that waited for her on the other side of this speech. She looked around at the familiar faces in the room and tried to summon the right words.

"I want you to know how much I've enjoyed working with you. And how honored I am to receive my recent promotion. But I'm afraid I can't accept it. In fact—" she turned to Harold, who was looking stunned "—I need to turn in my resignation right now. I'm very sorry." She looked down for a moment, collecting her jumbled thoughts. "You see, there's a ranch, in the sierras, and the aspen are changing color. And there's a cowboy…" She heard her own words and felt a fiery blush spread over her cheeks. She looked at the crowd of Taylor Advertising employees staring blankly at her. "Never mind," she told them. "It's complicated. Goodbye. And thank you." She handed the microphone back to Harold and whispered, "I'm so very sorry." And then she was gone, through the crowd of uncertain faces and out the double doors of The Metropolitan Club into the damp fog of the San Francisco night.

It took her precisely twenty-five minutes to pack and close up her apartment, and then she was in her car, heading across the Bay Bridge, the lights of the famous city skyline fading behind her. Her heart was pounding and her mind was racing.

She knew what she'd done was irresponsible. And probably completely crazy. But the wild beauty of the mountains was calling like a siren's song and the endless bustle of her life in the city seemed meaningless in comparison. Right now, nothing mattered more than witnessing the changes that another week of autumn had brought to the rough land she was coming to love. Nothing mattered more than seeing Jack again.

CHAPTER TWENTY-SIX

WHY WERE HER lights on at two in the morning? Why would the lights in the old ranch house be on at all? Samantha quickly turned off her headlights and parked her car a little way off to the side, away from the front porch.

Heart pounding in her ears, she carefully stepped out of the car and tiptoed around the side of the house. Her old friend the two-by-four was leaning against the porch, so she picked it up and carried it with her as she tried to look in through the dining room windows. Someone had thrown an old canvas drop cloth over the table and the surface was scattered with tools.

A whirring sound pierced the silence of the deep mountain night and Samantha jumped, her heart in her throat. Forcing herself to stay calm she listened. A drill? Who was drilling in her house uninvited? At two in the morning?

Samantha walked back to the porch and up the steps. Crouching down, she scooted to the living room window and peered over the sill. Lights were on here, too. There were cardboard boxes on the carpet and several pieces of lumber lying beyond. She heard the drilling sound again.

Carefully she opened the front door. The noise was coming from the downstairs bedroom. Samantha punched the numbers 911 into her cell phone and put it in her jacket pocket, so it would be easy to dial if she needed it, though at this point she was more mystified than scared.

She raised her two-by-four over her shoulder like a baseball bat, tiptoed across the living room and down the small hallway that led to the back of the house. At the bedroom door she peered around the frame. Jack was crouched over a piece of wood on the floor. Samantha stepped into the doorway.

Jack stood up suddenly and Samantha started, dropping her weapon in the process. It landed with a thud on the wood floor. Jack whirled around, drill raised as if he was holding a gun.

"Samantha! What the…" He stopped and lowered his drill.

"What are you doing in my house, Jack? In the middle of the night? Did something happen? Did something break?" Her tired mind was sifting through possibilities. Did Rob have accomplices? Was there more vandalism?

"Nothing's wrong. I promise." Jack put the drill down on the ground next to him. "I wasn't expecting you to come. I honestly didn't know if you'd ever come back at all."

"So...you decided to remodel? Jack, you don't own the place yet!" She looked around. The storage boxes that used to fill the room had been moved out and she could see that three tall windows let in light from the east side of the house. In daylight there would probably be an amazing view out to the valley floor.

"It's an office," Jack explained. "For you. So you can work here."

All the fear she'd felt coming into the house tonight, all the anxiety over the huge decision she'd made at the office party earlier, surfaced in her voice. "Jack, this isn't your choice to make! This is my career, my life. You can't assume..."

"Wait." He interrupted her almost-tirade. His voice was quiet. "I'm not assuming anything. You left, remember? You told me goodbye? Trust me. No assumptions." Jack ran his hand through his hair and looked down at her, his eyes dark, his face completely earnest. "I just wanted some way to show you that I believe it's possible for you to be happy here. With a busy, rewarding career. Have your cake and eat it, too, you know?" He looked tired, and sad, and Samantha's anger faded.

She walked toward him, wanting so much to put her arms around him. "Jack, you didn't have to..."

"Please, just look, Samantha." He took her hand and brought her over to a beautiful antique desk that had been placed near the windows. Someone had recently refinished it and the old wood gleamed with its new polish. Jack was pointing to a bulletin board behind the desk. It had been made from a huge old ornate picture frame and took up most of the wall. "Betty's idea. She saw something like it in a magazine, but we made it from a frame she'd found at a flea market a while ago."

"It's beautiful," Samantha said softly, touching the swirled wood.

"Look what else Betty did." Jack pointed to three pages pinned to the cork. On them were spreadsheets, with the names of people or businesses listed. In the next column it detailed the nature of their business. Phone numbers were provided.

"I'm not sure I understand," Samantha said.

"It's a list of everyone in Benson who has some type of business, and needs help publicizing it. Betty asked everyone she could think of if they'd like to hire you, and here are all the people who said yes."

"But there's got to be at least fifty people on here! Benson is a tiny town."

"It's not only town businesses on here." Jack pointed to one line that read "Sierra Fishing Expeditions." "They have a lodge a little south of here and they lead tours all summer and fall. Doug, who owns it, wants to expand into winter trips, but he needs help publicizing them. And these folks." Jack pointed to the middle of the second page. "They just started a family camp. Honestly, I saw their first attempt at an ad campaign and I can tell you that they need a ton of help. And look here. A friend of mine, Sandro, is working on opening a restaurant in town. Not just any eatery, though. A gourmet, destination type of place. That project alone could keep you busy for months."

"So you're saying I should open up an agency of my own. Out here." She looked around the room at what would soon be a beautiful office. Jack had been building her a bookcase tonight. She could see that now. "In this room."

"I'm not telling you what to do. I wouldn't do that. I know that in order for you to be happy here, you have to love the mountains, just for themselves, apart from me. Because they are the center of what it means to live out here, Samantha. I love this place. But Walt calls it the back side of nowhere and he's not far from the truth!"

Samantha laughed at that. "Walt's got a way with words, hasn't he?" Her heart was pounding again, but in a hopeful, excited way this time. "You and Betty didn't have to do this, you know."

"I had to try. I understand that maybe it's not right for you…"

"It's so thoughtful, Jack." Her arm came up to encompass the beautiful room. "It's so incredibly thoughtful. But it wasn't necessary. Because I came back. On my own." At Jack's puzzled look she went on. "Aren't you wondering why I'm here? At two in the morning? I quit my job, Jack. Tonight. In the middle of a big party, when I was supposed to be giving a speech. I quit my job!"

His slow smile started, the one she loved so well, with his sense of humor shining through. "Really? You quit right in the middle of your speech? I wish I could have seen that."

"Um, I might have mentioned something about a ranch...and a cowboy..."

"It sounds like one for the ages," he teased. Concern darkened his features. "But why? You just got promoted. You said yourself that your dream had come true."

"And you were right when you said there could be new dreams. I couldn't stop thinking about the mountains, Jack. I want to see the fall colors get brighter, and the leaves carpeting the ground at the end. I want to watch the world go white during the first snowstorm. For so long I just wanted my life to be predictable, safe and secure. But I don't want that anymore. I want a new kind of life, where I'm not sure what's going to happen next. Where there are adventures and mishaps and risks. You helped me see that, Jack. And so did Grandma Ruth, by giving me this ranch."

She looked over and he was watching her carefully, his expression a mix of hope and caution and desire. She closed the gap between them with quick steps and took him by the hands. "I got in my car and drove most of the night, and on the way I knew for certain that you are the other reason I need to be here. I love you, Jack. I love you so much."

His arms came around her and he held her close. His voice was muffled against her hair. "I love you, Samantha. I've loved you for a while now. I always will." They stood like that for a long time, holding on to what they'd almost lost, quiet with their thoughts.

Samantha broke the silence. "I can't change, Jack," she told him, still holding on tight. "Or at least I don't think so. I still love my beautiful clothes and shoes, and I know I'll visit San Francisco a lot to see my friends. I doubt I'll ever want to bake muffins or do crafts like Betty does. And, *yes*, I got scared by a goat the other day. But I know I want to be here, to live here, in the mountains with you."

Jack tipped her chin up gently and looked down at her. His eyes were as blue as a high mountain lake and glittering with humor and love. "I don't want you to change. I fell in love with a woman who wanders this ranch in high heels. Who pulled the bumper off her tiny car in an insane attempt to move a pine tree. I fell in love with a woman who tries to do everything herself whether it's possible or not. That's the woman I want. Why would I want her to change into someone else? Plus, Betty will happily keep us in baked goods, and I don't really like crafts. I just want you, Frisco." He paused, and kissed her slowly, lingering with his lips on hers. Then he grinned. "But I hope you'll still let me rescue you once in a while."

"Only if you wear your cowboy suit." It felt so good to smile again. Samantha wasn't sure she'd ever been happier than right now, poised between two worlds, ready to jump into the unknown.

Jack laughed and kissed her again, and she knew she was truly home. An owl called from somewhere up in the pines above the ranch. A soft and lonely sound. A mountain sound. Holding Jack close, Samantha sent a silent prayer of thanks to Grandma Ruth for her generous and precious gift. A bright legacy of laughter, adventure and love.

* * * * *

LARGER-PRINT BOOKS!
GET 2 FREE LARGER-PRINT NOVELS PLUS
2 FREE GIFTS!

HARLEQUIN

super romance

More Story...More Romance